HER TITANS

IRONHAVEN BOOK ONE

Genevieve Jasper

Editor: Rachelle Anne Wright
Cover Image: Mehdi Zegna

ONE

MADELAINE

"Left says *I'm unapproachable and not up for making friends*, and right says *I might rock your world if you impress me in the next five seconds*. Which one are you going for?"

I sigh, shooting a glare at Lia. "Neither, although closer to the right than the left." I throw both outfits down, ready to look through my wardrobe for the fifteenth time that night, wishing the outfit that perfectly matched my mood would appear in front of me.

"Then keep the top from the right and try it on with your ripped mom jeans, the black high-waisted ones." The ‘rock your world’ top she’s talking about is a strapless black corset with mesh panels. I do as ordered and add a belt to cinch the waist of them in. “Great, wear your black stilettos and you’re done,” Lia adds.

“Okay, that’s actually perfect!” I happily admit, loving the look of all black against my olive complexion. “You’re a miracle worker.” I shouldn’t have been surprised that Lia knew I needed a confidence-boosting outfit tonight. We met as fresh-faced teenagers Madelaine and Amelia, and as soon as we realised our nicknames were anagrams, decided we’d be best friends forever. Cue an armful of friendship bracelets and ten years of laughs. She could practically read my mind at this point.

“A phrase not said nearly enough for my liking. What’s got you so stressed, anyway? You can normally plan killer outfits in minutes and you’ve been faffing for nearly an hour.”

I fiddle with my hair while I think about how to answer. It is curled for once, and sits around my shoulders like a chocolate security blanket. I’ll definitely be playing with it all night.

“I think I’m ready to get back on the horse,” I tell her apprehensively.

Lia lets out an excited squeal and gets to her knees on my bed. "Yes, finally! I've been waiting to wing-woman your ass up for months!" Nine months, to be exact. That's how long it has been since I finally gained the courage to end things with Jed. The reluctance to end it had been that there was nothing glaringly wrong with our relationship, but there was nothing spectacularly good with it either.

"What are we looking for?" she asks as I plop down next to her. "They need to be top-tier to be your next boyfriend, obviously," she carries on without giving me time to answer. Not that I know how to.

"I was actually thinking of playing the field for a bit, having one of those wild phases everyone has crazy stories about."

"No offence, sweetie, but you are the opposite of wild."

I bristle, definitely taking offence. "What?! I can have one-night stands! I don't want to fall back into a dull relationship where I lose myself completely. It's taken long enough to find me again."

"I completely agree. It would be a travesty to lose this confident, sexy woman to that shell of a person you ended up as with Jed, but there is a middle ground between the two, you know."

I know Lia is right, and she's probably correct to be dubious of my wild streak, but even though I get what she's saying, the fact is that I am way happier single now than I was for at least half of my six-year relationship with Jed. I'm nervous to give myself to someone again when I am so content with who I am now, on my own.

"When was the last time we saw the top tier at Encore, anyway?" I deflect. "We're there all the time and I have never seen a man worth looking at twice."

"That's true," Lia ponders. "We could go somewhere else? We only started going there in the first place because we know Jed hates it."

"Nah, it's shitty but we always have fun and I feel safe there."

"Safe to be on the prowl, you mean," she says, waggling her eyebrows.

I roll my eyes. "Maybe we'll start with a kiss on the dancefloor and work our way up." I settle myself on the floor in front of the freestanding mirror to do my makeup.

"You need to relax. Getting ready to find a hookup is fun! Let me make you another drink."

"I'm not going out for a hookup, I'm just not completely opposed to the idea now."

"Yeah, well, Cinderella didn't ask for a prince either, remember?" She lightens the mood by using one of our favourite quotes.

"I know, I know. A dress and a night out."

"Maybe the jeans are a bad omen, then," she jokes.

I laugh, smudging my eyeshadow. Oops, I guess my smoky eye is extra smoky tonight. "Good. Hopefully, they'll stop me from making poor decisions."

"Hopefully not," she counters, standing up and smoothing her poker-straight red hair back behind her shoulders. She adjusts her tiny green bodycon dress and seriously looks like a temptress version of Ariel, the Little Mermaid. Lia knows she is seriously hot and likes to flaunt it, as she should. She teases every guy who looks her way and breaks hearts left, right and centre when they find out she is so loved up with her boyfriend of three years, Causus.

"Is Coze out tonight?" I ask. Caus lives behind me, and Lia met him the day I moved in. She was texting him later, and I read his name on her phone as 'Coze'. We found it way funnier than it actually was, but it stuck.

"Nah, he had his own thing to do. He'll meet me at mine later. Remind me to give you the spare key for his house."

We share a back fence, and I always use his house as a drop off point for taxis. You can never be too careful, and I'm always on edge going home alone late at night. This way, if a stalking serial killer trails me (as they do), they'll have the wrong address and will either find it empty or come face to face with 6ft of muscled bad-ass. Win-win.

"Thanks. Right, this is as good as it's getting," I claim as I stand up and spin to face Lia. "Passable?"

"Shut up, dork," she says, rolling her eyes at me. "You are a stone-cold fox, how are you the only person who can't see that?"

"So, is that a yes?"

"Seriously, Lai. How do you not know that? Guys queue up to hit on you every weekend. You're only self-conscious because Jed gave you like one compliment the whole time you were together."

"Are you hyping me up or bumming me out? Plus, the guys at Encore hit on every single woman in there, that means nothing. Come on, the taxi will be here in ten and you've promised me another drink," I say, heading out towards the kitchen.

I wiggle my way up to the bar next to Lia and she elbows me in the ribs. "Oh my God, check out the guy at 12 o'clock." I bite back my grumble from my smarting torso and look across the horseshoe bar. "He's not even top tier," she continues, "he may be an actual God. If you don't hit that, I will."

"No, you won't. You and Coze are so loved up it's sickening."

"Fair," she says with a moony smile. "But that just leaves you. Say hi!"

"I'm going to need a little more direction than 'say hi', it's been forever."

"You'll be fine, it's like riding a bike."

I huff and stamp my foot like a child but she stares impassively at me, so I grab my purse and make my way around the bar. This is fine, I can do this. Just say hi. Doesn't mean you have to marry the guy, Madelaine, chill out. But if he ignores me, I'll die on the spot. That's a promise. I pop myself in next to the guy in question, and

God is a very apt description. Surely he's a model. I could see him on a billboard somewhere, wrapped in leather and standing in front of a motorbike. What the hell was Lia thinking sending me over here? Yes, I get hit on as much as the next girl, but men are simple-minded. There is no way I am in the same league as this guy. He's going to laugh in my face. I contemplate slinking back to Lia with my tail between my legs when the bartender calls over, asking me what I want. Busted. I order a shot of tequila. Clearly nerves are doing a number on me, as I hate the stuff. They place it down in front of me, and I'm suddenly aware of the stranger's eyes boring into my skull. I take the shot, and with the amber liquid warming my throat, I turn and look straight into dusky green eyes. Don't knock Dutch courage, that shit is priceless.

"Hi," I blurt out. Nailed it.

"Hi."

"You're quite the starer," I reply, his gaze still on me. He doesn't react, his silence making me agitated. "Would you like a drink?"

"I think that's my line."

"I guess we're role-playing now, then," I say with an arch of my brow. I don't know where that came from, but I don't hate the confidence I gain from bantering with this guy.

His eyes flash and I heat, thanking the high heavens for my deep complexion that hides a flaming blush. Something in the back of my brain tells me to end this conversation and back away slowly, preferably without turning my back on him. Men like him are dangerous; I'm sure he could make me do things I'd never normally consider.

Before my brain can overrule my hormones, he answers me. "In that case, I'll have a whiskey."

"I would never order that, you're terrible at this game," I chide playfully.

His lips tilt into a full smirk, showing through ashy blonde stubble, which transforms his angelic resting face into one of pure sin. I want him to do it again and again. Making him smile is already addictive.

"Well, you're me, aren't you? So enjoy it."

"Okay then," I say, turning to the bartender, "he'd love a French martini, please."

We're silent while they make our drinks, me watching the bartender and him watching me. It makes my skin itch, in a good way. When the drinks are done I pay as he watches, amused. We both sip our drinks and wince.

"Maybe we should..." he starts, gesturing at our glasses for us to swap. "I never needed roleplay for a good time anyway."

It's sheer luck that I don't spit my drink straight out. He takes the whiskey glass from my hand and takes a large gulp directly over where my lipstick has stained the edge.

I feel a phantom tingling in my lips and wet them with my tongue.

His gaze zeroes in on my bottom lip, and the tension between us feels too much. I have to clear my head before I climb him like a tree right here at the bar.

"Nice to meet you," I say lamely before I walk back around the bar to Lia.

"What happened?" she asks the second I'm within earshot, but I can still feel his eyes on me. I down my drink before pulling her back into the crowd, away from his piercing gaze. I attempt to dance like nothing happened but Lia is having none of it.

"What happened?!" she echoes, and I sigh.

"Maybe it's too much, too soon. I don't know what I'm doing!"

"You think too much, you need a baptism of fire before you talk yourself out of it. Go with your gut for once and not your brain that only works at 250 miles an hour!"

I don't give her a reply and she rolls her eyes before we lose ourselves to the rhythm of the music and the thumping beat of the dancefloor, while I try not to think only of those sage eyes.

Lia and I walk out an hour later gulping in fresh air after the close heat of the club, and we wander a short way down the street towards the taxi rank.

"Oh, look," Lia says in a bored tone, pointing. "It's your wet dream car." An all black Hummer with tinted windows sits directly in front of the last waiting cab. I walk up to it and run my fingers softly down the side. She's right. This baby is my ultimate life goal. I've always wanted one when I am officially a Bad Bitch With Her Life Together™. As I caress the side, a voice from behind makes me jump.

"Do you want a ride, or are you happy to continue stroking it?"

Recognising the deep voice and blushing again at the insinuation, I spin to face the guy from the bar. He's bigger than he seemed in the dark club, closer to six and a half feet than six, with hair the same ashy blonde as his stubble. I normally don't go for man buns but this guy pulls it off, looking like a Viking in a three-piece suit. A type I never knew I had but definitely do now.

"You want two women to jump into a blacked-out gangster vehicle with someone they just met? Thanks but no thanks, even when the ride is that pretty." He may have been sex walking, but I have some preservation instincts.

"Pretty?!" While he's busy scoffing at the dent to his car's image, I wander over to the last idling taxi. I turn to Lia, opening the door with one hand.

"We'll get this-" but before I can finish my sentence, someone jumps in the other side and leans over, pulling the door shut again.

"Hey!" I shout, but the car is already peeling away from the curb.

"There's that problem solved," Lia grins, way too eager to get into the murder truck.

"We were going to hit the drive-thru on the way back," I say petulantly, gesturing at the car. "Plus, yours is way too big to get in." His lips twitch. Oh my God, what is wrong with me? Next week, I'll be the designated driver. Maybe.

"We'll work something out," he says. He opens the door for us to climb in and I jump at the guy already behind the wheel. "This is Jeremy," he offers as I take in the stern, older-looking gentleman who nods at us both. He has a definite authoritative air about him. I settle next to Lia, who is half asleep already, as the guy gets in the passenger seat.

Lia gets dropped off first, professing that she's tired and wants to get back to Caus, but she's full of shit and I vow she'll pay the next time I speak to her. As she gets out, she hands me the key which I had definitely forgotten about, which brings her minutely back from the best-friend doghouse. The guy swaps to the backseat when Lia leaves and I think of asking his name, but he hasn't asked mine. Maybe if I keep up these little invisible barriers, I'll have more luck acting wild. I'm lost in thought of how attached you can get to someone without knowing their basic information and staring blindly out the window when he interrupts my inner musings.

"Come here," he whispers. I'm torn between heating at his bossiness and raising my hackles.

"Er, excuse me. Do I look like some pet that obeys commands from where you're sitting?" Okay, hackles raised. His eyes flash but I catch Jeremy's smirk in the rear-view mirror, so I don't get too worried.

"Come here, please," he repeats. I scoot over an inch towards him but that's clearly not good enough as he lifts and pulls so my legs lounge over one of his and his hand roots itself on my thigh. He acts nonchalant as he starts skating patterns over my jeans that feel nicer than I care to admit. As we drive along, his hand inches slowly higher until his knuckles brush my zipper whenever his fingers bend.

We park up and I'm so focused on keeping my breathing even that I haven't realised we've reached Taco Bell. Wow, I must've really sounded childish if this is what he decided on, I don't remember admitting to my favourite guilty pleasure.

"What is it you wanted? Jeremy's going to go in." On any other day I could probably recite their menu, but tonight my brain is not working to full capacity with his hand so close to my centre.

"Anything. Surprise me?" I ask with a smile to Jeremy, regretting making a big deal about food now. Jeremy slips out and as soon as the door shuts, the God's hand is slipping through my hair and around the nape of my neck. I don't have time to think before his lips are on mine. The kiss starts gently enough, our lips exploring each other and getting into a rhythm. It deepens and becomes hungrier as his tongue slips into my mouth.

My brain screams at me to slow down, but the erratic beat of my heart and the steady thump of arousal between my thighs drowns it out. He lifts my hips effortlessly so I'm straddling his lap and his hands move up over my waist. We're still kissing frantically while he massages my breasts through my top.

I break away with willpower I didn't know I possessed but he moves his lips to my jaw, nipping along and down my neck. "Jeremy will be back soon," I say huskily, barely recognising my own voice.

He flicks the doors locked without pulling away and murmurs against my skin. "He'll get the message."

That doesn't sound massively fair, but it has been 9 months since someone has kissed me, let alone like this. To be honest, the building exploding and free tacos raining from the sky couldn't get me to stop, probably.

He undoes the clasps down the front of my top and presses his mouth to my free nipple, biting down slightly. I arch my back as the sensation travels straight to my core, rocking my hips and trying to create some friction between us, but my jeans restrict me.

"Who wears jeans to a club?" he grumbles, replacing his mouth on my breasts with his hand, kneading them in a way that has my breath hitching in my throat.

"They're to stop me from making poor decisions."

"How's that going for you?" he asks as he undoes them, slipping his hand into my underwear.

Any coherent thoughts of answering fly out of my head as his fingers run along my slit to my entrance. "Fuck, you're so wet," he growls, as he slips two fingers inside me. I tense at the intrusion and he slows, capturing my mouth with his and kissing me senseless until my body relaxes. He slowly pumps his fingers inside me while the heel of his palm rubs against my clit. I moan as his free hand grips my hair and pulls slightly, arching my back further as he runs his tongue around my nipple, sucking it into his mouth. The sting from my scalp and the warm pressure from his mouth along with the magic he is weaving in my panties has me quickly on the edge of release. He releases my breast, mumbling into my neck, “So fucking hot. Once you’ve come all over my hand, you’re going to ride my cock.”. His words tip me over and I detonate around his fingers, releasing a scream which he swallows, kissing me and continuing with his fingers until I’ve ridden the whole orgasm out.

In what seems like the blink of an eye in my addled state, he flips me back onto my seat, pulling my jeans and now ruined panties off. He pulls me back over his lap and my brain swims a little with the alcohol and the orgasms and the moving. I grip his shoulders as he grabs my hips to steady me.

“You okay?” he asks, worry in his eyes.

I nod and lean into him, kissing him this time, not wanting this to stop. It’s not long before he takes back control and he pulls my hips back and forth, rubbing his cock from my swollen clit to my entrance, lining himself up. Suddenly, the door handle goes and I freeze. His lips continue to kiss down my neck as he repeats, “he’ll get the message”. The door doesn’t burst open and the kisses reach the soft patch under my ear, so I find it hard to worry.

“If you make my tacos go cold, I’ll castrate you,” I mutter.

“Better get on with it then, haven’t we?” He grips my ass and squeezes, pushing me down so he slips partway inside me and I gasp at his size. He stops and grunts as my fingernails dig so hard into his shoulders, they must draw blood. The sound of our laboured breathing fills the car.

“Fuck, you’re so tight,” he groans and grips my hips even harder, surely leaving bruises. He gives me a second to adjust to his girth before moving underneath me with shallow thrusts, but he’s way bigger than I was expecting.

“Relax, baby,” he whispers into my mouth as he kisses me slowly, gently circling my clit with his thumb and causing pleasure to run through my entire body. He slips deeper inside of me until he’s fully seated and a growl emanates from deep within his chest. We sit like that for a second until I’m desperate for some friction and start rolling my hips a little, investigating the sensation. He takes this as encouragement and guides me up and down his length, pumping from beneath me at the same time.

They're hard, fast strokes, coming nearly all the way out before slamming all the way home again.

Shattering in a ridiculously short time, I bite down on his shoulder to stifle another scream. I'm not too embarrassed as he follows me straight over the edge with a groan, his pulsing cock and the feel of him emptying inside me lengthening my orgasm. I rest my head on his shoulder and catch my breath for a moment before sliding off him with a wince, his erection still semi-hard. Not wanting to put my panties back on, I wrestle with my jeans while he tucks himself back into his trousers. He reaches down and grabs my discarded panties from the footwell before I can, slipping them into his pocket. I wind both windows down to dissipate the smell of sex, and Jeremy notices from outside the restaurant. He hangs up the call he's on and before the God or I can make any awkward post-sex small talk, heads back to the car.

TWO

ATLAS

It's quiet as we drive towards her house. I'm currently not capable of coherent thoughts, let alone speech, although I wonder why she's so distant. The sex was incredible and normally that made women like limpets, but not this one. Half of my brain is cursing me for not using a condom. Quinn is going to kill me, he is always so paranoid about women using us. The other half of my brain just wants me to reach over, grab her, and impale her back on my cock, whether Jeremy is in the car or not.

She's the first woman I've fucked since Cara, but even as I think of them in the same sentence I know she's different. Cara was the last girl we'd all attempted to share, but it was a relationship of convenience for me. Max had started it and even he wasn't that into her. She definitely wasn't someone Quinn or I would've chosen for ourselves. That was the problem with sharing, there was never a girl for all of us. I hadn't even had a full conversation with this girl and I knew she was it for me. I wouldn't let her go. The question is, where do we go from here? She is mine, that's for sure. She just doesn't know it yet. However, it's hard to accept the fact she sits one seat over, studiously ignoring me. She hasn't even asked my name. Is she really okay with this just being a one-time thing? Like I'd let her get away that easily.

The bartender had said she'd never gone home with anyone apart from her friend, even with guys constantly hitting on her. Not that he was happy to relay that information, but our reputation helped us out more often than not, and this time was no exception. There was a reason I was the first to take her home. She had to feel the chemistry between us. So what is she playing at now? God, she's stunning. Thick dark hair with soft caramel skin. And those eyes. Almond and deep, they could easily hypnotise you. I'm so busy fantasising about the woman sitting next to me that I don't notice us pull up until she pops open the door.

"Thanks so much for the ride, bye!" she calls cheerfully, without looking back at me. She hops out and slams the door shut.

"Wait!" I call, but she's already at the front door. That's okay, I know where she'll be next Saturday. That bartender was useful, but maybe kept too close an eye on my girl.

Heading home, I think back to the argument earlier. Max and Quinn will love her, I can already tell. But Quinn was right, the drama that comes with sharing isn't worth it. I'm just thanking my lucky fucking stars I found her first.

The idea of sharing works well in theory. Three guys to give one girl all she could want, and to pick up the slack when the others are busy or being assholes, which we can be. Plus, you get to watch her being fucked. Group activities are fun for everyone! But theory is not actual life, and it never ends well. Our experience so far is that one of us always gets picked in the end, and we've never actually liked the girls enough to want their full attention. Plus, dynamics are always off when you try to go from a group relationship to a couple who live with the exes. Awkward.

Our move to Ironhaven signals a fresh start, seeing our own girls only. Although we've been so busy since we got here that we have had little time to meet anyone, and none of us have seemed interested, anyway. Quinn especially. Which surprises me, seeing as he was the advocate for separating our love lives and he loves to have a girlfriend to spoil. I walk into the house and make myself a drink at the bar before joining the guys on the couch.

"Where have you been?" Quinn asks.

"You keeping tabs on me now?"

"I thought you were checking out the new club, but you smell like sex."

"I did," I reply, annoyed he's so astute and reluctant to give him any more information.

"Fuck someone in the bathroom? That's one way to kick-start your newfound singledom," he smirks back.

"Car, actually." He's pissing me off. "And I'd say my single status is coming to a swift end."

"Fucking hell, you don't hang around. Who is she?"

"What's it to you?"

He rolls his eyes at me. "Chill, At. I'm not trying to steal her from you, I'll run a check on her if you're suddenly in love."

"As if you could," I reply, unable to let that one go. "But I'm not doing a background check on her."

"Why not?" Max interrupts. "We always do checks on our girls."

"Good thing she's not *our* girl then."

"Since when are you territorial?" Max continues. "You've never been fussed before."

"This is different. I don't want the sharing shit to scare her off."

"What's her name?" Quinn pipes back up. For fuck's sake, why can't he drop it?

"I don't know," I mutter.

He chokes out a disbelieving laugh. "So you don't even know her name and yet you're ready to throw down to keep her to yourself? Does she have a magic pussy or something?"

"Shut the fuck up, Quinn. I want to get to know her the normal way, it's boring as shit when you find out everything through a report. I'll know what she wants to tell me."

"Which at the moment is a grand total of fuck all."

I clench my fists, determined not to swing at him. He is like a brother to me, after all. 15 years of friendship can't be ruined by him mocking my connection with a woman I've only met once.

"How did you let her get away with giving you nothing?" Max asks, always the rational one, silently thinking it all through.

"I dropped her off, so I have an address. Which you're not having, Quinn," I add as he opens his mouth. "And I know where she'll be every Saturday, at our club."

"Can we all remember we came to Ironhaven for business and not to stalk ghost pussy?" Quinn adds. I glare daggers at him, and he shrugs cockily before leaving.

"Ignore him. You know he's still worked up about Cara," Max explains.

"Why? None of us gave a shit about her."

"He hates when he's chosen more than when he's not. It disrupts the status quo and exacerbates his trust issues. Cara spent months promising him the world, that she could love us all."

God, yeah. I'd forgotten how clingy she was.

"It turned out she was playing us both to stay close to Quinn. He feels guilty and betrayed," Max continues.

"Whatever, I've already forgotten about her."

"What's this one like?" he asks.

I'm hesitant, but finally admit it. "She seems pretty fucking perfect so far."

"What a great time to stop sharing," he mutters sarcastically.

I've spent the last seven days thinking of nothing but her, and yet my memory still hasn't done her justice. I watch her moving around the dance floor for an hour, waving off guy after guy offering her drinks. She's wearing black satin cuffed joggers that are cropped just above the ankle and strappy shoes that make her legs look a million miles long. A black strapless top leaves a strip of tanned abdomen on display. Fuck, I'm getting hard just picturing uncovering more of that golden skin. She heads over to the bar and a guy elbows his mates before following her over. I don't think so. I park myself at the bar next to her, but she's got her head turned, nodding at whatever he's saying to her. She rests her chin on one hand. It becomes quite apparent she's not involved in the conversation at all, he's talking at her while she nods along. The bartender comes over and I speak over the guy she's with.

"One whiskey, neat, and a French martini," I say as she stiffens, clearly recognising who's behind her. The guy harassing her looks over her shoulder with a disgruntled expression but pales when he sees me and leaves, murmuring a goodbye. My reputation does wonders. Good fucking riddance.

"Wow," she says, turning to face me. "That was quicker than I've ever gotten him to leave."

"I'm efficient," I reply. "How many times have you tried to get away from him?"

"Every Saturday for the past six weeks. God may like a trier, but I certainly do not." She rolls her eyes but my blood heats and I'm considering going to find this guy when the drinks appear in front of me.

"Taken a liking to them now, have you?" She nods towards the pink cocktail and I slide it over to her.

"For you."

"Thanks," she grins before picking it up and disappearing back into the crowd. I stand there, slightly bemused. Surely that's not it? Is she actually expecting us to be just a one-night thing? Not if I have anything to do with it.

She dances with her same friend from last week for hours until the club quietens down, and like a sad sack I wait around for the chance to speak to her again. Finally, they head to the bathroom. I hang about in the corridor and when they emerge I step forward and catch my girl's hand, stopping her from passing. They both spin to see who's grabbed her and her friend smirks when she sees it's me.

"Can I borrow her for a second?" I ask, pushing her back into the bathroom.

"Take as long as you need," her friend offers as I shut the door and lock it behind me.

"Rude, much?" she asks, putting her hands on her hips.

"Me? Were you just planning to ignore me all night?"

"We spoke earlier," she replies, eyes still defiant. I step towards her and for each step I take, she takes one back.

"Let me give you a lift home. This place shuts soon," I offer, desperate to extend any time with her. I step forward again, and she bumps against the vanity behind her.

"No thanks. Coze is picking us up. We don't make a habit of getting more than one lift from strange men who don't even tell us their name."

"Who's Coze?" I ask, leaning forward and putting my hands on the counter on either side of her, caging her in and putting our mouths inches apart.

"Who are you?" she counters. I could have a lot of fun with this sass and my dick twitches at the thought.

"Atlas," I concede.

"Well, Atlas, this isn't a good idea," she says, putting her hands on my chest. She pushes lightly, with no actual force behind it. "Especially since the last time, neither of us remembered a condom."

Shit. "I'm clean," I blurt out, suddenly desperate to ease her worry. I still can't believe it. "I've never done that before. You make me lose my mind a bit, you know."

Her eyebrows raise slightly and as her fingers curl in my shirt, she closes the gap between our mouths. I let her explore a little until she tentatively licks my lips and I lose what little control I have left. I press my body against the full length of her and feel her perfect tits pressing against my chest. She slides her hands up over my shoulders, wrapping her arms around my neck and I lift her so she's sitting on the edge of the countertop and I'm settled between her thighs. The car hadn't afforded enough flexibility to be this close, and I'm heady with the feel of her lithe body wrapped around me. There's no gentle lead-up. Even with her earlier feeble protests she's not hesitating, and there's no way I will either. We both know how good this can be and want to get there as quickly as possible.

This wasn't actually my plan. I wanted to pull her aside and talk, but when she ignored me that calm approach went out the window. She brings out the feral in me. I run my hands over her hips, tugging at her waistband until she lifts, allowing me to get rid of her trousers and panties. Seriously, what is with the awkward clothing? Not that it's stopped us either time we've been together. I start undoing my trousers when she takes over, rolling down my zip and pulling me out into her soft hand. I nearly come on the spot like an overexcited teenager. She raises a brow at my gasp.

"Condom?" she asks.

My face must fall because she smirks slightly. "If you give me an STD, I will castrate you."

"That's the second time you've threatened to make me a eunuch, I must be doing something wrong." I pull her legs higher around my waist and she leans back on her hands as I line myself up with her, rubbing my tip in her wet folds.

"Practice makes perfect," she says with a challenge in her eyes. Fuck, she's sexy. I thrust my hips towards her, and she rolls her head back with a gasp as I enter her up to the hilt. I don't give her time to get used to the fullness this time, her breath catching as I pull out and ram in again and again. There's no way I'm lasting very long, watching her brow furrow and mouth pop open in an 'O' of pleasure. I use my thumb to rub circles around her clit and feel her tightening around me as she lets out a husky moan, "*Atlas.*" My name has never sounded sexier and I follow her over the edge in seconds, filling her with my cum. We stay like that, leaning against the counter with her legs wrapped around me, my length still inside her while we catch our breath. After a minute she sits up and pushes lightly against me until I step back, slipping out of her.

"Hang on a second," I say, running the tap next to her and putting myself away, but she's already down and heading to the cubicle.

"I've got it." I stand awkwardly outside as she cleans up. She's so closed off again as soon as we've finished. Neither of us can deny how explosive we are together when our bodies are involved, but surely she can't think that's all this is? She seems to have no interest in knowing anything past my name. I pop her panties in my pocket just as the cubicle door opens. She exits and begins pulling her trousers on, looking at me suspiciously when she can't locate her underwear.

"Okay, seeing as my trousers are doing nothing to stop my poor decisions, I have to say it out loud. This won't be happening again." She heads to the door without giving me a chance to answer and mutters, "I need to find a new bar."

"What's wrong with this one?" I laugh, trying to prolong the conversation as she's trying to make a speedy exit.

"It's got a shit cocktail list, clearly French martinis cloud my judgement," she says with a pointed look and then she's gone. I decide to let her go. Let her think she has some say over this, but really, she's already mine.

THREE

MADELAINE

Work on Monday absolutely drags. I love my job, but some days seem to last a week, especially when I can't stop my mind wandering to amazing orgasms in incredible cars and dingy bars. My mood switches between feeling euphoric when I remember the last two Saturdays and being confused as to who I've become. I'm not the girl who has one-night stands. As much as I tried to convince Lia I was, I wasn't convincing her or myself, really. I feel like there's an angel Madelaine on one shoulder, and a devil Amelia on the other who is kicking Madelaine's heavenly butt. Am I just trying to prove the point that I can be wild?

Even as I think that, I know it's not the case. I actually wanted to sleep with a stranger. Not that there's anything wrong with that, but I've never been brave enough. To be honest, I've never been so attracted to someone that I couldn't wait to get to know them and find a bed before I mounted them. With Jed, our relationship didn't have this fiery passion. We got together so young and then stayed together because we hadn't found a reason not to be. Yes, we had sex, because it was what couples did. I never initiated it or felt sexy around him. Atlas awakens something in me that I didn't even know was there. He makes me feel brave, powerful, and so sexy that I can make a guy like him lose control. Yes, I know I'm not hideous, but most people aren't and Jed never hyped me up. I guess he was as used to me as I was to him. Like furniture that you're so used to being there, you don't even really see it anymore.

I'm brought out of my inner monologue (accompanied by tiny violin) by Kacey wandering out of the office next to mine, followed by her client. My former assistant almost exclusively uses her outside voice inside, so you can't help but eavesdrop on her conversations. I refuse to feel bad about it. Jason recently gave her the opportunity to be a trainee architect, which I'm super happy about. We used to be close but since she moved up she's had this weird competitive energy which I can't entertain; there's room for every successful woman in the workplace.

"I just need this restaurant to be incredible, Kacey. I'm surprised I snapped it up at all with the rate the Titans are claiming real estate around here," the client says in a voice far too whiny for someone his age.

"I know, as if we need more criminals around here," she agrees as they walk to the elevator waiting at the bank. Kacey returns when she's dismissed her client and plonks herself in the chair opposite me without invitation.

"Mr Kane moaning about real estate again, it's not the Titan's fault he takes a full month to make the tiniest decision." She rolls her eyes, changing her tune completely from moments ago. I studiously ignore her, but she ignores me ignoring her and continues on, our usual routine when she wants to gossip.

"Apparently they've moved into the city and are taking over all the businesses. Everyone thinks it's a front for their dodgy activity."

"Everyone thinks, or everyone knows? It sounds like an excuse for Mr Kane's terrible business sense," I say. I wouldn't normally speak unprofessionally about a client, but he was a hideous sleaze and was always making slimy comments about Kacey working for him *personally*.

"Well, my friend Sarah's friend Jessica heard from her nail girl Jade that they're fitter than gods themselves. Said she'd let any of them do criminal things to her."

I stare at her blankly, trying to unpack that sentence as she continues on her third... or fourth-hand gossip tirade. "The Vipers aren't happy about it, apparently. Mr Kane says we'll be lucky if there's not a gang war on our streets within weeks."

"This isn't a movie, Kace. We're not surrounded by heroes and villains."

"You should hope so, cause they'd all be villains from what I've heard."

Jason saves me from having to find a response to that, thank God. "Hey Lai, got a minute?"

"Yeah, of course." Kacey stays in my spare seat, studying her nails. "In your office?"

He rolls his eyes at her. "I guess so."

I follow him to his office and shut the door behind me.

"We've got a new pitch, and I thought I'd give it to my star if you want it," he says, getting straight to the point.

My turn to roll my eyes. "Flattery means something bad."

"It's just a refurb in town. Plus, I know how much you love the place."

"Where?"

"Encore."

"Oh, cool. What's the bad news then?"

He attempts to give me puppy dog eyes but can't quite pull them off, so I stare at him flatly.

"They want to start the refurb within the month so pitches are due ASAP, and I'd like them in by Wednesday so they don't have a chance to find someone else before they see ours," he reams out in one breath.

"Jesus, two days? You're lucky I love that place. And you, but you owe me." I stand, actually excited to get stuck into a new project so close to my vodka- and dance-loving heart.

"Add it to the list of favours you've clocked up. Good thing you never cash them in or I might go bankrupt. I'm sending the deliverables to you now," he says, turning to the computer and clicking away before I've even left.

I head back to my office buzzing with ideas about the refurb. *Could I add a new cocktail menu to the requirements? It took me weeks to coax a French martini out of them.* Kacey is, of course, still lounging where I left her. "Kace, I've got a big job on so I need to get back to work, if you don't mind?"

"Fine, I'll go hang with the other minions," she says petulantly

I ignore that comment. "Bye, Kace."

It's Saturday night and I am so far past tipsy. It's Lia's birthday so we've dressed up and completed a cocktail bar crawl that ends here at Encore, of course. I'm dressed way out of my comfort zone in something skin-tight and tiny, although the high neck offsets some of the flesh on display. It's sleeveless, and the section that would normally sit over my left thigh and hip has been replaced with sparkly tassels. I love it and it didn't take Lia much guilt-tripping to get me to go all-out for her big day. My hair is sleek and down my back, with my signature smoky eye darker than normal to compliment the black dress. Finished off with my Louboutins and I feel a million dollars.

I feel Atlas's presence on my back and smell his smoky aftershave before I see him. The drinks lift my confidence so I press back into him, continuing to sway my hips to the music when I should be running in the other direction. Devil Lia - 3, Angel Lai - 0.

"I didn't think I'd see you tonight," he murmurs in my ear.

"I'm sure you've been pining," I reply sarcastically, spinning to face him. I don't know what it is, but he makes me want to constantly agitate him. He cuts off any more potential sass with a forceful kiss that doesn't end until my arms are around his neck, my body pressed against his. He breaks apart from me and attempts to pull me along behind him but in my inebriated state I trip over my own feet and nearly face plant the floor. His hands appear suddenly on my upper arms, steadying me.

"You're drunk," he says, amused.

"You're observant," I fire back.

He changes course and instead pushes me against the wall slightly off the dance floor, in a more secluded corner.

"I'd like to see you try to sass me with your mouth filled with my cock."

God, that's hot. He kisses me again, running his hand up the outside of my thigh. I arch into him, feeling the evidence against my stomach that he's just as turned on as I am. His words light a fire inside me, and feeling reckless I reach between us and stroke him through his trousers. His considerable size is still obvious through his clothes. He pulls my hand away while still stroking the bare skin of my hip. That feels massively unfair to me, so I wiggle my hand from his and grab him again.

"Not that I wouldn't happily fuck you right here and make everyone watch, but you're way too drunk," he says against my lips, too reluctant to pull away from the kiss completely.

"You don't seem like a guy with solid morals," I pout childishly.

"Ouch," he replies, grabbing my hip so that his thumb grazes under my dress and along my bikini line. "No underwear?" he asks, and it's a wonder I can think straight with my fuzzy alcohol brain short-circuiting every time his thumb sweeps over the sensitive skin where my underwear should be.

"Maybe somebody else already pocketed them." Okay, so sarcasm is muscle memory at this point.

"You'd better hope that's not fucking true, baby." There must be something wrong with me because the murderous look in his eyes makes everything down south clench.

"Where have you been?" he asks. I roll my eyes, not about to explain myself to a man, but he doesn't let me get away with it. "Keep it up, baby. I'll happily spank that attitude out of you."

Lia interrupts while I try to pick my jaw up off the floor. Dirty talk is definitely a newfound turn-on for me.

"Lai, there you are. Photo time!" she squeals.

I grab Atlas's arms and try to step in front of him for the obligatory prom photo, but I really am quite drunk as he so helpfully pointed out, and I pitch forward. At least I trip on his feet this time, much more respectable than tripping on my own. He catches me around the waist and I laugh.

"Maybe we should sit," he suggests, walking me back a few steps to the sofa lining the edge of the room. He sits and pulls me into his lap, where I happily settle myself, crossing my legs in between his thighs.

"Thanks," I beam down at him, getting a returning smile that could rival the sun. I don't think I've seen him smile properly before, a smirk normally playing on his lips.

"You should smile more often," I tell him.

"There are plenty of ways you could make me," he returns.

"Okay, all done," Lia declares, having apparently been snapping pictures the whole time. She hands the phone to me, but Atlas intercepts it and takes it from her.

"Birthday nights have to be documented, it's the rule," she explains to him.

Atlas scrolls to a photo of us from seconds before, me perched in his lap, him with one arm around my waist and the other hand in the space my dress leaves on my thigh. I'm speechless as I stare at the photo of us smiling at each other while eye-fucking. I can't believe it's me in that photo. I can't believe it's us. He swipes to another, from when I tripped. I'm leaning forward, laughing my head off while he grabs my waist from behind, looking down at me. His gaze is soft, adoring. It's too much for my brain to handle right now. Did that drunken fumble mean more than I realised?

"I'm going to the toilet," I blurt, standing from his hold and practically running to the bathroom. Lia follows me a couple of minutes later and finds me leaning against the counter, effectively hiding.

"What took you so long?" I ask, whining.

"He wanted me to send him the photos," she shrugs.

"So now he has your contact details?"

"Calm down, loon, I airdropped them. You want to make a run for it?"

"No, it's fine. I don't want to end your birthday because of my freak-out."

"A completely unnecessary freak-out. Those photos were so hot! But I'm ready to call it a night anyway, this place closes soon and Caus just texted to say he's home."

"If you're sure?" I ask, feeling guilty.

"Absolutely. Let me order an Uber and we'll see if we can convince them to go through the drive-thru. It is my birthday, after all."

I laugh at her, feeling my freak out disappear thanks to my incredible best friend.

FOUR

MAXTON

"I can't believe no one in this entire room can track down one woman," Atlas yells at the guys sitting around the conference table in our office. We've already been over the fact that "Lay" is not enough of a lead to find a person, so everyone wisely stays quiet.

Atlas glares daggers around the table. "What about the address?"

"Sir, that's not her address," Gus bravely offers.

"What do you mean? Jeremy and I dropped her there ourselves."

"But it's not registered to her, so it doesn't help," he practically whispers.

"Whose house is it?"

"Connor Jones. It was bought in his name three years ago."

Shit, did she have a boyfriend? Atlas's head looked close to exploding.

"Everybody out," he dismisses them, voice like ice.

As soon as the door shuts behind them, he grabs an abandoned glass from the table and throws it against the wall.

"Chill, man. It won't be the first time a girl's gone searching for some extra-curricular activities when her boyfriend's not satisfying her," Quince says unhelpfully.

"If she has a boyfriend, he's dead," Atlas spits.

"At, even we don't kill people for dating women we've fucked," I pipe up.

"I, for one, am relieved it's just a hidden boyfriend she's being secretive about and not something more sinister, especially since you can't seem to fuck her with a condom on."

"Shut the fuck up, Quinn," Atlas rages.

"I'm just saying-"

"Quince, enough. At, there's not a lot we can do right now, so chill."

"I'll chill when I've got her. Let the guys know that for every day they don't find her, I'm firing one of them. They should thank their lucky fucking stars I'm not breaking bones."

Atlas hasn't seen her in ten days. The last time he caught her she disappeared, and we've had to unexpectedly speed up the refurbishment on the club since then, so it's been shut since. It's a big warning sign that his mood is linked to seeing this girl he doesn't even know the name of. I don't blame Quince for being suspicious.

Jeremy chooses that moment to knock and enter, holding an envelope.

"What?" Atlas barks.

"Stop being such an asshole," I shoot at him. "What's up Jeremy?" I ask my second.

"There's suspicious activity at the Encore building site, I'm taking a few of the guys over there to check it out."

"Alright, I'll meet you there."

"Me too," Quince adds. "Anything to get away from this angry fucker." He jerks his head at Atlas, who flips him the finger in return.

Pulling up to the site twenty minutes later, all hell has broken loose.

"What the fuck's going on?" I ask Jeremy as he ambles over to us, calm in a storm of chaos.

"Max, Quince." He nods his head respectfully. "The security team for the contractors contacted us when they noticed something odd with the camera feed. Turns out it had been looped. I've fired them all, what a simple fucking trick to let through." I nodded, glad he'd already taken care of that. "We came down to see why anyone would've bothered with that on a building site and found a bomb in the primary room." He delivers that as if he's reciting what he had for breakfast. That explains the buzzing atmosphere around us. "It's real but was deactivated before being placed here. It was left showing one second left," he adds nonchalantly.

Quince and I both just blink at him for a minute but Quince recovers quickest. "I'm not telling Atlas." *Fucker.*

We spend a bit of time walking around with the guys, checking to see if anything else has been tampered with and looking at the bomb. It was only about the size of a carry-on, with a flashing one.

on the mini screen and a wire chopped at the back. Leaving the crew there to finish the building sweep and bomb disposal, we head back to the house, where we find Atlas still in the office. After updating him, we sit around discussing our theories. We've got a lot of great guys in the inner workings of our organisation, but we always discuss everything between us three first.

"Vipers?" Atlas offers the obvious suggestion.

"Bit subtle for them," I answer. "They don't tend to give second chances."

"And why would they pick that random bar to warn us about?" Quince asks. "We've flipped loads of businesses since being here and none of the other openings have been threatened."

"Another business associate? We know people aren't happy with how many properties we're buying up," I admit.

"No one would dare," Quince threatens.

"Hopefully we'll have something soon. Jeremy's bound to be combing the place."

Jeremy enters as if Atlas has summoned him. *Speak of the devil.*

"We found this under the bomb when it was moved," he says grimly, passing a photo over to Atlas.

"Motherfucker," he roars, ejecting from his chair and throwing his fist into the wall behind him.

Quince pulls the photo from Atlas's fist and whistles as he takes in the woman on the front.

"Fucking hell, At. No wonder she's made you crazy."

I take it from Quince and read the scrawled handwriting along the bottom. 'Ours'.

"So back to the Vipers?" I ask.

"Told you she's dodgy."

"Shut the fuck up, Quincy," Atlas and I both shout. "How can these people find her and none of our fucking useless lot can?"

"Because they already know her, duh."

At's jaw clenches as he holds himself back. "So they follow her to a bar and watch her with me? It doesn't make sense," he spits out between gritted teeth.

"If she's a Viper, then they'd have dealt with her themselves for sleeping with the enemy, not be sending obscure threats to us," I agree.

"So who, then?" Quince asks. "You said she was pretty popular. One of her disgruntled suitors, pissed off she put out so easily for you and not them?"

"Who knows, but whoever is daring to try and take her from me now must have a fucking death wish, and I'm going to fulfil it." He storms out of the office, slamming the door shut behind him so hard frames fall off the wall.

We've commandeered two of the new booths in Encore. I haven't seen the place since the bomb hoax, it now looks incredible. The primary room has two curved sides, one holding a row of booths and the opposite one holding the DJ stand on a stage. The dance floor sits in the middle with the entrance and cloakrooms off to one side. The bar is now nearly the full length of the wall opposite the dance floor, with a corridor that leads to the bathrooms and store rooms. A mirror covering the entire back of the bar holds shelves containing every drink imaginable, with 'Encore' in warm neon settled in the middle.

Atlas has circulated her picture to the guys and everyone has an eye out, but so far it doesn't look like she's here. His jaw clenches a bit more with each passing hour. We're not expecting anything to happen here tonight, not when the bomber gave us a very clear warning to stay away from her. But Atlas wasn't able to track her down, so he's desperate to see her.

Quince is off chatting with the manager and I can't take the tense atmosphere at the table much longer. Politely declining our server's offer, I decide to go to the bar to get a drink and detour via the bathroom. As I exit, I'm completely lost in thought and bump into the person walking in.

"Oh shit, sorry!" she exclaims. It's her, and she's phenomenal.

"No, my fault," I say automatically. I can't help but stare at her.

She gives a confused look, almost certainly noticing the recognition in my eyes. "Well, yeah, actually it was. I take it back. Why are you coming out of the ladies?"

"I'm not." I step back, revealing the men's sign.

"Ah, the ladies used to come first. I should've remembered they'd changed."

“So it is you who deserves the blame. How about I buy you a drink to soften that blow?”

“Sure,” she says, amused. “I’ll have a pretty Instagram-able cocktail, please.”

I head to the bar and order a rainbow layered daiquiri, sadly desperate to impress her. She finds me just as it’s put in front of me and takes it as I hand it over.

“I’m Maxton, by the way.”

“Thanks, Maxton,” she says, smiling as she slips back onto the dancefloor and gets swallowed by the crowd. Having been thoroughly dismissed, I head back to the table. Quince is still MIA and Atlas visibly relaxes when I let him know she’s here. We stand at the railing, watching her dance with her friend for a while. She's wearing a t-shirt style dress that seems see-through but when you look beneath it, it blurs what's underneath. As she moves under the lights it shows an hourglass body in a skintight black cami dress. Her friend locks eyes with Atlas and whispers in her ear, pointing up to us. She heads up the stairs to our booth and I try not to stare at her incredible legs in those sky-high heels. Eyeing me warily, she approaches us both.

"Of course you two know each other. How did you know who I was?" she directs at me.

"I didn't," I lie unconvincingly. I'm not even sure why, she's clearly observant enough to know I recognised her. Cool, calm, and collected Max has officially left the building. This Max is horny and dense.

Her eyes narrow at us and she turns to leave, but Atlas catches her before she can flee. "I need to talk to you."

"What you need is to get your hands off me," she retorts.

"What's got you so pissy?" he asks, dropping his grip on her arm.

"I think one of you as a stalker is enough, can you not enlist your friends to be my keepers?" she says, looking at me. "Wouldn't want to double your security bill."

"I'm sure you're worth it," I tell her truthfully.

"Oh, I definitely am."

"I'm serious. I'll give you a lift home later," Atlas interjects.

She eyes him warily. "This better not be your 'I've given you an STD' talk," she says, earning chuckles from the guys behind.

He sighs at her, keeping quiet.

"Do you ever think you might get what you want more if you bothered to ask, rather than order?" she asks primly.

"Seems to be working out okay for me so far," he replies with an arch of his brow.

She crosses her arms, but the sexual tension rolling off them could turn a nun into a nympho.

"Come on," he insists. "It's important."

"Okay, fine, I'll find you later."

"Or you could stay here," he says, winding an arm around her waist.

"With you and Tweedle Dee? No thanks."

She wriggles out of his hold and returns to the dancefloor while I chuckle. "That makes you Tweedle Dumb."

"Fuck off, Max," he laughs, his mood improved infinitely.

The guys chat between themselves, but Atlas and I spend the rest of the evening staring at her, transfixed. I know someone has warned us to stay away, but I don't know how that's going to be possible. She's like a magnet wandering around the room, attracting people into her aura. She can barely move without another guy approaching her, which I don't blame them for, but At looks like a tiger ready to pounce. I'm sure the only thing keeping him in his seat is the fact he doesn't want to jeopardise her leaving with us.

Quince finally comes back a little while later. "Any luck?"

"Yeah, I'm giving her a lift home."

"You mean I am?"

Atlas ignores that, knowing full well that Quince is our designated driver. Jeremy's off tonight, and we don't trust anyone else to drive us.

"Why are you even getting involved with her? The bomb shows she's bad news," he continues.

"No, the bomb shows someone else wants her, and I'm not surprised. But we've never let anyone threaten us before, and we're sure as fuck not going to start now," Atlas rants.

Quince gives up on going over this argument again. "I'm going to get a drink."

"It's table service," I remind him.

"Yeah, but Atlas isn't over there," he replies childishly.

We both roll our eyes at him as he wanders away from us.

FIVE

QUINCY

They haven't noticed she's at the bar, or they'd have questioned me further. I only just recognise her from the photo Atlas forced us all to memorise. You could tell she was gorgeous in that, but in real life, she practically glows. I slide in next to her as she looks to see who's coming to chat her up next. Her full lips are already parted, probably to brush me off, but she stops when she sees me and they tilt into a reluctant smile instead. She's only a few inches shorter than me in her heels and I don't see any recognition in her eyes, but maybe she's a brilliant actress.

The Vipers probably train them young. I smile at her in return, ready to dance with the devil.

"Can I buy you a drink?"

"Sure, thank you," she replies easily, not at all surprised by my abruptness. It's not a shock to me that she probably gets that offer a lot.

"You're welcome." I am nothing if not polite, whether or not this woman is a temptress spy. "What are you drinking?"

"Surprise me?" she asks, handing me the menu. "The new cocktails all look amazing."

Challenge accepted. I take the menu in one hand and stick the other out for her to shake.

"My name's Quincy, what's yours?" Time to get the information.

She looks quizzically at my outstretched hand before smiling and taking it in hers with a shake. "Madelaine." Now Lai makes more sense.

"Nice to meet you, Madelaine."

"Likewise, Quincy." I like the feel of her name in my mouth almost as much as I like hearing mine from hers. No one ever calls me Quincy. I'm not even sure why I introduced myself with it; I'm normally Quinn or Quince.

The bartender comes over and I find I don't want to let go of her hand. I reluctantly let go and point to a cocktail. "And a mocktail version, please," I add.

"No alcohol for you?"

"I'm designated driver tonight," I say with a grimace. "I'm sure I'll get another chance."

"Yeah? Do you come here often?"

"Not really, but it looks great now it's reopened." I keep to myself that the only other time I've stepped foot in this place, it was completely gutted and had a bomb sitting in the middle of it.

She gives me a weirdly proud look, which I can't quite decipher. Atlas said she was here all the time before, maybe she's pleased it's officially cool now that it's not such a shit-hole.

"What is it that you do?" she asks conversationally when I continue staring at her. I'd planned to charm her into spilling something useful on my way up here, but now it's like my brain is blank. A fully grown man, tongue-tied by a pretty girl. Okay, stunning girl, but still fairly pathetic on my part.

"Finance," I answer succinctly. "And you?"

Before she can respond, a woman taps her on the arm from behind, and she turns slightly.

"We're ready to go, Lai. What about you?"

"Okay. Atlas is here, so I'll grab a lift home with him. Do you want me to walk you out to Coze?"

"No, I'm good. Security is insane tonight, I'll be fine," her friend replies while rifling through her bag. It's about the size of an envelope, how she's lost anything in there, I'm not sure. She finally locates a key and hands it to Madelaine.

"Nice to meet you, Quincy," Madelaine says, getting ready to leave the bar and happy to end the night now that her friend's not staying. At that moment, the bartender puts our drinks down in front of us. She gives me an awkward look, then turns to the stranger on her other side.

"Here, I just got this, but I'm leaving. It's come straight from the bartender, it's good," she reassures her and the girl thanks her profusely.

"It's the thought that counts, right?" she asks, before pushing onto her toes and pecking me on the cheek, rendering me speechless. "Thank you." She flashes me a coy smile and follows her friend into the crowd. I watch them hug goodbye, then Madelaine heads over to where

Max and Atlas are sitting. I head to the exit to wait for them out by the car, knowing Atlas will leave straight away now that she's ready. Sure enough, a couple of minutes later they all head out together, and she slows when she sees me standing next to the Hummer.

"Quincy," she says with a glare, her eyes colder than they were at the bar. "Another minder for me, Atlas?"

"Something like that, Madelaine." I nod my head to her, not in a massive hurry to warm her up to him.

"Madelaine?" he asks, looking between us. "How did he get your name?"

"He asked," she says simply. She jumps into the passenger seat before anyone can object or get her door for her. She gives me an address and then spends most of the ride quiet. Her attention remains engrossed in her phone until we're not that far from her destination.

"So, what did you want to talk about?" she asks without taking her eyes off her phone.

I'm surprised at how restrained Atlas has been so far, but he's clearly over that now that she's invited the conversation. "Do you live alone?" he demands, like a creep. Madelaine must think the same because her fingers pause over the screen.

"Why, are you planning on breaking in?"

"Answer the question." She remains quiet, and it's clear she's going to do the opposite of that. Brave woman, taunting one of us.

Atlas sighs, clearly knowing what she's waiting for. "Answer the question *please*, Madelaine," he says with an edge to his tone.

"Yes," she says with a slight smirk that he thankfully can't see from his seat behind her. Her determination to provoke him amuses me and I have to stop myself from smiling at her.

"You sure about that?" he presses.

"Yes," she says, clearly done with this topic and going back to text.

"Who's Connor?" Atlas asks, not letting it drop.

"How would I know?"

"He owns the property you live in."

With this revelation, she forgets the phone and whips around in her seat. "What the fuck? What's this about?"

"It's about you living with a man in his house when you claim to be single," Atlas says, temper flaring, as I park opposite said house.

"First, I don't claim to be anything. I don't remember you stopping to ask me questions before you impaled me on that monster cock of yours. Second, my living arrangements are none of your business." She spins back around but freezes with her hand on the door handle as we all notice the flames in the background of her house. She stays rigid in her seat for a long moment, staring transfixed at the flickering light and shadows. Suddenly, she comes to and jumps out of the car with a gasp, rushing across the road and up the front steps of her home. She fumbles with the lock then speeds inside without shutting the front door behind her.

We're all out after her, curious about her haste, and follow into the house moments after her. It's weirdly bland and impersonal for such a vivacious person, but I don't have much time to look around as she rushes through the house and straight back out the patio doors.

"Fucking hell, Madelaine. Weren't you born with survival instincts?" Atlas calls after her. She ignores him, crossing the huge back garden and letting herself through a gate in the fence that separates her property from the one currently on fire. As she rushes through, a police officer spins and catches her as she tries to pass him. He clutches her around the waist as she flails wildly, struggling to get free.

"Hey, lady. Calm down," he shouts to her, but she's not listening. The guy is not that big and is clearly struggling to contain the wild woman. With a pointed look at his hands around her waist from Atlas, he hurriedly lets him take hold of her. His eyes widen as he recognises Atlas and looks behind him, taking in all three of us, but wisely chooses not to say anything.

"Get the fuck off me," Madelaine screams. "That's my house!"

"What?!" Now is clearly not the time to be asking her questions, but I have so many. *I knew she was hiding shit! Why not give a guy you've fucked multiple times your name?* Now it's obvious she didn't want to be found. It can't be a coincidence that her secret boyfriend lives behind her, but why have your fuck-buddy drop you at his house? We need so many answers. Atlas sees Madelaine is in no state to be explaining herself and tries to get some sense of the situation instead.

"What happened?" he asks the police officer. There are more people milling around, some pointedly not looking in our direction, but no firefighters yet so the fire rages out of control with black smoke billowing into the sky.

“Neighbours say it came out of nowhere,” he shouts back, his voice loud enough to be heard over the crackling of wood and the roar of the flames. “The first thing they knew was an explosion which we think was the car, and by the time they looked the entire house had gone up. Seems to have caught everything within minutes.” He directs all of this at Atlas, which enrages Madelaine even further.

“Why are you talking to him? This is my house!” The police officer looks to Atlas, who nods, which makes Madelaine huff. The police officer explains that they’re assuming an accelerant had been used because of the speed of the fire, so deliberate arson is likely. Madelaine stops fighting in Atlas’s arms and visibly deflates, looking suddenly very vulnerable and young.

“Can you come to the station and give a statement?” the police officer asks.

“Not now,” Atlas barks, but she doesn’t even appear to be listening and surprisingly doesn’t object to him answering for her. Now that she’s subdued, he lets her go to swap cards with the officer. The sound of sirens is growing closer when Madelaine turns and walks back through the gate, her arms wrapped around herself in comfort and her face hidden by a cascade of hair. We follow her and Atlas takes the keys, staying behind to lock up the doors as Max and I follow her to the Hummer. She leans against the door, watching the dancing orange flames for a moment until she lets her head fall back and closes her eyes. I take the opportunity while she's oblivious to take in her face. She is stunning, that can't be denied. Long, fluttery eyelashes, full pillowed lips, glowing caramel skin. She's doing a pretty good job of playing the part of the dejected homeless girl, but I've been with too many women putting on the act of a loving girlfriend to believe everything they show us. Footsteps approach as Atlas walks towards us, stopping right in front of her. His eyes search her face.

"Are you okay?" She doesn't answer, just shrugs and he grabs her hand, tugging her into his arms. They stay like that for a while, a shockingly intimate moment between them, until he leans into the passenger door to pull it open and guide her into the car. She gets in silently and he clicks her seatbelt, bending to pick up her phone that must have been dropped into the stairwell in her rush to get to her house. We all jump in after her, the stench of smoke following us and filling the car, and I pull out just as her phone vibrates in her hand. She stares at it as it rings out. When it immediately starts up again and the screen flashes Lia, Atlas reaches forward to take it from her. I turn up the music as Atlas explains the recent events to who I'm assuming is her friend from the bar, and since I haven't received any different instructions, we head home.

SIX

MADELAINE

I wake up in a dark and unfamiliar room, with sunlight peeking around the curtains. My phone is charging on the bedside table so I reach over to check the time. Nearly lunchtime already, I never sleep this late. There are also around a hundred messages from Lia so I call her back straight away, not bothering to get up first.

"Lai?!" she answers frantically.

"Morning," I mumble, my voice rough with sleep.

"Thank God, I thought you'd been murdered. I tried to get Atlas to drop you at mine but he was having none of it."

"It's fine, I'm still alive so far. Doesn't sound like it's them out to get me anyway."

"Yeah, Atlas filled me in. What the fuck? What are you going to do?"

"Right now? I don't know. What's the first step of getting your life back together when everything you own is gone?" I ask her, slightly melodramatically but I feel like it's justified.

"Shopping?" Lia asks hesitantly.

I smile at the turn in her tone, melancholy to cautiously hopeful in the blink of an eye. "Yeah, that seems right."

"I'll meet you at our coffee spot in an hour?"

"Perfect, this is why I love you."

"One of many, many reasons."

I laugh again and hang up, already feeling lighter. I reluctantly heave myself out of the massive bed I've found myself in and pad over to the curtains, pulling them open. The view is incredible, it's like I've woken up in a national park. Were we still in Ironhaven? I didn't recall driving for that long last night but I wasn't in the right frame of mind to be paying much attention. I don't remember much at all between the flames and waking up just now.

I spin slowly, taking in the stunning room which is full of different textures in natural beiges, creams, and bright whites. I collect some clothes that I'm hoping were left for me and don't belong to someone else and wander into the bathroom, emptying the huge tub and admiring the rest of the marble and gold fixtures. A memory invades my brain, of Atlas running it for me full of scented bubbles before feeding me as he tried to get me to relax. Was that right? It seemed real but he didn't seem like that kind of guy. How much damage could shock do to your brain?

I push those thoughts aside and get ready, making a mental note of what I need today. I figure two weeks worth of clothing and toiletries, some work makeup, shoes, and underwear should cut it. This leads me to thinking about actual errands I need to run and my head begins to swim. I message Jason and ask for tomorrow off, calling in a favour and apologising for the late notice. He replies quickly, saying he hopes everything's okay and that he has good news for me when I'm back.

I venture out of the room and wander along the hallway towards the sound of someone moving around. The doors are all shut down here but as I reach the end it opens up into one big space. The lobby and front door are to my right, and on my left is a huge open plan kitchen diner. The whole back wall is glass that looks over a large patio area with a pool. Wow. Where am I?! The kitchen itself is all white with a huge oak dining table opposite, a counter with bar stools sitting between the two areas. The source of the noise is an older lady unloading a dishwasher.

“Good morning, Miss,” she greets me. “Would you like anything to eat?” She doesn't appear to be surprised to see a strange woman wandering unescorted through the house.

“I’m good, thank you. And Lai is fine,” I reply with a small smile, still taking in the gorgeous surroundings.

“Lucy,” she replies and offers me her hand, which I shake. “Are you sure I can’t tempt you? These are just about finished.” She pulls out a dish of baked eggs from the oven and my mouth waters.

“They do smell delicious," I admit. "Do you know where Atlas is?”

“He left for lunch already,” Maxton replies from behind me, making me jump.

“Oh, thanks.”

Lucy puts two plates on the counter and excuses herself. I guess she took my admission as a request.

"How are you feeling?" Maxton asks as he sits down next to me. Suddenly I feel awkward in this space. He obviously feels at home here, is this his house? I feel self-conscious, being alone with this handsome guy. He's huge, both in muscle (which you can tell is stacked even through his shirt) and in height. I'm only 5'6 so the difference was about eight inches in my heels, but he bears down on me now that I'm barefoot. He's definitely the tallest of the three. I am wildly attracted to him, with his eyes almost black against his deep brown skin, and his black shaved faux hawk seems to beg me to run my nails through it. This attraction was okay when I thought I was flirting with a stranger at the bar, but now I know that he's Atlas's friend, I feel weirdly guilty. Added to the fact that he isn't flirting back, just keeping an eye on me like a child, I bristle internally.

"Better this morning, now I've got plans to sort my shit out." I start my breakfast, not wanting to talk anymore, but moan when I taste the first bite. This food is incredible. Screw the Hummer, hiring Lucy may now be at the top of my life goals.

Maxton clears his throat next to me, “Need any help?”

“No, I’m good, thanks. I’m about to Uber into town to meet Lia. I just wanted to thank Atlas before I went, but can you pass the message on?”

“Jeremy will take you,” he says, getting up and leaving before I can argue. I finish my breakfast and he returns while I’m washing my dish.

“I don’t need Jeremy to take me, I can Uber just fine.”

“Jeremy’s there for security, he also conveniently happens to have a car.”

“Why would I need security?” I ask, whipping round.

He shrugs. “You can chat to Atlas when you get back.”

“I’m not coming back. I'll just grab a hotel room for the night, then I’m arranging something more permanent tomorrow.”

“Atlas won't want that. And like I said, he wants to speak to you.”

“Then Atlas can come to me. Unlike some people I know, I don’t follow his commands,” I say with a pointed look.

“Fine,” he replies as if he’d rather be doing anything other than having this conversation. “You can have that argument with him, but Jeremy is still taking you.”

I concede with a nod because his mention of security freaks me out slightly with the memories from last night filtering back to me, but I won’t admit that to him. I run back to the room, grabbing my phone and bag from last night. It looks odd with this casual outfit I've been provided, or maybe accidentally stolen, but it has everything I own left in it. That currently encompasses my bank cards, ID, and keys to a burnt down house. Wow, let's not focus on that, now is *not* the time to panic.

Jeremy is waiting for me just outside the front door, standing like a sentry.

“Morning, Jeremy!”

“Morning, Miss.”

“Please, we’re going to be pals. Call me Lai.”

“Yes, Miss Lai.”

I roll my eyes but say nothing and a small smile appears on his lips. He walks me across the driveway to a closed garage with the Hummer pulled up out front. We jump in and I google the distance to the coffee shop, half an hour away. So we are still in Ironhaven. How they've got this much land in the city, I do not know. Messaging Lia to let her know we'll be a bit late, I settle in for the drive, moving my mental shopping list onto a google doc on my phone. I'll share it with Lia so we can divide and conquer in the shops, as I have a lot to get and not a lot of time with it being a Sunday. She knows my style better than I do most of the time, anyway.

We pull up to the coffee shop and I thank Jeremy. We're in the high street, which is set out in a square and Jeremy offers to meet us at each corner to offload any bags. Have I mentioned that I love him? Maybe I'll poach their entire staff at some point. I find Lia with both of our usual orders waiting at our favourite spot, two huge armchairs in the corner. She stands to give me an enormous hug and I hold on for a little longer than normal.

"You okay, Lai?"

"Yeah, I think so. It's just a lot to process."

"True. But if anyone can handle it and come out thriving, it's you," she says with a reassuring smile. We finish our drinks and I catch her up on who the guys at the bar and on the platform with Atlas turned out to be. On the way out I grab an iced coffee that I'm pretty sure ends up being at least 50% sugar with all the cream and caramel I add. I have no idea what Jeremy drinks but hopefully this is a safe choice. We drop it off at the car for him, hoping he has a sweet tooth; we'll be pals in no time.

"Okay, you didn't tell me Jeremy is seriously hot. Is that a requirement to work for Atlas or something?" Lia whispers as we walk away.

I sneak a peek back through the car window and have to admit Jeremy is not bad to look at. His hair is dark, scattered with grey, and he definitely pulls off the silver fox look.

"You have met him before," I remind her.

"Yeah, but I must've been too drunk or too tired to notice those muscles," she says with a wiggle of her brows.

"I would've thought he was way too clean-cut for you."

"I dunno, the military vibe is working for him. Although I am more than happy with my own tattooed bad boy."

I shake my head and laugh at her, not wanting to delve too deep into how hot she found Jeremy or Caus, to be honest. We shop for hours, dropping our bags off at every corner, which really should be a service people provide. I would happily pay for that shit. I don't even know half of what Lia has picked and we finally finish after being ushered to the tills in our last stop with three baskets full. We decide to stop for an early dinner so put our names down at a great little tapas place we both love. There's a brief wait for a table, so we sit at the bar and order a round of drinks.

"Cheers to a successful trip," Lia says, raising her glass. I grin at her and tap my glass to hers as her eyes glance over my shoulder and her answering grin gets even bigger. I turn around, curious, and find myself staring straight at Atlas's pecs. Not the worst view, admittedly, but unexpected.

"Hi, ladies. Atlas," he offers to Lia with an outstretched hand.

"Amelia," Lia replies with a smile, shaking it. "Don't mind me, I'm just popping to the restroom."

I narrow my eyes at her retreating back. "What are you doing here?" I ask Atlas as he takes Lia's vacated stool.

"You told Max I should come to you."

"This isn't what I meant, I'm a little busy."

Ignoring my plea, he continues. "You're not staying at a hotel tonight."

"Last time I checked I was a fully grown adult who could make their own decisions, but thank you for your input." I'm mature enough to recognise when I am cutting my nose off to spite my face. Yes, someone had set fire to my home yesterday, but I am still a strong, independent woman. Also, it was just too hard to believe that I'd actually been targeted. Me! What?! I'm a delight! How many enemies could an architect make, really? But being mature enough to recognise the signs was as far as I went, apparently. I was not about to right those personality flaws. "I've got stuff I need to do in the city tomorrow, anyway."

"That's fine, Jeremy can take you."

"I'm sure Jeremy has much more interesting things to do than chaperone his best pal around." I try not to chuckle at Atlas's confused expression.

"He's a fully trained member of our security team, second only to Max, so it's one of those two, or Quinn."

Not wanting to be alone with either Max or Quinn, I sigh, which Atlas must take as a concession. "Great, I'll see you at home later." When I open my mouth to argue further, he leans forward and cups the back of my head, kissing me until I can't think straight. "Enjoy your meal," he says, with way more coherence than I can muster right now and leaves before I pull myself together. Lia returns within a minute, clearly having watched most of that exchange.

"Call yourself a best friend, abandoning me with him?!"

"Oh please, you'll be adding that to the list of reasons you love me soon enough," she replies, smirking.

While we wait for the bill, stuffed with delicious food and more than a few cocktails, I go to Google hotels but find my phone missing.

"You didn't pick up my phone, did you?"

"No, it was next to you on the bar when I went to the toilet," Lia explains. "Maybe they've still got it up there?" Even as she suggests it, I know Atlas took it when he left. That controlling fucker, making sure I have to go back to him. I wouldn't bother if I didn't need it for my meetings tomorrow, but I have enough shit to sort out without adding shopping for a new phone to my list.

Lia and I leave the restaurant, hugging as we separate, and she heads to meet Caus. Jeremy is opening my door for me as I stomp towards the car, which is unnecessarily dramatic considering Atlas isn't here to see me flouncing. It causes me to stumble and practically fall into the passenger seat. Maybe I had a few more cocktails than intended with dinner, but at this point of my weekend, they're practically medicinal. Jeremy checks I'm okay before climbing in and we head back to the house.

SEVEN

THE STRANGER

I gave them a warning and they blew it. I thought they might, they're too cocky for their own good. It's why I was ready when I got the message that she was leaving with them. Them! The fucking Titans. Can't they see how easily I could ruin them? The visual of the bomb nearly out of time was so cinematic. At least they're adding a thrill to our love story.

Wait until she hears everything I've been through for her. To prove that she's mine and I deserve her. It's time to show them what I'm capable of: complete and utter destruction. Maybe she'll see why spending time with the Titans is such a bad idea. I wander around the house, spilling gasoline as I go.

It's a shame, really. The house is so warm and inviting. It smells like her, and the photos of her and Amelia smile at me as I move around the room. I loved to come here and relax when I was stressed. Being around her things calms me, like I'm being soothed by her, wrapped in her embrace. It's probably a good thing I can't stick around to watch the aftermath. It would hurt me too, to watch it all burn. But the risk of being spotted is too high. I don't know where Causus is, and he'd recognise me in seconds.

EIGHT

MAXTON

"She seemed okay when she left this morning," I reassure Atlas. "Maybe quiet, but she might not be a morning person."

"Yeah, she seemed alright earlier. I left her at dinner with Lia so hopefully they're having fun."

"I'm sure she's just peachy," Quince replies, heavy on the sarcasm.

We're all sitting around the dining table, our default gathering place when we aren't working. It makes sense for us to have our workspace within our home where we're secure, but we still try not to live and breathe work.

Especially with what we do. You need that separation to remain sane.

"What is your problem?" Atlas asks him and I sigh, readying for this argument again.

"I don't trust her."

"Tell us something we don't know," I counter. "Your trust issues have been building for years."

"Yeah, thanks to beautiful women like Madelaine, I'd like to point out."

"Well, innocent until proven guilty, I say," Atlas declares.

"Since when do you say that?"

"Since I met Madelaine."

"God, you're sickening. Am I the only one who can see all the dodgy vibes she gives off?"

"Like what?" I ask, humouring him.

"Like refusing to give her name to avoid a background check."

"She didn't refuse. She told you the first time any of us straight out asked her, and why on earth would she think we'd do a background check?"

"Oh, please. You mingle with the Titans, you get checked out. Everyone knows that," Quince insists.

"I don't think she knows who we are," Atlas says.

"As if. If she has any connection to the Vipers, then she knows."

"Exactly, so maybe she doesn't have a connection to the Vipers."

"How do you explain the photo?" Quince asks, not giving up for a second.

"Why would they try to hurt her with the fire?" I ask him, ignoring his question. None of it makes sense to me, which is making me edgy, seeing as security is my responsibility. Nothing is adding up, but I don't believe she's playing us.

"They didn't though, did they," Quincy continues. "They burnt everything in minutes when she wasn't at home."

"And what's the point of that? To send her a warning now that we've had ours?"

"She hasn't mentioned receiving any threats or knowing a possible reason for the fire to me," Atlas states.

"Oh yeah, 'cause she's been so forthcoming with information so far. She seems to get way more out of us than we get from her," Quince says bitterly. "She even has a whole backup home to cover up her real life. That's not normal, At."

None of this is new information and doesn't seem to bother Atlas in the slightest. "I'm sure there's a reason for that."

"Good luck getting that from her."

"Whatever, Quinn. She's staying."

"Excellent. Invite her into our home. Definitely not exactly what a Viper spy would want. Did you even need to convince her to come back?" he asks.

"I'm pretty sure the only reason she came back last night without a fight was that she was practically comatose," I say. She hadn't seemed massively keen to spend any more time in our company in the car.

Atlas takes a phone out of his pocket and waves it at us. "I can be very persuasive," he smirks, replacing the phone.

"She has turned you into such a psycho, At," Quince complains.

"Nah, she's just brought it out of him," I correct.

Atlas ignores us both and gets up to make us each a drink. He always has one when he gets back from the weekly lunches with his family. Says he needs to remind himself he's a man after suffering through his mom's babying. I'm surprised she doesn't hand-feed him.

"What happened when we got back, anyway?" I ask him, recalling him going back and forth to the room we gave her.

"Nothing. Like you say, she was practically comatose. Great actress if she is pretending," he aims at Quince. "She just kept listing the things she doesn't have anymore. I mean, her whole life had just gone up in flames."

"If that was even her actual house," Quince mutters.

Atlas ignores him and continues while handing out the whiskies and taking his seat again. "Jeremy found her some pyjamas and clothes from God knows where and I ran her a bath, tried to get her to relax and eat something."

"I'm surprised you didn't try to get her in your bed."

"Fuck off, Quinn, she was in shock."

Just as Quince unwisely opens his mouth to bitch back at Atlas some more, Madelaine walks through the front door. Atlas spins around to face her and must have a shit-eating grin on his face, because her eyes narrow when they settle on him.

"I don't know what you're looking so pleased with yourself for. You managed to trick a woman into going back to your house, well done," she says with an eye roll. "Where is it?" she asks, walking over to us at the table.

"Let's chat first," Atlas bargains.

She walks to the other end, sitting opposite us like a board meeting. "Okay, what do you want?"

"I meant me and you."

"Now or never, Atlas."

She's lucky he seems to worship the ground she walks on. No guy would get away with talking to him that abruptly.

"Fine. I want you to stay here until we've spoken to the police and worked out what the fire was all about. This place is secure, and then you're not putting Amelia at risk or staying alone in a hotel where anyone can get to you."

He clearly has her attention after mentioning Amelia, and her jaw tightens. "All valid points, fine." He looks shocked but recovers well. "I've got the day off to sort things out tomorrow, but then I'll be back at work for the rest of the week."

"What is it you do?" Quince asks, jumping at the chance for more answers.

"I'm an interior architect."

"Madelaine, from LLI?" I ask her.

"Yeah, how did you know that?"

"You did the bar refurbishment," I say, as understanding dawns on me.

"Yeah. It looked good, right?" she says proudly. It had looked great, we'd just asked them to work with us on a few more projects. She was insanely talented. Brains and beauty, she is going to ruin us all.

"We own that bar," Quince tells her.

"Clearly that bar does better for itself than it seems, then," she replies, looking around at our home. I guess she's realised we all live here by now. It took us a while to find something and renovate it to our needs, but we all love it. "Anything else?" she asks Atlas.

"Yes, you should be my girl."

"No, thank you. Are we done?" she finishes, bracing to stand, but Atlas isn't letting that lie.

"What do you mean, no?"

"Do you need a dictionary definition?" she sasses. The things I'd do to that sassy mouth.

"I want to know why you're saying no, Madelaine," he spells out.

She shrugs at him. "Maybe I'm just not that into you."

"Liar."

I feel like I'm at a tennis match watching these two go at it, my eyes swinging from left to right as they trade blows.

"Fine, I'm not looking to give anything a go with anyone. I'm quite happy having my wild phase, thank you."

"Your wild phase?"

"Yeah, you know. That time where you can do whatever you want whenever you want without worrying about another person?"

"Do whatever, or do whoever?" Atlas asks through gritted teeth.

"Both," she says, not backing down from his gaze even though it must be molten. "Everyone else seems to have had one, and now I want mine."

"Why haven't you had it before?" Quince jumps in, always desperate for answers. Atlas is rigid in his seat, but

I'm on the edge of mine, loving how open she's being right now.

"I was in a really long relationship before. I actually meant for you to be my first one-night stand," she directs at Atlas.

"Sorry to ruin your fun," he sulks, which makes me chuckle. I can't tell if he's mad she's not dropping to his feet or if he gets off on her pushing back at him.

"What does this wild phase include?" I ask her, my pants in danger of getting too tight as I think of a wild Madelaine.

"I guess it's time to go with the flow and not overthink my decisions. Be happy with the person I am, see what kind of person I'm attracted to. Basically, to experiment and explore life." Her eyes dart to all of us, checking our reactions. I'm sure there'd be a blush under that beautiful bronze skin.

"You don't need to see what kind of person you're attracted to," Atlas pipes up, cockiness returning. "I'm the type of person you're attracted to. Check that off the list."

"Yeah, but I was attracted to Maxton and Quincy too until I realised they were your henchmen. Maybe I should expand my horizons," she quips back.

Atlas shifts in his seat while Quince and I give him matching glares.

"You can't do this experiment with one person?" he asks Madelaine, avoiding looking at us.

"No, that defeats the point. In my last relationship I wasn't me, I was half of a couple," she explains.

Atlas mulls that over for a second while Quince and I continue to stare daggers into his skull.

"A proposition, then. While you're staying here, you give this a chance. Trust me, I am more than willing to let you use me to explore your wildest fantasies. When you're ready to leave for your own place, if you want to move on to greener pastures, then fine," he offers Madelaine.

She thinks about that for a long minute while we all sit there, watching her. "I'll think about it," she finally says, standing this time and going to leave, but Atlas grabs her arm as she walks past him.

"You've got until the end of tonight. I don't enjoy waiting."

I might want to kill my best friend for getting to her first, but even I have to admit the sexual tension pours off them in waves. He pulls her phone out of his pocket and places it in her hand before letting her go. She says nothing else as she walks off to her bedroom.

"What was that about?" Quince asks as soon as she's out of earshot. "You didn't sound like you'd let her move on earlier."

"Yeah, and like fuck am I going to now. She just needs a push to realise how great this can be. If not, I'll lock the fucking door."

"Who said romance was dead," I mutter.

"I'll give her romance, if that's what she wants," he replies.

"Doesn't seem like it right now," I say, quite enjoying her stripping Atlas down so easily.

"Well, I'll let you know how it goes while you both enjoy the friend zone," he jokes.

"I can't believe she admitted finding us attractive and confirmed she wouldn't go any further because she's already slept with Atlas, in the same sentence. What a rollercoaster," Quince sighs, rubbing his hand down his face.

"Surely you're not disappointed, Quinn? God forbid you fall for the Viper spy," Atlas adds, taking his chance for a jab at Quince.

"Of course not."

"How did your grilling go, by the way?" I ask him, registering that he'd gotten hardly any information from Madelaine again.

"Fuck off, both of you," he mumbles as he leaves the room, tail firmly tucked between his legs.

NINE

MADELAINE

Monday morning comes around and the slight ache behind my eyes reminds me of the drinks I consumed at dinner last night. I remember our last conversation and groan, rolling my face into the pillow. Did I really explain my wild phase to the guys? Did I truly admit I found Maxton and Quincy attractive? Fucking hell. Probably best to front it out and pretend I see nothing wrong with it. I can't deny, even to myself and sober, that I find them all as attractive as each other. Even Quincy, who hasn't been welcoming at all. He's the most like my normal type out of the guys, with his shaggy brown hair and eyes nearly the same colour. Plus, glasses on a guy just do something to me. He gives serious surfer vibes but with a nerdy twist, and he would have been my ideal teenage fantasy. Being leaner and probably just over six feet, he's not as daunting as the others. He's the one you would think was the friendlier of the three, though that hasn't been my experience so far.

After spending ten minutes mourning my pride, I get up and ready for errands and Jeremy meets me at the car before we head to the drive-thru. I chickened out and crept past the kitchen on my way out, so I am ravenous. Food is what I need, and then I'll be back to my boss-bitch ways. I get a breakfast wrap that saves my soul and even convince Jeremy to try it, breaking down our barriers with sugary coffee and hash brown goodness.

The police station takes forever and I'm not sure why, as I know nothing and have a pretty solid alibi. They seem to ask way more questions about the guys I was with rather than anything related to the fire, but maybe I just have them on the brain. Finally, we finish with the insurers and I check my phone as we get back into the car to head back to Atlas's house. I've got a couple of missed calls from Atlas, little shit must've swapped numbers when he had my phone. Just as I decide to speak to him when I get back, seeing as we're on the way anyway, he calls Jeremy, who answers through the car Bluetooth.

"Hi, sir," Jeremy answers.

"Hi, is Madelaine in the car?"

I make a pretty obvious chopping gesture against my neck, but clearly Jeremy hasn't read the rule book on best friend loyalty yet, as he answers affirmatively.

"Madelaine, I said you had the night to decide, and it's now the following afternoon. What's your answer?"

My face heats. Thank God Jeremy doesn't know what he means.

"We're on the way back. Can we talk about this when I get there?" I ask him.

"You've had long enough. I'm sure Jeremy is happy to stay on the line while you decide whether you want to use my body to explore..."

"Oh my God, Atlas," I shout. My face is on actual fire and I cover it with my hands. You could get a tan from the furnace coming from my blazing cheeks. "Fine, yes," I splutter, wanting this conversation to be over.

"Great. Jeremy, put your foot down. See you soon, Madelaine," he says as he disconnects the call.

“Sorry,” I mumble to Jeremy.

“Don’t worry about it, Miss Lai. I’m used to him getting his way.” We share a conspiratorial grin and my embarrassment melts away. We pull into the garage this time, as there are only two cars in there. I stroke along the low curves of an Aston Martin.

“That’s Atlas’s second car, the other is Lucy’s,” Jeremy explains to me.

“Wow, Atlas must pay well. Maybe I’ll work here.”

“That was actually a divorce present, but yes, he treats us all very well.”

As we walk through the front door, Atlas is coming through another to the right.

“Thanks, Jeremy,” he says, bending and lifting me over his shoulder without hesitation.

A squeal of surprise slips past my lips. “Atlas! Put me down!”

He smacks me on the ass instead of replying and I yelp but stop my futile struggling. A minute later, I’m laid down on the bed of the room I’ve commandeered the last two nights. He leans over me, caging me in with his hands on either side of my head.

"How was your day?" he asks. I take a second to study his face while he's this close, and he really might be one of the hottest men I've seen in real life. His ashy blonde hair is rumpled and those green eyes stare into my soul. He raises a brow and I realise I haven't answered.

"Fine," I squeak. Sexy. He smirks and leans down to kiss me, slow and tender until I open my mouth with a sigh and he tastes my tongue with his. He teases me, overwhelming me with another deep, panty-melting kiss until I wriggle underneath him, needing more.

"I'm happy to let you use me to explore but I've been thinking about this for three weeks, so you can explore next time," he says as he whips my oversized t-shirt and bralette over my head. He starts a trail of light kisses along my jaw. I go to start on his shirt buttons but get distracted by him nipping down my throat and collarbone, so my hands move to his biceps. I press my chest up slightly as he nears my nipple, but he skims his mouth over the curve of my breast and down my stomach until he reaches my waistband. He pulls my leggings and underwear off and separates my legs so I'm laid out in front of him, completely naked.

"Fuck, baby. You are spectacular." I heat at his words and try to pull my legs together, but he frowns slightly and pushes my knees apart. He runs his hands from my ankles to my hips, making me shudder as he situates himself between my thighs on his haunches.

"You don't have to hide anything from me," he croaks as he runs a finger along my seam. I stare at him leaning over me fully clothed with his hand between my legs and am more turned on than I think I've ever been. He continues running a finger from my entrance to my clit and back again, making me tense with anticipation. He leans over, kissing me as he rubs circles around the bundle of nerves. When I think I'm about to come embarrassingly fast, he moves his fingers up to my breasts, rubbing my wetness over one nipple. Lapping at it with his tongue, he sucks it into his mouth before repeating the process on the other side. I'm nearly panting as he pulls himself out of his trousers. "One day I'll make you come using just these perfect breasts," he murmurs as he coats his cock in my arousal and presses the tip to my core.

I tug at his shirt, wanting to feel actual skin and not cotton, but he grabs my hands in his and holds them above my head. Leaning on his forearms, he gently pushes in, and

I wrap my legs around his waist, groaning as he slides deeper. "Fuck," he groans as he seats himself fully inside me. I can think of nothing but the feel of him as he pulls back and then pushes in slowly again, our faces inches from each other, my breathing getting more ragged. The slow pace is driving me wild.

"Atlas, please," I whisper into his mouth, and a growl comes from his chest as he picks up the pace, pumping his hips with restrained fervour. It doesn't take long for the pleasure to build inside me and as he releases a hand to rub my clit I explode, releasing a low moan, clenching around him and making him join me in oblivion. He lets my hands go and sags slightly so that I can feel his weight on me.

"Are you okay?" he asks after a minute, when all we can hear is our slowing breaths.

"Yeah, just waiting for my brain to rewire."

He laughs. "So, trying again. How was your day?" I chuckle and bask in the lightness of our conversation. Everything has been so intense recently that it's nice to just be ourselves. I find myself wishing for more of it, then scold myself. *Do not catch feelings for your first one-night stand, Madelaine, you'll make a mockery of the sacred wild phase.*

"Okay, thanks. Got some decisions to make with the insurers and I gave the police my statement. How was yours?"

"Okay, just work stuff," he replies vaguely. I know we're having this very normal conversation with him still inside me, but I'm okay with that.

"What is it you do, exactly?"

"Well, at the moment we're focused on buying up failing businesses and refurbing them. Or rather, our very talented designer is refurbing them. I can't believe you designed the bar, it's incredible."

"Does this count as a completion bonus?" I joke.

He chuckles and his cock twitches inside of me, hard again. "Good stamina, noted," I tease, as he gives a few lazy pumps of his hips. He smirks at me before pulling out abruptly and flipping me over. He pulls my hips up so I'm on my knees and then presses my chest to the bed before slamming back into me from behind.

"Fuck!" I cry, as in this position his every stroke hits deeper. I grip the duvet in my fists as unintelligible sounds fall from my mouth. He thrusts relentlessly, hands squeezing my hips as he pulls me back to meet every one. As I build, he wraps an arm around my waist and pulls me up until my back is pressed to his front and he sits back on his feet. I have a bit more control in this position and I take it, lifting slightly on my knees and dropping back down into his lap, reveling in the tightness my closed thighs give. He grips my throat, and I let my head fall back against his shoulder, every muscle clenching delightfully with the light squeeze of his hand around my neck.

"Shit, baby. You like that?" he murmurs huskily into my ear. I clench again, and Atlas groans. "Come for me, baby."

Such an unnecessary command, as I couldn't stop myself if the room was on fire. Wait, too soon? Stars explode behind my eyes, and after a couple more hard thrusts Atlas comes for the second time, holding me close. We fall over onto our sides, breathless and with limbs like jelly. I'm coming back down to earth when I catch his shirt-covered arm lazily wrapped around my waist. The fact that he's still dressed comes to the forefront of my brain.

"How come you get me completely naked but you haven't taken one thing off?" I chuckle.

He stiffens slightly but I ignore his weirdness, opting to head for a much-needed shower instead.

I'm happy to dive back into work and some semblance of normalcy the next day. Jason's big news is that the club owners loved the refurb and have kept us on for a handful of other projects they're starting. I decided to keep the fact that I'm currently lodging with these club owners to myself, for the time being. Not that I think Jason would have an issue. They clearly hired us again before they knew who I was. But I can barely explain the situation to myself, I can't face trying to rationalise it to someone else as well.

There's way too much work for just me to handle this time, so I bring Kacey in to help. We spend the next few days touring the venues and discussing ideas. She has some brilliant concepts and I'm reminded of why she got promoted in the first place.

Wednesday comes around and Kace and I are heading for an early afternoon meeting with Jason to lay out our plans.

"I can't believe we work for the Titans now," she says wistfully.

"Hate to burst your bubble, Kace, but I've met the owners of the club and they're just business flippers. You might have to pin your hopes of a gangland romance on someone else." I almost feel bad about her dejected expression.

We walk into the meeting room and I freeze in the doorway, causing Kacey to bump into me from behind and drop everything in her arms.

"Sorry!" I exclaim, spinning around to help her collect her things. Atlas gets up from his chair to help pick up the spilt belongings and smirks when he's at eye level with me. I glare at him and elbow him in the ribs as we stand without drawing any attention. Yes, that does make me feel better.

"Madelaine, Kacey, this is Mr Grayson, the client for this project. This is Madelaine Noxx, the project lead, and Kacey Mane, an assistant architect here at the firm."

Atlas reaches a hand out and Kacey throws herself at it, shaking it vigorously. "So nice to meet you, sir," she beams.

“Clients don’t normally come to meetings this early in the project,” I state abruptly. Jason gives a bemused look at my tone, but Atlas answers before he can say anything.

“I thought I’d drop by on this one.”

“The timescales are so brief again on these projects that it’s probably a good idea to combine some meetings,” Jason protests.

“Great idea. Lovely to meet you, Mr Grayson.” I hope I’ve redeemed myself and Jason forgets my slip up later.

We all take a seat and go through our ideas, Jason and Atlas both giving feedback and requests. The meeting is thankfully short as they both seem happy with our visions and have minimal changes.

“Great, we’ll complete our designs and then send it on to the project teams for the next phase.”

“That’s great. Thank you, Madelaine,” Jason beams.

Kace and I get to our feet, ready to say our goodbyes and leave when Atlas stands, too.

“Miss Noxx, have you got a minute?”

“Of course, My Grayson,” I answer, not having much choice but to be polite.

"In private?"

My eyes tighten involuntarily. "Certainly." I leave the office and he follows me to the other side of our floor and I gesture for him to enter my office, which I am sadly proud of. I feel like I've achieved something by having an office to myself. It also has a gorgeous little balcony that lets beautiful light through the double doors. You may only be able to fit two people out there at a push, and the view is a dingy back-alley no one ever uses, but still, the pride is there.

I follow behind him and stand just inside the doorway, the door still open.

"How can I help you?"

"I can't decide if I like this submissive, agreeable Madelaine or if I miss the feisty version," he says, walking towards me.

"Atlas, I'm at work."

He reaches behind me and pushes the door closed. "Best be quiet then." He grabs the nape of my neck and kisses me senseless.

"We need to discuss your work clothes," he says when we come up for air, pulling my skirt up to my waist and shoving my underwear down. I don't know what has come over me, but I step out of them as he frees himself from his trousers, hard and ready.

"Your opinion has no relevance to my work clothes," I reply as he lifts me into his arms. I wrap my legs around his waist, thanking my lucky stars this office has no internal windows.

"I definitely prefer the feisty version," he murmurs into my hair as he pushes me back against the door and slowly slides inside me.

My mouth drops open at the sensual slowness and he claps his hand over my mouth, the domineering act causing me to tighten around him.

"Unless you want me to fuck you hard against this door and let everyone hear exactly what we're doing, you need to stop that."

I can't help myself. His words make me heat and I moan into his palm.

He growls deep in his chest and spins, carrying me over to my desk with one arm wrapped around my waist and sits me on the edge. Pushing my chest back so I'm laying down, he keeps one hand over my mouth and the other moves to grip my hip.

"Hold on, baby." I realise belatedly that he means it literally when he slides out and slams back into me, causing my body to arch and a scream to slip out against his hand.

I grip the edge of the table as he keeps up his hard and fast rhythm, and it's not long before I'm right there. He releases the tight grasp on my hip to reach between my legs and circle my clit, sending me spiralling into an orgasm that he follows me into a few pumps later.

I lay there for a second, listening to us both pant, until the fact that we're in my workplace comes flooding back to me. He pulls out of me as I sit up and puts himself away while I straighten my clothes and cross back over to the door to collect my underwear.

"You should go," I say. "I need a clean up ASAP."

He doesn't get to reply as the door swings open, Jason striding in through the unlocked door as I hastily shove my lace panties behind my back.

"Oh, sorry Madelaine. I didn't realise you were still in a meeting."

"That's okay, we just finished."

"We certainly did. It's been a pleasure, Miss Noxx," Atlas says as he walks behind me, heading to the door.

Kacey calls for Jason from her office door, which distracts him long enough for Atlas to risk sliding my panties out of my hand as he passes. I retreat back behind my desk and am sitting to hide the shaking of my legs by the time Jason's attention is back on me.

He doesn't stay long, thankfully, just wanting to congratulate me on the plans. I rush to the bathroom as soon as he leaves to do as best a clean-up as possible. Just as I'm attempting to sneak back to my office, trying not to look like I just got pounded, Kacey rushes over to me.

"I'm glad I caught you. What the hell?" she exclaims. "I told you it was the Titans!"

"What are you talking about?" My brain isn't fully functioning yet.

"The guy in our meeting, Mr Grayson. Even without seeing the tattoos, I'd recognise him," she insists.

My brain is officially malfunctioning and my post-sex glow disappears like smoke, replaced by simmering anger coursing through my veins.

"Sorry, Kace. I've got to go." I head back to my office and seethe in silence until it's a respectable time to leave, my productivity having careened out the window.

Jeremy picks me up as usual. We've bonded through our trips to and from everywhere, and once he pulls out into traffic, I can't keep it in any longer.

"Jeremy, what do you know about the Titans?"

"I'm not sure what you're asking, Miss Lai."

What a cop-out. I give him a suspicious look, but he keeps his eyes resolutely on the road and drives us home.

TEN

ATLAS

I stroll back into the house after my meeting with Madelaine in a great mood. Of course, Quinn is there to fix that. He and Max are standing around the kitchen island discussing something that's put a frown on Max's face.

"Do I even want to hear this?" I ask, joining them.

Max sighs. "Quince did a background check on Madelaine."

"What the fuck?"

"Well, I didn't tell you what it said, did I? So enjoy courting her the fucking old-fashioned way."

I glare at him. "You know that's not the point."

He glares defiantly back at me, not giving anything away. Quinn is normally the chill one out of the three of us, always laughing and joking. I know the reason he's so caught up in investigating Madelaine is that he is scared of how great she could be for us. Until he sorts his shit out, he won't get me on his side.

"Fine. What did it say?" I ask, curiosity getting the better of me.

Quinn's face looks smug enough to punch. "Absolutely nothing."

"So what's the problem?"

"Quince thinks that's even more suspicious than seeing red flags," Max explains.

"It is! There was no extra information at all. It's like she didn't even exist until three years ago, and since then she's been a ghost."

I have to admit that's odd, but do I want to rile him up?

"Yes, that's unusual, but it could be several things. Maybe she had trauma when she was younger, or maybe she's in witness protection."

"And these aren't things you'd want to know?" Max asks me, genuinely curious. I know he's way more open to believing Madelaine is innocent than Quinn is right now.

"As I've said before, I want to know what she wants to tell me. If that makes me naïve and puts us in danger, call me out on it when it happens. Until then, she's getting the benefit of the doubt from me."

"Shit, you really like her," Quinn remarks, his shock clear.

"I do, and I think you do too. You're fighting it, but that's your problem. Fuck this up for me, Quinn, and we'll have a huge one."

He agrees to my terms with a nod and Max thankfully changes the subject, asking for an update on how Encore is doing. We chat mindlessly for a bit, the atmosphere much lighter now that we have cleared some air between us. A while later, we all grab drinks and a seat in the lounge off of the kitchen diner. The front door slams and I call "in here" to who I'm assuming is Madelaine back from work. She blows into the room like a hurricane and I immediately feel better. Our conversation eases and I smile as she comes towards me, but she holds up her hand as I reach out to her.

"Take your shirt off," she commands, no joking in her tone.

"Err, what?" I ask, thoroughly confused.

"Take it off," she repeats, giving me nothing.

"I think that's our cue, Max," Quinn murmurs, going to stand.

"No need, I'd love to admire the art on *all* of you," she says, standing in front of us with her arms crossed. We all freeze, like naughty schoolboys being questioned by the head-teacher. To be fair, I wouldn't be against a little role play with Madelaine in that figure-hugging pencil skirt. No. Focus, Atlas. Our art. *She knows about our Titan's tattoos. Fuck.* I don't know where to go from here and I'm not the only one, as we all just stare at her.

"So you're happy to ambush me at my work and make me look like an idiot, fuck me in my own office, but you don't want to strip for me? You're happy to act like you're doing me a huge favour protecting me, when it's probably your fault that I need protecting? Insist I stay here with you all acting like generous wankers, when I've never had to worry about my home burning down until I met the fucking *Titans?*" She's shouting by now, flailing her arms around. She normally speaks with her hands, gesturing to enhance her point and I love how expressive and fully involved in a conversation she is, though it does not bode well for me that I'm on her bad side. "You know what, I don't need this," she says, spinning on her heel.

"Madelaine, let me explain," I assert as I stand, and my words stop her in her tracks.

"Oh, now you want to explain? Why didn't you try that earlier?"

"I didn't want to give you a reason to go," I shrug, perfectly happy with my reasoning. I have no intention of losing her now that I've found her.

Her eyes widen as she absorbs what I've said. "Oh my God. I've stranded myself with a psychopath. How did I not see this coming?" she asks, almost to herself. "I've waltzed into a horror film. This house is where I die," she says, turning and wandering through the doorway, away from us all.

"Where are you going?" I follow her out and feel the guys behind me, even though they're both staying quiet while she fumes. I guess neither of them owes her anything yet.

"None of your fucking business," she yells back at me. "The time for exchanging information has well and truly passed."

"Just try to leave this fucking house, baby." Okay, so I could've approached this better, but the thought of her walking away from me is not something I'm keen to experience.

"Watch me," she says with a glare as she storms off. She walks down the corridor that leads to the bedrooms, it's that fact that stops me from grabbing her. If she'd walked towards the front door it would've been a different story.

"Calm down, man," Max says from behind me. I spin to face him and Quinn.

"You think I should let her go with all this shit going on?"

"Let's not pretend it's the threats that are making you so crazy," Quinn adds.

"Of course not," Max answers me, pretending Quinn hasn't spoken. "I just think you could've delivered that message better. Obviously, she's pissed. We kept it from her because we knew she would be." There's tense silence while I take in Max's words. "At least Quinn should believe she didn't know who we were after that performance," he adds, trying to lighten the mood.

"I'm going to order some food," Quinn says instead of replying to Max. We all take a seat along the island and sit quietly, waiting for the delivery, each lost in our heads. I calm down and think over the argument again. She found out we were the Titans from someone else when she's been staying with us for days. I get why she's pissed off, especially when I've asked her to give me a chance while she's here. But Quinn's also right, she keeps shit from us. I might not demand answers from her, but surely that means I don't have to reveal everything either. Plus, I liked meeting a girl who wasn't desperate to be on her knees for me because of who I am. It's been nice to get to know her without her knowing all the shit we do.

Even without all that, she's amazing. She's witty, funny, ambitious and crazy talented, plus she's any man's dream to look at. I know I can't just let her go. I won't. The door goes a short while later, pulling me out of my thoughts as the food arrives.

"I'll go let Madelaine know," I say as Quinn gets up to collect our dinner.

"Be chill, Atlas," Max warns.

"Yeah, yeah." I walk away from the kitchen and along the hallway that houses all five bedrooms. I knock on the door and get no answer from her. No surprise there. Her stubbornness matches mine, after all. "Madelaine, we got food. You need to eat, even if you're mad." Still no response. "We won't even talk to you if that's what you want," I shout through the door, knowing full well that won't happen. Nothing.

I try the door and it's unexpectedly open, as is the window as I go in, but I can't see Madelaine. I wander into the bathroom even though that door is open too and see the bottles that normally clutter the counter are gone. The open rails of the wardrobe are also empty, of Madelaine and any clothes. I run out of her room and back to the guys.

"She's gone!" I shout at them as I rush past.

"What do you mean?" Max asks me as they both abandon the food and rush after me.

"I mean she and all of her shit are gone." I try her phone over and over, but it rings out every time. "How the fuck did she get past us?"

We search the property for an hour, assuming she couldn't have got out any other way than by leaving through the bedroom window. We know she doesn't have a car, but would she have asked a friend to come and get her? If she could even get that far. She didn't go through the main gate, there are two guys there most of the time and neither of them had seen her.

After exhausting all of our first options, we head back inside, ready to go to the office to watch the CCTV. We step into the foyer and freeze, all of us piling into each other with our mouths agape. Madelaine is sitting at the dining table, finishing a plate of Chinese food, the cartons Quinn ordered open all around her. We wander further in and she rolls her eyes as we approach, standing and heading over to the sink. No one says anything as she washes her dish and goes to walk past us back to her room, ignoring us all.

My patience has run out by now and I grab her by the arm, swinging her around and pressing her against the wall. I'm desperate to touch her.

"Do you think that's funny?"

"Well, not 'ha ha' funny," she answers nonchalantly.

"We've been frantic for a fucking hour, Madelaine," I tell her, my mouth an inch from hers.

"Maybe that'll teach you not to order me around like a dog." Her eyes are burning as she holds my gaze, pushing me back a step. I'm not even mad at her, I just can't stand the thought of her not being here. I'll tell her anything at this point. Fuck Quinn's suspicions. "You can't control me."

"I'm not trying to control you," I insist. "I'm trying to protect you."

"Why are you so obsessed with protecting someone you've only just met?" she asks.

"Good question," Quinn mutters under his breath.

"I know this is it, you're mine. I'm just waiting for you to realise it. And I will protect you from now until the end, whether you want that or not."

"Jesus, you're insane," she protests, but her tone is lighter and her eyes dance. She definitely doesn't hate what I've just said.

"Maybe, but I'm right."

"Who do I need protection from?" she belatedly asks, seeming to just process everything I said.

"Maybe we should clear some things up," Max offers, and her eyes flick to him, softening further. Interesting.

"Great idea," Quinn adds. He heads back to the table and helps himself to some food. Max and I join him with Madelaine retaking her seat, but eating is the last thing on my mind right now. When no one offers any information, Madelaine sighs and leans forward, clearly ready to get some answers.

"Who are the Titans?" Seems as good a place as any to start.

"Us three head it up, and we have people who work for us. You'll probably never meet most of them, just the house-based staff."

She nods, satisfied with that answer. "And the clubs we're refurbishing are legit?"

"Yep," Quinn replies. "I can show you the books if you'd like."

"That won't be necessary," she says, overly polite. "Did the fire have anything to do with you?"

"Hang on, why are you getting all the questions?" Quinn interrupts. "Surely it's our turn."

"Okay," she says, unfazed, picking at a spring roll.

"Why did it take you so long to give us your name?"

"People are creepy. They think once you have a conversation you owe them something. I got used to not saying it unless asked directly."

"And the fake address?" Quinn pushes.

"It belongs to Lia's boyfriend, Coze. They stay at hers most of the time because she has the cutest German Shepherd cross Springer Spaniel puppy that can't be left too long. Her name's Rue, and she's absolutely mental." I have no idea where this is going, but we all let her carry on uninterrupted. "She'd chew everything in sight if she got too bored, so she needs people around. Anyway, going back to 'people be creepy', I don't like giving my address out to taxi drivers or intimidating men who give me lifts home and orgasms in their blacked-out Hummers. So I give Coze's address and pop through the back gardens. If anyone tries anything later, they either come upon an empty house or a huge, tatted Coze, who can definitely handle himself."

Max and I both give Quinn 'told you so' looks and he seems suitably sheepish.

"Any more questions?" Max, who had been relatively quiet until now, asks. I think Madelaine exonerating herself has buoyed him up.

"Am I safe here? Was the fire linked to you?"

I let Max take this one, being head of security.

"You are 100% safe here, Madelaine. I promise. We won't let anything happen to you. And about the fire: probably. We got a photo of you warning Atlas off so it can't be a coincidence that it happened the night you saw each other again."

She freezes, startled by the casual mention of the photo. "It showed nothing incriminating," Max tells her, noticing her unease. "Just a shot of you in the middle of the day in the city."

"Okay," she rallies, and reflects for a minute or two. "I need time to process. I don't know what else I want to know." I'm surprised she hasn't quizzed us on what it is we do or our reputation, but if she's happy with what she knows then I am too.

"Actually, what is it that you do?" Oh.

"We flip businesses. Choose great locations that are run down or not being used effectively, and refurb them," Quinn explains.

"No, as the Titans. What do you do?" My ease was clearly premature. "I don't want to be staying with sex traffickers or anything as awful as that." She rubs her arms in clear discomfort.

"Nothing like that at all," I promise her. "Our businesses are most important, they make up the bulk of what we do."

"But not everything?"

"Not everything," I agree.

"If there's anything you need to know, we'll tell you," Quinn tells her. She cocks a brow at that, clearly remembering what's gotten us to this conversation in the first place. Quinn tries his best not to let a smile slip. "Starting from now."

"I can work with that," she agrees. "Anything else from me?"

"No more questions," I confirm.

"Well, that was much more productive than the empty background check," Quinn quips. *Shit*. Madelaine's face crumples and she has my heart in a vice, it aches at her expression.

"You ran a background check on me?" she asks, hurt clear in her voice.

"It's standard procedure," Quinn tries to reason.

"Good to know I'm nothing special, then," she says with an arched brow. "If we're all done, I'm going to chill in my room." She avoids eye contact with us all and leaves, none of us trying to stop her this time.

As soon as she's gone, Max and I both turn on Quinn. He drops his head into his hands, looking mortified. "Fuck, I'm so sorry!"

"You should be. It was going so well!" Max says. He never gets annoyed, he's unflappable and rational. The fact that he's angry over Madelaine's hurt speaks volumes.

I add nothing else, but get up and head to her door. Knocking but getting no answer, I try the handle and find it locked. I'm not worried she's running this time, after everything that's just been said, but I weirdly don't like the idea of her going to bed feeling let down. How ridiculous does that make me? I run a huge business and am worried that some woman is pouting in her bedroom over me, yet I don't want my obsession with her to stop.

ELEVEN

QUINCY

Madelaine seems to have cooled down a bit since our big conversation. I didn't see her much yesterday, but she wasn't outwardly glaring at me so I'm taking that as a positive. No doubt Atlas and Max have both apologised about the background check already and I know I should too, but I want to do it without the peanut gallery watching.

This morning gives me that chance as she needs to catch a ride into the city with me. I normally visit a bunch of our businesses on a Friday and it doesn't make sense for Jeremy to drive Madelaine if I'm going anyway. It sounds like an excuse, even to me, but I'll take extra time with her wherever I can get it. The guys are right, I can see how special she is, but that's part of the issue. Even with our previous girlfriends who I hadn't exactly been invested in, I'm always all-in. As soon as we realised what they were doing, lying about wanting to be with all of us to stay close to one, or when they chose between us, we all had our feelings and pride hurt. Mostly me. Knowing that we could all be seriously into this girl makes it so much easier for her to break us. Not that she seems to have even entertained the idea of being with more than just Atlas. Would that make things worse? Surely a woman couldn't tear us apart.

I walk from my bedroom down towards the kitchen, hearing music from that direction. Lucy hardly makes any noise, we joke she's like a cleaning spectre. I turn the corner into the open kitchen diner and see Madelaine and Lucy dancing around the island to an upbeat Whitney Houston song. Lucy looks as if she's reluctant to let go and enjoy herself, but I hope she knows we wouldn't mind it at all. Madelaine isn't having any of it, grabbing her hands and waving their arms about as she sings along to the words. Her hips shimmy and I'm transfixed for a second on her ass shaking to the rhythm. Then she spins with her eyes closed and I see the pure joy on her face.

She's ethereal, lost in the music and her Friday morning fun. She's effortlessly gorgeous on a normal day, but seeing her like this makes me want to make her feel like that all the time. She's completely herself, laughing and smiling. Carefree and light. It's been pretty intense since she got here, but I know this is the true Madelaine. She spins Lucy away from her on her arm as if they're ballroom dancing and Lucy lets go, freely laughing at their antics, until she catches sight of me over Madelaine's shoulder.

"Morning, Quincy," she says through laughter. "This one's a bad influence! I'm way behind."

Madelaine spins to face me as Lucy talks, caution edging her eyes and pushing the glee out slightly. I feel that hit in my gut.

"Don't be silly, Lucy. It's great to see you so happy. I'll grab food on the way to work. Good morning, Madelaine."

"Morning, Quincy," she says, looking around for someone to save her. Lucy has shuffled off, leaving us to it.

"I'm working in the city today, so I'll drive you in. Jeremy's gone with Max and Atlas. If you're ready now, we can stop for breakfast on the way?"

"Okay," she says, tempted by food. I love that she loves food, I hate when people pick at salads.

She grabs her things and I lead her out of the house and over to my car in the garage. "No Hummer?" she asks, stroking my Audi.

"Nah, that's pretty much Jeremy's, or for when we're all together."

I drive to a pancake house. It's ten minutes away from our place and a slight detour from the city, but I had to bring her here. It's a favourite among us three and we used to drive here even before we lived in Ironhaven. We settle into a huge booth, a top-choice seat that you have to choose even with only two, and a server quickly comes over to take our order.

"Hey, Quinn. Long time, no see," she greets me.

"Hey, Mandy. We're busy men, you know that. This is Madelaine," I offer, gesturing towards her sitting opposite me.

"Lai, please," she replies with a smile at Mandy.

"Morning, Lai. What can I get you both?"

"I'll have my usual with a black coffee, please," I say, not even looking at the menu.

"I'll have the same but with an apple juice, please," Madelaine echoes, handing the menus back.

"It'll be right up," Mandy says as she leaves us to it.

We sit in comfortable silence for a minute. "Are you not going to ask what the usual is?" I say when the curiosity burns at me.

Madelaine shrugs. "I like most things. I would've got lost in that menu for days, I don't do well with too many choices. As long as it's not seafood, I'm good. Though I would have to disown you if you chose seafood for breakfast."

I smile at that. I know it's just a saying, but I'm happy to pretend she's claimed me.

"Not seafood," I promise. "I'm glad I got you alone. I wanted to apologise for the background check. It wasn't a reflection of you, I can be a suspicious bastard at times."

"Apology accepted," she says lightly.

I relax, relieved. "I thought I was going to get more of a hard time than that."

"Why? You're apologising, just don't doubt me again," she says in a mock-serious voice, waving her knife at me jokingly.

"Deal. Fresh start? I swear I'm more fun than I have been."

"Fresh start," she grins.

At that moment Mandy brings our plates over, and Madelaine's eyes go wide as saucers. She places a plate in front of each of us, heaped with their special. A full fried breakfast of sausages, bacon, eggs, beans, hash browns and mushrooms, with pancakes and maple syrup, and waffles with fruit and chocolate spread.

"Oh my God, I'll be falling asleep at my desk!" she exclaims, laughing.

I laugh too. "There's no way you're eating all that."

"I thought you weren't doubting me anymore," she says with a raised brow.

"Touché." I catch Mandy as she goes past and ask for a side plate, moving my hash browns onto it when it arrives.

"Who's not eating all of it now, huh? Eyes too big for your belly?"

I laugh at her fighting words. “I just don’t like them, I normally swap with one of the guys.”

“What kind of psychopath doesn’t like hash browns?! I’ll swap with you. What do you want?”

“It’s fine, it’s not an issue.”

She acts like I haven’t spoken, sliding the hash browns onto her plate. “I’m picking, then. You can have my mushrooms, I can’t stand them. Not really a fair swap, but you snooze, you lose.”

I laugh at her seriousness on the subject and feel more relaxed than I have in weeks, maybe months. Definitely worth the detour. We eat in companionable silence and my God, she finishes the lot. “Where do you put it?!”

“Well, you’re not exactly obese yourself,” she counters. “I’m sure I’ll find a way to burn it off.”

I don’t know if she meant for that to sound so suggestive, but my mind goes there immediately and I have to shift in my seat to get comfortable again. We pay the bill and leave, settling back into the car, and I drive us into the city. “Are you sleeping?” I ask when we reach her office and she’s still quiet.

"I think the medical term is a food coma," she groans, getting out and grabbing her things from the back seat.

I laugh, doing way more of that this morning than I've gotten used to recently. "Send me a message when you're done later, I can be here in ten."

"Great, thanks! See you later."

I'm in my second meeting of the day and paying about as much attention as I did in my first, i.e., none. The managers could've told me they'd been robbing the place blind for months and we're going into bankruptcy and I would've nodded and smiled. I can't stop running through breakfast with Madelaine. I'm like a teenage girl after their first date, playing it back over and over. Five o'clock seems so far away. I decide to head over there at lunchtime, knowing neither of us will want to eat anything after our mammoth breakfast, but we can still take a break and grab a coffee or something.

I suffer through my third meeting watching the clock the whole time and drive back over to Madelaine's office around one. My car is waiting at the lights opposite when I see her leave through the front doors and jump into a taxi. I should've called her and said about coming, she must have other plans. I call her through Bluetooth, hoping I can squeeze in some time with her after. Maybe she's just popping out.

"Hey," she answers. "Everything okay?"

"Yeah, fine. Just wondering if you want to grab a coffee on your break?"

"Oh," she says, surprised. "I'd love to but I'm swamped today. I don't think I'm going to leave my desk, let alone take my break." Weird.

"Okay, I'll just pick you up later then."

"Actually, Jason's heading that way after work, so I'll jump in with him. Saves you waiting around for me." Weirder.

I follow her. I reason that Atlas would have my head if anything happened to her on the day I act as Lai's security, but really, I'm suspicious. Why did she lie? Where is she going?

The taxi goes right out of the city and after we've been driving for about 45 minutes, I realise where we're heading. The prison. I call my assistant and let him know to cancel my afternoon appointments, I'll never make it back in time for them now. Madelaine exits the taxi and heads into the building entrance. I sit outside in my car for an hour, stewing over what's happening.

What is she here for? For work? Surely not. More likely to visit someone. But why wouldn't she tell any of us that? Why outright lie? Unless it's someone we wouldn't want her visiting. Someone against us? I'd just accepted that she was who she said she was, an innocent woman who happened to get caught up with us, and this happens. I feel so stupid, and angry. But if she's working against us, the warnings make little sense. I can't figure out any of it and it frustrates me. I can't believe I was letting my guard down for this woman, swallowing her 'don't doubt me' shit, for her to do what every other woman does. Betray us.

I head home, deciding that ambushing her outside a prison full of officers isn't the best decision. Better to wait for her to come to me.

I'm sitting at the island when she walks in, having wound myself up for the past couple of hours.

"How was work?"

"Fine, thanks," she says, walking past me to grab a drink from the fridge.

"They need many interior designers at Riverbend?" I ask facetiously.

She whips around and narrows her eyes at me. "Are you following me?"

"Why were you there, Madelaine?" My voice rises as I speak.

"None of your business." Her flippancy infuriates me, and I jump up and grab her arm as she tries to leave.

"I should've trusted my instincts. I knew you were hiding shit from us," I yell.

"Get your fucking hands off me," she fumes, volume dangerously low.

"Do as she says, Quince." Max's voice comes from the doorway, deathly quiet.

I let go and she shoves against me, both of us turning to see Atlas and Max stood there. Our raised voices must've drawn them out of the office.

"You're just accepting this shit as well, are you?" I direct at Max, my fury unleashed now. "She let you fuck her, too? Her pussy really must be fucking magic."

Before I can even register he's moving, Atlas is in front of me with his fist in my face. I stagger back, pain radiating from my cheek, and catch myself on the counter. "You don't talk about her like that, ever," he hisses at me.

"Everyone calm the fuck down," Max calls.

She goes to walk off again and I step in front of her.

"You're not going anywhere until you explain why you were there."

"Where?" Max asks.

"Riverbend."

"You're such a fucking hypocrite, Quincy," she accuses.

"Me, the hypocrite? It was only yesterday you were crying that your fuck-buddy hadn't told you his complete life story, and now you've got even more secrets."

She's practically vibrating with fury. "Did I ask for his whole life story? Any of yours? I wanted you to have let me know I was bunking up with fucking criminals. Yet you expect me to tell you everything. Get fucked," she shouts, shoving me again, but this time I'm ready and stand solid as she pushes into my chest, infuriating her even more.

"Madelaine, just tell us and all this can be avoided," Atlas sighs.

"It could be avoided if Quincy didn't have a fucking stick up his ass. You don't get any information that you decide you want, I don't give a fuck how many trust issues you might have."

Max chuckles behind me. So not the time, dude. "Well, now Madelaine's put Quince in his place, can we move on?"

"Jesus, someone wants to get laid," I spit bitterly.

"You're fucking unbelievable," she says as she leaves us and heads to her bedroom.

Atlas heads after her. "Lai..."

"Don't you dare 'Lai' me. You're going to stand there and let him treat me like that? Stay the fuck away from me," we hear from around the corner.

Atlas sighs as he comes back to the kitchen. "Well, that could've gone better. 48 hours without pissing her off. A record, surely."

Max makes us all strong drinks and we sit in silence. So that definitely escalated, but she's so fucking difficult. We're used to women giving and saying whatever we want them to. Even now I think back to those Stepford girlfriends and realise how fucking boring they were. Madelaine has way more fight in her than all of them put together, and I love that about her. Her fire and her balls. There's no rational thinking on my part when she's pushing back. I want to make her submit to me, but I have the feeling I'd hate that if it ever happened and she lost her spice.

I have no idea how long has passed when Madelaine leaves her bedroom and walks past us towards the front door. She looks spectacular in a tight, black silk dress that drapes at her chest, showing the swell of her breasts. She has skyscraper heels that show off her slender caramel legs and the super-thin dress straps show off her arms and collarbones. Fuck. Why am I pissing off a woman that looks like that? I have to remind myself that she's a lying traitor who wants to bring us all down. Yep, that's definitely what she is.

"Where are you going?" Atlas asks with an edge to his voice, jumping up from his barstool.

"Dinner with Lia," she replies curtly. "Don't worry, this isn't my running away outfit."

"I'll drive you," he offers.

"Jeremy is waiting outside." With that, she walks out.

Atlas slams his fist down on the counter. "This is your fucking fault, Quinn. And why isn't she mad at you?" he asks Max.

"Probably because I stuck up for her," he explains.

"Atlas hit me," I deadpan.

"Yeah, when you mentioned fucking her. He let you run your mouth the rest of the time, even tried to convince her to spill her secrets to placate you."

"Fuck," Atlas says. "When did you get so wise?"

"Trust me, for a girl like Madelaine, I'll pay attention."

TWELVE

MADELAINE

I rant about the Titans for a full thirty minutes, my flow uninterrupted as I rage to Lia. She's very good at being a best friend and lets me get it all out, only piping up to agree that yes, Quincy is a butt-munching dick. I finish describing how I would pay Atlas back with a very creative use for cocktail sticks with an enormous sigh.

"Okay, that's it. I'm done talking about them," I promise.

"Good, I'd say they've already ruined enough of your birthday," Lia says. "Let's restart now. With gifts!" She produces a bag from under the table with a flourish. We both love birthdays, especially with how close together ours are. We'd usually go all out but with everything going on at the moment, I opted for a quiet dinner with just us two. We've dressed up and come to a place that we've been dying to try for ages. It's a set menu of about 12 mini-courses and we're two down so far. Obviously every course deserves its own cocktail, so I'm already praying for my head tomorrow.

I take the gifts from Lia and admire the wrapping. It's stunning, as always, and I'm careful as I tear into the paper. I'm not one for keeping it, but I'm also not a savage. Inside the first box is a stunning silver chain with an M and my birthstone. It's slightly chunkier than the dainty jewellery I normally wear, and the clasp is at the front where the charms sit.

"Oh my God, Lia. It's gorgeous, I love it!" I exclaim.

"Good," she grins. "I saw it when we were out shopping and thought it perfectly matches you now, slightly tougher than before but still beautiful."

"You're going to make me cry," I complain.

"No, no tears! Birthdays are for photos, not tears," she claims and pulls her phone out, snapping a photo of me admiring my necklace. “Next, next!” she chants and I laugh at her, replacing the chain and starting on the second gift. It’s a larger, flatter box and inside is the most stunning lingerie, a black bodysuit as thin as tissue paper and completely sheer. The bottom is a high-waisted thong with two lace strips that run from the waistband up to a thin halter neck, covering your breasts. There’s a ribbon that runs around the back to hold them in place and that’s it. I don’t think I’ve ever owned something so sexy.

“Wow!” I breathe.

“We are all about your confidence glow-up over here, and cannot wait to hear how Atlas swallowed his tongue when he saw you in this before even getting to touch you. Just what he deserves,” Lia says smugly.

I burst out laughing at that imagery. “Thank you so much, Lia! It’s absolutely gorgeous, they both are.”

“You’re welcome,” she smiles at me proudly. “They’re from Caus, too, although he didn’t actually pick them,” she reassures me. “You know he loves you just as much as I do.”

“The big brother I never had,” I agree. I don’t exactly believe in love at first sight, but I swear Caus and Lia both had hearts in their eyes when they first met. We’ve been a little trio ever since, especially when I was trying to avoid the monotony of my relationship. He works in project management and is super busy working crazy hours, so Lia and I still get a lot of time as just us two, which is great.

I pop the gifts away just as they bring us out our third course. The amount of food I'm going to be consuming today should be illegal. First that huge breakfast with Quincy, and now these courses. Remembering breakfast makes me sad. Such a brief time of me and Quincy being okay, but it was great. Now look where we are. No, I'm not dwelling on psycho men tonight. I'm enjoying my birthday with my best friend.

"How was your visit today?" Lia asks. She's one of the few people who know about my sister.

"It was good, I love to see her. I hate that she limits the visits, but I understand. Whatever is best for her, after all."

"Yeah, and she knows you're always there for her, whether you see her twice a year or twice a day."

I smile, her words cheering me up. We spend the rest of dinner chatting and laughing, getting progressively louder and more obnoxious as each cocktail takes hold. Basically, having a great time.

When we're finished, Caus picks us up to drop me home. Home?! When did that happen?

"Thanks so much for the gifts, *Coze,*" I tell him, hugging him as he meets us at the door of the restaurant.

"You're welcome, *Lie,*" and I smile at my nickname.

When Caus found out about his nickname he returned the favour, saying my name should be pronounced 'Madeline', like a 'normal person' would pronounce it. He opts to call me 'Lie' like in Madeline, instead of 'Lai', like Madelaine. We've never grown out of it, and I love it.

He drives me back to the house and pulls up on the street outside.

"Is that a security gate?" he asks.

"Yeah." I roll my eyes. "Just let me out here, it's probably easier," I say.

"Okay," he agrees, "we'll watch you in."

I say goodbye to them both, Lia getting out of the car to hug me, and head through the gate. The guys on watch are trying to get a look into the car but there aren't any lights on inside it. “It’s fine, they’re just my friends,” I explain and they nod as I head towards the house. I’m home and free in my bedroom without having run into anyone when there’s a knock at my door. I sigh, preparing to ignore Atlas on the other side, but it’s not him that calls out.

“Hey, Madelaine. I just wanted to check that you're okay,” Maxton says from the other side with the only voice I’m happy to hear right now.

I open the door and there he stands, holding two Slurpees.

“Hey, I brought a peace offering,” he says, showing off the drinks.

“I don’t remember it being you that needed one,” I say with a smile. “How did you know I like these?”

“Jeremy spilled about your trips to 7-Eleven on the way home.”

“No loyalty, that one,” I joke. “You bought me two?” I’ve never seen Maxton drink anything nearly that sugary, mainly water or whiskey.

“Thought it was a good excuse for me to have one too,” he admits.

I fake gasp. “You’re secretly a sugar fiend.”

He laughs at me and I take the offered drink, savouring that first glorious sip.

"What are you up to?" Maxton asks.

"Probably just going to watch a movie. If I try to sleep now, I'll vomit."

"Had a good night, then?" He raises his eyebrows, and I nod. "Want some company?"

And I find I do. I want some company, and I want that company to be Maxton. He's got such a calming presence, he soothes me. Plus, he doesn't seem to talk much other than when he's around me or the guys, but when he does he's wickedly funny.

"Sure," I say, stepping back and gesturing for him to come in. "What's your favourite movie?"

"I haven't watched a movie since I was about 13."

"What?!" I exclaim.

"I'm a busy man," he explains as he wanders into the room, shutting the door behind him.

"So I've heard. We'll go with a classic, then. Miss Congeniality."

"Sounds right up my street," he says with an eye roll.

"Hey, don't you dare bash Sandra Bullock on my watch, Maxton."

I head into the wardrobe to change into some pyjamas, realizing how flimsy they are when I come out to Maxton's gaze. He looks away quickly, settling himself on the bed on top of the covers.

I snuggle underneath them on my side, flicking play on the movie.

For all my objections about falling asleep, I do just that about half an hour in.

I rouse when I feel the weight shifting as Maxton gets off the bed and flicks the TV off. I can't be certain if I imagine it in my sleep, but I'm almost sure I feel his lips press a kiss to my hair as he murmurs "Goodnight, Madelaine."

I wake up Saturday morning with a pounding head, very much self-inflicted, and practically crawl to the kitchen. Guzzling water by the glass and popping a few pain relief tablets, I notice the weather is gorgeous. None of the guys have appeared yet so I decide to test out the outside area, silently thanking Lia for picking up a bikini when we went shopping. I get ready in my room and take a towel, my phone, and some headphones out, as well as grabbing a drink on my way back through the kitchen. I absolutely cannot face food right now. I haven't been out here yet, but it's lovely.

An enormous pool takes up the centre, with loungers running along the side closest to the house. There's a hot tub in the patio corner and a seating area with a BBQ. The whole thing looks out over a manicured lawn that goes on forever and wraps around the house, giving me the view from my bedroom. I choose a lounger in the middle of the row and settle myself in for the long haul. Saturdays with no plans are my favourite.

I must fall asleep in the sun because the next time I open my eyes, a very shirtless Maxton is stretched out on the lounger next to me. My mouth parts slightly with an exhale. Jesus Christ, I think I just combusted. Thank God for my sunglasses, which hide my eyes popping out of their sockets.

I knew he was hench but I haven't seen him without at least a shirt and trousers on yet. He is ripped. And that tattoo! He has a big chest piece done in all black outlines, no shadowing at all. It's so striking and fits him perfectly. I can't see exactly what it is from here and I'm soon distracted when he reaches over for his drink, showing me his back. I watch the muscles as they ripple as he moves and I swallow, my mouth suddenly dry. Laying back down, his abs flex and I squirm in my seat, suddenly very hot and bothered, and I can't blame the sun for it. He looks over and I pull my headphones out.

"Hey," he says. "Sorry, I didn't mean to wake you."

"No, you're good. I didn't mean to sleep, I'm lucky I haven't burnt."

"Do you want some sunscreen?"

"Oh yeah, it's not one of the things I thought to buy."

He hands it over and I apply it to my front still feeling his eyes on me, not helping with the hot and bothered situation.

"Need a hand?" he asks when I twist into a pretzel to try to reach as much of my back as I can.

"Thanks." I hand him the bottle and turn to face away from him.

As soon as his hands touch my skin, I realise my mistake. This is delicious torture. He rubs slowly all over my back, diving to the band of my bikini bottoms, under the strap holding my top together, and up over my shoulders. I'm lost in the feeling of being caressed by Maxton when the patio doors sound and Atlas emerges. I jump, guilt flooding through me.

"All done," Maxton says easily, and I lay back against the lounger, giving him a weak smile. Atlas walks around from behind us, and I almost swallow my tongue. He's just as big as Maxton but less defined and he's covered from wrist to collarbone in tattoos. I didn't even notice he had any with his clothes on, even after Kacey mentioned them. His whole body seems to be one piece, the design flowing seamlessly down his torso and along his arms. The centre piece is of a kneeling man holding a globe and the whole thing feeds from there, all in full colour. They're stunning. I take more than a moment to just watch him as he wanders along the loungers to reach us and takes the one on my other side. I'm in a Titan sandwich and I'm acutely aware of how little material is covering me right now. Lia's choice in a bikini is skimpy, to say the least, not surprising at all. He leans forward so his lips touch my ear. "I only get jealous outside of the group," he whispers instead of a greeting. What the fuck does that mean? I can ogle Maxton? He can touch me?

"Can I apologise for yesterday?" Atlas asks in a normal volume after leaning back.

I'm really trying to focus on what he's saying, but my God, these men are killing me.

"If you want to."

"I'm sorry," he says with sincerity. "I trust you to decide what to tell me. And I know you can handle yourself, but I'd have killed anyone else who spoke to you like that so I shouldn't let Quinn get away with it."

Okay, as far as apologies go, that was pretty good.

"Apology accepted," I tell him.

"That's it?" he asks.

"She's surprisingly forgiving when you apologise," Quincy adds, coming through the door and leaning on the back of my lounger. I tilt my head back to look at him upside down. Still gorgeous, although he's got a shirt on, which is a shame. I wouldn't have minded the trifecta of half-naked Titans.

"On your first go round. After that, you're on your own," I tell him and he grimaces.

"What are your plans tonight?" Maxton asks, diverting us away from another argument.

"Lia's trying to convince me to go to the club but I'm not sure I can face another night of drinking."

"We'll come with you," Atlas says. When I give him a suspicious look, he continues. "It's our place, we need to check up on it."

I roll my eyes. "I'm sure you do. We'd meet at The Lounge first, though."

"Quinn will go with you."

"Great, hiring out the babysitters now?" I ask sarcastically.

"Okay, time to give that sassy mouth something else to do," he says, bending down and picking me up in his arms. I squeal and protest but truthfully, I've been ready for this since I woke up to Maxton's bare chest. And Atlas is a man of his word, I'm way too busy moaning to give him any more sass.

THIRTEEN

QUINCY

I'm in my bedroom getting ready to go out, and my head spins with thoughts of Madelaine, constantly. I have to admit to myself that if she turns out to be betraying us I'll be crushed, even though I've kept her at arm's length. She's wormed her way into my chest, and I don't want her to leave. Whether I let my guard down and trust her or not, she's gotten me. And I do want to trust her. That's half the problem. My gut wants to trust her, but my head lists the reasons why I shouldn't. I've got no real say, though. I've fallen into her orbit, just like Max and Atlas have.

I'm slipping on my jacket when there's a knock on the door and there she is. She's in a white, high neck, long sleeve dress completely covered in lace, looking like the sexiest angel I've ever seen.

"Oh, sorry. I thought this was Atlas's room."

"You don't know where his room is yet?"

She shrugs. "We use mine."

"Everything okay?"

"Yeah," she replies, looking awkward. She's barefoot and is only just over half a foot shorter than me without her heels.

"What's up, Madelaine?"

"I need some help to zip up."

"Let me." I gesture for her to spin.

She does so and her dress hangs open at the back, only just high enough to cover her ass. I grab the zip and the tightness of the dress means the tip of my thumb trails up her bare spine as I do it up. I feel myself getting affected by our proximity and all of her smooth, bare skin, a couple of shades deeper after her day in the sun. As the dress closes all the way to the nape, she shivers.

"Thanks," she mutters and practically runs from the room. Dammit. I really should've taken the opportunity to apologise, rather than ogling her. I know a simple sorry won't work this time. She's already warned me and that's fair, but apologising is a good place to start.

Atlas drives us all over in the Hummer and he and Max drop us outside The Lounge. Madelaine rushes inside to greet Lia, and I amble in after her. I think it's probably best not to crash their drinks too hard, so I situate myself at the bar, ordering myself a drink. This place could definitely benefit from an upgrade. I try to focus on the business part of my brain but an hour or so passes and I'm getting really bored of watching Madelaine brush off guy after guy. Okay, maybe less bored and more really fucking irritated. She's got her hair in loose waves and is wearing clear stilettos that make her legs look endless, the white colour of her dress making her bronze legs pop. Two new guys waltz over and that's my limit reached. I walk up behind Madelaine and they pale when they spot me over her shoulder. "Are you two ready to go?" I ask the girls while looking straight at the guys. Madelaine cranes her neck to face me as the guys stutter between themselves.

"Sorry, I didn't realize they were with someone," one says. Madelaine rolls her eyes as the guys leave.

"Fine, let's go," she concedes as she and Lia down what's left of their cocktails. "But you owe us both a drink."

"I'm sure I can manage that."

I follow them both out of the bar before Lia pops back inside to use the bathroom.

"Can we talk?" I ask Madelaine as we wait outside in the fresh air.

"Sure, what's up?" she asks flippantly.

"Come on, Lai. I hate this."

"I didn't cause it."

"I know, but-"

"The last I knew, you still thought I was lying. Does 'Madelaine' mean I'm in trouble and 'Lai' signify that you're over it? I need a way to track your mood swings," she bites sarcastically.

"I don't think you're lying. I just hate not knowing things," I try to explain.

"Look, Quincy, don't you think you've ruined enough of my evenings this week?"

That blow hits true. "That's not fair."

"Actually, I think it is," she says, clearly finished with this conversation. Just then Lia comes back out, giving us a questioning look, but Madelaine smiles at her. “Let’s go.”

Atlas, Madelaine and I are on the way back to the house and she is merry, to say the least. I’m still sulking so I sit quietly in the back watching her, but I don’t think she’s even noticed.

“Lia says I’m cutting off my nose to spite my face. I’m pushing too hard against you because of Jed.” The many drinks have loosened her tongue, but she won’t care. I love that she stands by everything she says, she’s not the type to say things she doesn’t mean in the first place.

“What do you say?” Atlas asks. She thinks about that for a minute, her nose scrunching up adorably as she mulls it over.

“I say I do like you. But how do I not lose myself again?” she asks, genuinely curious.

“You trust me to not take too much,” Atlas tells her as he pulls up inside the garage. She thinks that over as we walk into the house and into the kitchen. Atlas lifts her and sits her on the side of the island, while I lean against it.

"That's pretty profound, you know," she says with awe in her voice that makes me smile despite the pity party I'm in.

Atlas laughs as he hands me a glass of water and comes to stand in front of her, handing her a glass, too. She ignores it completely, trying to undo his shirt buttons around his arms.

"What did I tell you about drunk chicks?" he asks, amused by her.

"Are you turning me down?" Her brow furrows.

"Fuck, no. I'm trying to be respectable and you're making it really fucking hard."

"It, or you?" she says, snaking her hand down the front of his trousers.

"Okay, let's get you to bed."

"Now you're talking!"

"Not me, you. If I lie down with you like this, I'm going to do something I regret."

"Okay, I'll control myself but I'm not tired yet. What about a movie?"

Atlas laughs and rests his hands on her thighs. "I'll watch a movie with you."

He's so intimate with her, and I feel a burning envy in my chest. I've got no one to blame but myself.

"Where's Maxton?" she asks. She calls us all by our full names and she's nearly the only one to do so. Even Atlas gets his name shortened by others the majority of the time. "We need to show him all the movies."

"He had something to do at the club," At explains.

She pouts and looks dejected. Great, she likes both of them and can't stand me. Good job, Quince.

"I'm going to head to bed, 'night you two." There's no way I can sit and watch those two act like teenage lovers and paw over each other for an hour and a half. We all have a 'no drunk sex' rule but that doesn't extend to some heavy petting. They echo my goodnight and I slump into my room. I hate that I'm so jealous of my best friend. He touches her so easily and she's so receptive to it. I want to be the one to hold her, to stroke her hair away from her face and look after her when she's inebriated. What have I done?

In the morning, I head out to the pool where Lai and Maxton are already sitting. We never use this area normally, but I don't blame him. I'd also follow her anywhere, in that bikini.

"Can I apologise?" I ask, sitting on the edge of the lounger next to her.

"I'm getting déjà vu," Max mumbles with amusement.

Ignoring him, I carry on. "I really am sorry. I lose my head a bit when I think someone's hiding stuff."

"That sounds like a 'you' problem," Lai responds.

"It absolutely is. I'll work on keeping my shit together. And this is totally the end of me quizzing you." I can't tell what she's thinking with those huge sunglasses on. Her eyes are normally so expressive and it puts me on edge, not being able to see them.

"You've called a truce before, Quincy, and I believed it. Then you ambushed me with more shit. I can't handle this back and forth."

"No more. I'll prove it to you," I swear, desperate for another chance.

"I'll wait for you to do that. Also, second round apologies normally come with a gift," she jokes. "Edible, preferably." I smile and let out a sigh of relief, my shoulders relaxing. I'm not out of the woods yet, but she's giving me the opportunity to make it up to her, and I won't blow this one.

We spend the morning sunbathing in peaceful quiet, and Atlas comes out to join us for lunch. We're sitting at the outside table finishing up an amazing Ploughman's that Lucy produced when Lai decides she wants to take a dip. It's even hotter than yesterday and the cool blue water does look inviting.

"Don't expect me to save you when you seize up and drown," At calls to her as she walks to the edge. Max and I both give him disbelieving looks. We all know there's not much he wouldn't do to save her, under any circumstance.

"That's a myth," Lai calls back to him before diving into the water. We all watch her go, trying to keep a visual on her underwater until she pops up in the middle. "Come on, I didn't realise cramp was the thing that scared the Titans," she says with a smirk. Atlas, Max, and I all exchange looks, knowing she has us hook, line and sinker, and jump out of our chairs, jumping into the pool at the same time. I come up for air to the sound of Lai laughing and I feel so light.

"You're all like rocks," she chuckles.

"We can be fast when we need to be," Max promises.

"Race!" she calls, lifting herself up on the side of the pool. We all get out and line up while she counts down, ready to dive in as she shouts go. Lai is way more streamlined than any of us and takes the lead in the beginning as we all break the surface. Our strength would put us ahead in no time, but I'm really not invested in this race and grab her foot just in front of me instead. She goes under laughing and comes back up spluttering.

"Dirty tactics!" she shouts, treading water.

"Where's your ref?" I ask her, laughing. She gestures behind me, and I turn like a fool. Pushing herself up on my shoulders, she sinks me into the water and dunks my head for good measure before pushing away. When I come back up, she's a couple of metres away, laughing at me, her eyes twinkling.

"That's how we're playing it?" I ask, stalking towards her. She swims backwards until she bumps into Atlas behind her.

"Hey! You're supposed to be on my team," she protests.

"I don't remember having that conversation," Atlas chuckles.

"Maxton!" she calls to him as he floats on his back to the side of us. "I need rescuing."

He laughs without up-righting himself. "That you most certainly do not, Madelaine."

I'm half a meter away from her, wondering what to do now. If I touch her anywhere other than her ankle, I'm going to have a very visible issue on my hands. I'm saved from making that decision by Jeremy heading out onto the patio.

"Sorry to disturb you," he calls. I feel Lai tense when she realises the position he's just caught her in, but Jeremy doesn't bat an eyelid. He's sure to keep his eyes away from her, even with most of her body concealed by the water. "We just got a parcel."

We all swim over to the side, lifting ourselves out. Atlas hands Lai a towel, knowing she'd feel uncomfortable being so underdressed in front of Jeremy. She doesn't have an issue with us seeing her like that, but she really respects the friendship she's got going with him.

"What do you mean, 'we got'?" Max asks.

"Lucy went to the supermarket and when she went to load the groceries in the trunk, this was in it. It's addressed to Madelaine," he finishes, looking at her now that she's covered up.

"I don't want it," she says, punctuating her claim by taking a step backwards. "That's creepy as fuck."

"It's not explosive or contaminated, we've already checked it out," Jeremy tells Max, handing it over. He rips it open and we all take in the panties sitting inside.

"Oh my God, they're mine!" Lai shrieks, grabbing the box from Max. "What the fuck? Have they been in my room?!" She's freaking out, understandably.

"They're the ones I took from your office," Atlas tells her. "I thought I'd misplaced them or you got them back without me realising."

"So, how did this freak get them?" Max asks.

"Let's take this to the office," Atlas tells us. "Do you want to come, Madelaine?"

"No way," she exclaims. "I'll chill out here. Burn these, please," she asks, handing over the parcel to Max.

Atlas holds Lai's stricken face in his hands and murmurs something unintelligible to her as the rest of us head inside. She visibly relaxes and I'm struck with a wave of that overfamiliar jealousy. One day, I'll settle her like that.

"We can't go at the Vipers with no evidence it's them," Max commands. "Seems more like a scorned lover to me, anyway, and we're walking a thin line with the Vipers as it is. We don't want to trigger a war. It'll be mutual destruction at this point, they're just as powerful as we are."

"Fuck off. Silas and his VPs are like, 100," I scoff. They have a different structure to us; we run the Titans jointly whereas they have one leader and three vice presidents.

"Yeah, but their sons aren't. From what I've heard, it's them practically running the show from the shadows right now."

We've been in the office for hours. Jeremy ran us through CCTV from the supermarket parking lot but the feed was clearly looped. We've gone through security for everyone, most importantly Lai, here and when she's out. Now we were going round in circles discussing possible culprits, but really we just have to wait for them to hit again instead of being proactive, as we have little to go on.

"Right, I'm done," I declare. "I was much preferring our lazy Sunday to this frustrating shit."

"Okay," Atlas agrees. I was finance anyway, I can get away with ditching. "We'll finish up soon." I nod my acknowledgment and leave, heading towards the kitchen, where I can hear Lai's voice. Much better. I find her sitting at the island, chatting to Lucy.

"Hey," I greet them both.

"Hey," Lai replies, and Lucy gives me a smile. "I'm just quizzing Lucy on everything she does around here."

"Keeps us alive," I say, only half joking, and taking another bar stool.

"Not at all," Lucy rebukes. "I only need to keep the place tidy, but I'm an early bird, so I usually provide breakfast. And then lunch because they're always busy. It's been so nice seeing you all actually take some time off." She gives Lai a fond look but carries on when Lai looks embarrassed. "They normally like to sort their own dinners, though I'll do something special for their birthdays, shall I?" she asks me.

"Their birthdays?" Lai asks before I can respond.

"Yeah, Max's is Wednesday and At's is Thursday."

"Wow, August is a popular month, isn't it?"

"I guess," I shrug. Not that unusual for two people to have close birthdays.

"What do you do?" she presses.

"Not a lot, we're not massively into birthdays. Dinner would be great, thanks, Lucy."

"Can I plan something for them?" Madelaine asks enthusiastically.

"If you want." I smile at her excitement.

"Great. Although there's not much time," she adds pensively. "If only I knew someone who owed me, who could help."

My smile grows even bigger. "I'd be happy to help you," I say, and I mean it.

FOURTEEN

MAXTON

Monday passes uneventfully and I head home, hoping Quincy hasn't managed to piss Madelaine off in the last twenty-four hours and cause her to camp out in her room. Thankfully it doesn't look like he has and I find her at the dining table surrounded by paperwork when I get in.

"Hey, *belle*," I say, making her jump. She looks up with a small frown on her face that gets replaced by a big smile when she sees it's me. I feel like the Grinch, my heart just grew three sizes.

"Hey," she replies. "What does *belle* mean?"

"It's *beautiful* in French," I say, which makes her smile widen even further. "What are you up to?" I ask, sitting down next to her.

She sighs and puts her pen down. "Just insurance stuff. I have to list everything I owned that was in the house and the car, or at least everything I want to claim for." She pulls a face. "I've been here forever. Then I have to decide whether I want a payout or a rebuild. Same for the car, replacement or cash."

"You know who would be great at this?" I ask her but she obviously knows who I mean as she rolls her eyes, making me smile. I've been doing a lot of that since she moved in. "What do you think you'll decide?"

"I have no idea. I loved that house, it was my first proper home after my dad died. It was so special but rebuilding it won't be the same, will it? I think it's tainted now, even if we find whoever did it. I'm not sure if I'll ever feel safe there."

"I'm sorry to hear about your dad."

"That's okay, you didn't do it," she replies with a weak smile. "As for the car, I guess whichever makes the most financial sense. It was just a reliable runaround, there was no sentimental value."

"Atlas is the one you need to speak to about cars," I tell her.

"Yeah, somehow I don't think the payout will stretch to a Hummer, but I'll bear it in mind," she says as she laughs. That might be my favourite sound.

"Speaking of, he wanted me to tell you he's got business shit to do tonight so will be back later."

"Yeah, Quincy's out too."

"Doing what?"

"Running some errands for me," she says, looking very pleased with herself.

"I would make the most of that, it doesn't happen often. What other tasks has he got before you forgive him?"

"I think I have forgiven him, he's pretty hard to stay mad at. But don't tell him that. I wasn't even that mad, more hurt. Stupid, really."

"It's not stupid. He told you he trusted you and then accused you the very next time something came up."

"But why do I care so much about what he thinks? I'm sure most people don't get upset about the housemate of the guy they're sleeping with not liking them," she tries to joke.

"Is that who he is to you?"

She meets my gaze with a deep look, warring emotions flashing in her eyes.

"Whatever. He's not even here, and he's getting all the attention! Looks like it's just me and you for dinner, what do you fancy?" she asks, collecting all the paperwork.

"I don't mind," I reply, not putting any thought into it. I'm too busy thinking about an evening alone with her.

"Choices!"

"Huh?"

"It's a game Lia and I play. 'I don't mind' is the most infuriating answer ever, so if you say it and someone else says 'choices', you have to give them two options to pick from."

"Okay, pizza or Taco Bell?"

"You don't eat that shit, that's cheating!" she complains.

"I eat it!" I definitely don't, but I know they're her favourites.

"Shall we be super chill and eat it in the lounge? I can enlighten you with Legally Blonde, another classic. And Atlas isn't here to moan about crumbs."

I laugh at that. She knows us all so well already.

"Done."

Madelaine orders dinner and I let her choose for me. Her eyes widen when given free rein, so lord knows what will turn up. She goes to change into pyjamas but thankfully has a shirt on over the skimpy ones I saw before. It's Atlas's shirt, and I have to adjust myself when my mind wanders to her wearing my shirt, with nothing underneath. I'm knocked out of my fantasy by the food arriving, and it's my turn for my eyes to be like saucers when I see the amount the delivery guy is carrying. I take it back into the lounge and lay it all out on the coffee table while Madelaine grabs us drinks.

"The only thing that could make this better is a Slurpee," she declares as she comes through the door, and I have to agree. I used to be addicted to them as a kid but hadn't had one in years before I delivered them to her door the other night. It rekindled my Slurpee obsession.

Her gaze falls on the mountain of food. "Oops, I shouldn't be trusted when I'm hungry. Let's blame this on wanting to comfort eat my stress away."

"How long have you got to decide for the insurers?" I ask.

"Until the end of next week, I've got some time."

"If you didn't rebuild, what would you buy?"

"No idea. I can't think of setting roots down anywhere while that creep is still out there. What if I settle in somewhere and he finds me? I wouldn't be able to stay."

"Do you feel safe here?" I ask, needing her to say yes.

"Yeah, I do, but this is temporary. You guys have been generous enough as it is."

I shrug, not saying anything but knowing that if any of us get our way, she won't be going anywhere.

Heading to the kitchen early Wednesday morning, I'm jolted out of my half-asleep state by the last thing I thought I'd see today.

Bobbing over my normal seat at the dining table are three enormous balloons. The biggest is a solid gold sphere with 'Happy Birthday Maxton' written on the front with a floating present and cake on either side. I'd forgotten it was even my birthday. None of us guys ever really make a fuss, so the culprit is obvious. I stand there taking it all in: the balloons, the table confetti and the gifts sat on the table.

Madelaine shuffles in rubbing her eyes but perks up when she sees me.

"Happy Birthday, Maxton!" she grins.

"How did you..." but Quince interrupts, jumping on my back and scrubbing my hair.

"Happy birthday, dude!" I throw him off just as Atlas joins the party, coming up behind Madelaine. He wraps his arms around her waist and settles a kiss on her shoulder.

"Happy Birthday, Max."

He looks up and takes in the birthday supplies. "Is this what you got up in the middle of the night for?"

"Yeah," Madelaine says, still grinning. "You stay up so late," she directs at me. "Lucy will be here to make breakfast in five so I'm going to get ready and then we'll do gifts after." She wriggles out of Atlas's arms and makes to leave.

"Thank you, *belle*," I say before she can leave.

She meets my eyes for a beat, then leaves.

"Fuck, man. She's going to ruin us all," Quince says when she's gone.

"Not this shit again, Quince," Atlas moans. "It's way too fucking early." I take a seat at the table, the balloons bobbing over my head. If only our enemies could see me now.

"I don't mean that. I mean, look at the way Max looks at her. These gifts are way too sweet to come from your best friend's fuck buddy. I already want to rip your head off whenever you touch her, now I've got to beat Max too?"

"Err, Max doesn't get to touch her," I complain

"You're a lot closer than I am."

"Whose fault is that?" Atlas chips in.

"Yes, I know. I'm working on it."

"I think we can all tell she likes you, Max," Atlas continues. "Jury's out on Quinn, but I'm still not doing anything to scare her off so if that means you two live the rest of your lives with blue balls, then so be it."

"I don't think she's down for the polyamory shit. You should see the guilt in her eyes whenever she thinks she's overstepped," I tell them.

"Does she know you're both okay with it?" Quince asks.

"How the fuck do you bring that up?"

I sigh, wishing I knew the answer to that. "How did she know it was my birthday, anyway?"

"Lucy spilled the other day so heads up At, she knows yours too."

"Do we know hers?" I ask.

"It would've been in her background check, but I didn't bother to look. Whether she was a Capricorn or a Pisces wasn't the most pressing issue at the time," Quinn says sarcastically.

We're distracted from our conversation by Lucy coming in the front door.

"Oh, you're up already? You're never up yet! I'll get breakfast sorted. Happy Birthday, Maxton," she says.

"No rush, Lucy," Atlas says. "I'm going to go get ready for work."

"Me too," Quinn adds, and they both leave.

"Thanks, Lucy," I say to her.

"Balloons, eh?" she asks. "You three don't normally decorate for birthdays."

"It wasn't those two. You know they can barely function as it is. It was Madelaine."

She laughs. "I assumed as much."

I'm lost in thought as Lucy prepares breakfast. Quince is right, we are all in way over our heads with Madelaine. How has she got us all wrapped around her little finger so easily? Would she be into being with all of us if we broached the subject with her? Has she really not contemplated a polyamorous relationship, or is that something she wouldn't do? So many questions are running through my head. I sit there mulling them over and over until the others come back in.

"Morning, Lucy!" Madelaine calls as she crosses over to the table to join me.

"Good morning, Lai. Breakfast will be in ten, okay?"

"Great, thank you!" The others both take their usual seats so Madelaine is opposite me, with Atlas next to her, and I've got Quinn next to me. She grabs a large, thin gift off the table, handing it to me. "Open! They're only silly. What do you get the guy who has everything, huh?"

"I'm sure they're perfect," I tell her, and I know they will be because she chose them for me. What is happening to me? I'm not normally this soppy. I tear open the paper and stare down at the square frame. The print inside shows 'The 100 best movies of all time' and a sharpie rolls out the bottom of the wrapping.

"You can already cross two off," she smiles apprehensively but it doesn't quite reach her eyes, like she's worried this gift isn't great. I pick the sharpie up and cross over the films we watched together recently.

"Thank you, *belle*, it's amazing."

"I'm glad you like it. You'll have to open this one next." She points at the second gift on the table and I lean over to rip the paper off. I chuckle as I unwrap a Slurpee machine. "So maybe this is 50% birthday gift, 50% necessary purchase?" She smiles.

"Saves me running to the garage every time Quince pisses you off," I say, earning a laugh from Madelaine and a glare from Quince. "Really, thank you."

She beams at me, happy her gifts have gone down well. "Any birthday plans?"

"Nope."

"Nothing?"

"Just working, we really don't do birthdays," I reiterate.

She rolls her eyes. "Nothing fun at all?"

"We could do a movie night, start in on this poster? I'll even make you a Slurpee," I offer.

Her face splits into a wide grin. "I'd love that."

"I'm there," Quince pipes up, and Atlas chuckles.

I'm saved from whacking him by Lucy bringing the food over. She loads the table with waffles, pancakes, fruit, and bacon. This might be my favourite birthday yet.

FIFTEEN

ATLAS

Max and I come out of the office a little later than usual, having gotten caught up with something at work. We walk into the kitchen diner to see Madelaine and Lucy putting the finishing touches on a bonafide feast.

"That smells delicious," I say truthfully. "What have we got?"

"We tried our hands at some Togolese foods," Madelaine beams proudly. "We've got Gboma Dessi, Djenkoume, grilled Togo chicken, and Ablo. Then some grilled veggies and hasselback potatoes, just in case we butchered the rest."

"I can't believe you've done all this, it must've taken you ages." Max is clearly pleased she's done the work to cook from his native culture, but as usual, she shrugs off her efforts.

"It was mainly Lucy, to be honest. I've had the simple day at work."

"Oh, please. You've been researching for days."

"Well, thanks to both of you. Where's Quince?"

Madelaine suddenly looks guilty. "He's caught up in town. He ran in to get me some things and it's gone a bit haywire."

I chuckle at her culpable expression. "Don't feel too bad, he deserves to miss out on this amazing feast."

"You all save him some," Lucy scolds, heading back to get some drinks.

We all sit and devour the meal Madelaine and Lucy have made. Everything is delicious. Lucy has the foresight to make up a plate for Quinn before we can consume the lot and hides it in the fridge for him later. We roll into the lounge afterwards to watch a film from Max's print while our food settles. As soon as the credits roll, Madelaine jumps up and runs out into the kitchen area, while Max and I give each other curious looks. Just as I'm about to go after her she returns with a birthday cake, covered in chocolate icing with a drip and swirls of more icing on top. A curly candle sits on the top.

"Happy Birthday!" she tells Max, for maybe the fiftieth time today. "Make a wish!" He gazes up at her standing in front of him with pure adoration in his eyes, his wish obvious to me. He blows the candle out, and before he can say anything, Madelaine pushes the cake up into his face with a laugh. I cackle next to him. The second his face comes away covered in icing, she seems shocked that she did it. Max has a matching shocked expression under the layer of chocolate. Madelaine slowly lowers the cake into his lap and takes a step back.

"Run, *belle,*" Max says in a low voice.

She backs up as he hands the cake over to me, a lovely face-shaped dent in the middle, and stands. She giggles and makes it to the door, taking one last look before turning and fleeing. Max goes after her and I put the cake down on the coffee table and follow them out. They're standing on either side of the dining table, Max stalking her as she uses it as a buffer.

"Okay, let's talk this through as adults," she tries to reason.

"Adults? I'm covered in icing." This makes her release a laugh again, which she tries to stifle. I wander over to the kitchen area, leaning on the island and taking in the show, a smile around my lips. Max is always so cool and collected. I love that Madelaine brings out the fun in him.

"It's your birthday, icing is a necessity," she coaxes, reaching the head of the table.

"You're not helping yourself," Max explains. That's when she makes a run for it, darting between the table and the kitchen. She's within arm's reach of me and clearly hoping for a rescue when Max scoops her up from behind. He does a full spin with her in his arms, both of them laughing, and deposits her on the island next to where I'm leaning. He steps between her thighs, placing his hands on either side of her while they grin at each other. The island helps with the height difference and they're pretty much eye level. We're all so close that as Madelaine breathes, I can see her breasts brushing against Max and her pupils dilate. I'm hard as steel in seconds. As she registers the positioning her amusement dies and tension fills her posture.

"Don't overthink it," I say, turning into her and gripping her face in my hands. She pulls back slightly.

"But I am. This doesn't feel right without talking about it. Going with the flow will give me an aneurism."

Max smirks while gazing at her like a lovesick puppy. God, I hope I don't look like that, but I'm almost certain I do. "Okay, what do you want to know?" he asks as he reaches for some kitchen towel, cleaning his face.

"What's happening here?"

"Whatever you want," I tell her truthfully, releasing her.

"Have you done this before?"

"We've shared a girl before," Max admits.

"As in, one of you joins in with someone and their girlfriend?"

"Not exactly."

She looks confused at our cryptic answers, but I'm suddenly terrified of scaring her off.

"Is this too wild for your wild phase?" I ask her.

"Is this a phase? Do you get to pass me around for sex until you're ready to swan off and get a different girl?"

"Not at all," Max reassures her. "You must know how At feels about you. And me, too. What do you want?" Max asks her.

Her shoulders tense even more and in a small voice, she answers "I don't want to upset anyone."

Max visibly stiffens, and I know he's expecting her to shut this down. To choose one of us, just like the other girls who all eventually have.

"You won't, baby," I reassure her, "but we all need to be open with each other."

She looks at us both with cautious eyes. "I want to be Maxton's girl, too. Or at least, to try."

"You do?" Max blurts.

"Yeah," she says with more conviction now that it's out.

"Does that mean you were already officially my girl?" I ask, teasing her.

She rolls her eyes at me. "As if I ever had a choice."

I lean forward, kissing just behind her ear where I know she's ticklish, and whisper "Then let's show you how well we treat our girl." I bite her earlobe and pull her face towards me, kissing her deeply and showing her exactly what I think of this conversation. I kiss down the side of her neck along her collarbone and Max steps back so I can wrap her legs around my waist.

"We're going to give Lucy a heart attack if we stay here," I say, picking her up off the counter and carrying her to my room. It's the same layout as the one she has, just a different colour scheme, opting for blues and browns instead of whites and creams. Max sits on the edge of the bed and I drop Madelaine into his lap. She shifts so she's straddling him, their mouths an inch apart. They pause, eye contact sizzling while they wait for the other to make the first move.

Madelaine strokes Max's cheek with her thumb, cupping his jaw as he closes the distance, finally kissing her. He grips the back of her head and deepens the kiss until she rocks her hips in his lap. I pull Madelaine's top and bra off, as well as my shirt, and Max runs a hand up the curve of her waist, caressing one breast with his hand before breaking their kiss to take the other in his mouth. She arches her back as he sucks and gropes and a moan escapes her.

I tangle my hand in her hair, pulling her head back and kissing her from behind. Max swaps his hand and his mouth, twirling the now wet exposed nipple in his fingers, and she moans into my mouth. I can't take much more taunting, so I undress the rest of the way and sit next to them. Max stands Madelaine up, removing the rest of her clothes, and she climbs into my lap. I line myself up and slip inside, pulling her down by her ass to take my full cock. She gathers a rhythm and Max licks his lips, now as naked as the rest of us, watching and stroking his length in his hand.

I can't believe Madelaine is into this. The sensations and thoughts are too much and when she speeds up I lay back, every extremity buzzing with pleasure. Max stands up and positions himself behind her, pushing her chest forward lower against mine and bringing her ass up so I slip out. He must plunge straight in again as Madelaine's eyes close and a moan falls from her mouth. Fuck, that's so hot. All I can see is Madelaine's face twisted in satisfaction and her breasts rocking with every thrust Max gives her from behind. I grab two handfuls of her ass and pull her off of him.

"Have you ever had anything in this perfect ass before?" She shakes her head, eyes shining. "Soon we're going to claim that too." Her eyes widen and I slam her back down on me and thrust up into her. It doesn't take me long, and I'm pouring myself into her with a groan as she looks down at me with a lustful expression. Max takes back over, sliding back inside her as I reach underneath, swirling circles around her clit. She explodes with a scream, taking Max along with her as she pulses around him. She collapses on top of me and he lands on his back next to us.

Not one of us says anything for a few minutes, lost in bliss and trying to catch our breath. I feel the proof of what we've done start to leak out of Madelaine and onto me, so I wrap my arms around her and stand, taking her into the adjoined bathroom. Max stays where he is, leaving me to check on our girl, and she's quiet as I settle her on the counter before turning the shower on to let the water warm.

"What are you thinking about?" I ask her, brushing some of her loose hair off her face.

"I kind of feel like I should feel guilty, like I just cheated on you."

"I was there, baby, I don't think it counts. Did you like it?" I ask, suddenly worried she's regretting it.

"Yes," she replies simply.

"And you like Max?"

"Yes," she says again, with a smile.

"So you're happy?"

"I'm happy," she confirms, smile widening.

"And Quinn?" I have to ask. Her expression saddens.

"Quinn can't decide whether he hates me or not on a daily basis."

That's not what I asked and we both know it, but I don't press her any further.

I wake up on my birthday alone and drag myself up to go and find my girl. Wandering into the open area, I see I have the same treatment as Max did yesterday. Two gifts sit on the table in front of my usual seat, with three new balloons floating above. I hope these are the things Quinn had to pick up for her. I would pay good money to see him struggling down the street with those. Three clear globes read Happy Birthday Atlas, with the first containing smaller black and gold balloons, the second filled with confetti, and the last with huge streamers coming from the base.

Madelaine walks in with Quinn, who nods at me. "Happy birthday, man."

Madelaine practically skips over to me, and I can feel my matching grin to hers stretching across my face as I thank him. "Happy Birthday, Atlas," she says with a chaste kiss, but I grab her chin and turn her face back to me, getting lost in her taste until her muscles relax and she sighs into my mouth.

"Thank you, baby." She pulls out of my arms and hands me the first gift just as Max walks in.

"Happy Birthday, At," he says, chirpier than he's been in months. I smile my thanks as he wanders over to Madelaine. "Morning, *belle,*" he says and before she can answer he's pressing her to him and kissing her senseless.

"No way!" Quinn bursts. "I'm out running errands all around town like Driving Miss fucking Daisy and you're all getting it on?" We all laugh but ultimately ignore him, and I unwrap my first gift, holding the canvas in my hands.

"What's that?" Max asks Madelaine, but I answer for her.

"It's a French martini and a whiskey." And it was, a simple watercolour of both drinks in the middle of a white background. "Where did you get this?"

"I painted it, obviously. Very specific requirements to get from the high street," she says sarcastically. I narrow my eyes playfully at her sassy mouth but tell her truthfully, "I love it."

"Good." She smiles and swaps the painting for my second gift, glancing quickly at Quinn and Max. I take the lid off the shallow box and gulp when I see the red underwear sitting inside. I pick the panties up. They're solid satin in the front but the back is a lattice of ribbon with a bow that would sit right at the top of her perfect ass.

"That's a preview," she says.

I reach out to pull her against me, whispering in her ear, "here's a preview for you." I show her exactly how she affects me by pressing it into her stomach. Her breath hitches as her lips part and I take my opening, kissing her until I hear two matching groans. I break away from her to see both of my friends subtly rearranging themselves and laugh. I have a feeling this thing between us all could be really great.

SIXTEEN

MADELAINE

I've spent the morning at work in a complete daydream, with a huge grin on my face. I'm even annoying myself with how happy I am, but I can't help it. Happy that Maxton likes me back. Happy that Atlas is okay with it. Happy Quincy seems to be keeping his word. I can't fully let my guard down around him yet, but I really hope he proves himself to me. I walk towards my office and see Anna, our receptionist, giving me a quizzical expression and smiling. Last night definitely blew my little wild-phase mind. How did going out hoping for a one-night stand land me two boyfriends?

"There's someone on the phone for you," she calls as I pass her. "I knew you wouldn't be long so they're waiting on the line."

"Okay. Thanks, Anna," I reply. I can't pop out and pick up some lunch without coming back to more work. I open the door and freeze, my brain not computing what I'm seeing.

The guy spray-painting my wall turns and looks me dead in the eye. He's dressed in head to toe black with only his eyes uncovered, dead and soulless. He steps towards me and this jolts me out of my shock. I scream before he gets any closer and he turns through the open balcony doors and jumps to ground level. Anna runs in behind me, closely followed by other members of the team, clearly alerted by my scream.

"What the fuck?!" Jason says as they all stare at the 'MEA' on the wall, the message not complete.

"Are you okay?" Anna asks me when I stand there in silence.

"I don't know," I reply honestly.

"I'll get security up here," Jason finishes and ushers everyone back out. "You take a seat, Lai, out here."

Nodding, I sit down at the reception desk, numbly following his instructions. I notice the light on the phone flashing, reminding me of the client waiting on the other end. I take a deep breath and bolster myself. Now is not the time to break.

"Hello, LLI, Madelaine speaking."

"Madelaine, it's Max." My resolve shatters and I let out an enormous sigh.

"Maxton," I say, relief clear in my tone. I am a strong, independent woman but I can admit to needing a bit of support sometimes.

"What's up, *belle*?" he asks, instantly on alert.

"There was someone in my office."

He says something mumbled to someone he's with, and then he's back with me. "Jeremy's on his way up now. We'll be there in ten, okay?"

"Don't tell Atlas, I don't want to ruin his birthday," I say ridiculously.

"Madelaine, as if I could keep anything about you away from him. I've quite liked my life recently," he jokes, making me smile and relax slightly. "Do you want me to stay on the phone with you?" he asks.

"No, it's okay. Security will be up in a minute, I should go. See you soon."

I look up as Jason appears in front of me. "You shouldn't be answering client calls, Lai, even you need to take a break sometimes. I think this situation warrants it."

Okay, I have to have this conversation with him now. I know Maxton is on his way, and the chances of him being alone are slim. They'll all come barrelling in like rhinos and there's no way I can keep this quiet any longer.

"Actually, that was Maxton. So technically, yes, a client, but I've also been staying with him." He says nothing, stunned into confused silence. "And Atlas," I continue. "And Quincy."

"Better known as the Titans?" he asks when he's found his voice.

"I guess. But I swear we got the contract and the renewal before any of us knew the connection. Our relationship had nothing to do with it," I blurt.

"Calm down, Madelaine. You're a fully grown woman and one of my best members of staff. I trust your judgement and your integrity."

I deflate in relief. The last few minutes have been a rollercoaster, and it's knocking me for six.

"Okay, good, because they'll be here in ten and they're not exactly wallflowers."

It was definitely more like five and I worried about the speed they must've reached to get here. Jeremy arrived just as Jason and I finished talking, along with the building security, who he promptly banned from my office. They were pretty happy to not have any more work to do and slunk off, leaving Jeremy to survey the scene. He decamped me so I moved my things into a conference room, which is where the guys find me when they appear. They all rush towards me, but I hold a hand up.

"I'm fine," I insist. "I'm over the initial shock. Plus, I am still at work, so please don't make a huge scene," I implore.

They all back off but don't look the slightest bit happy about it. "What happened?" Quincy asks, the first to get his question in.

"I came back from grabbing my lunch and found some guy in my office, mid-wall scrawl. I screamed, and he ran."

They all fire questions at me for the next ten minutes, a more in-depth interrogation than my statement to the police. No, I didn't recognise him. Yes, he must've come in through the balcony. How would I know what he was going to write? The more answers I didn't know, the more anxious I was getting that Quincy might flip, and I kept glancing at him to see his reaction. Which should have been ridiculous. I knew my truth, and if Quincy couldn't get past his issues then it was his problem, not mine. Even with my inner pep talk, he must notice my concern as he strides over to me. He leans over me in my chair, pulling me into his arms and in a gentle gesture, presses a soft kiss on my hair.

"I'm on your side," he says insistently, pulling back to look at me. "I swear."

Relief floods through me, and I smile up at him.

"Now, shall we get going?"

"Going where?"

"Home."

"It's barely the afternoon, I'm not going anywhere."

"Madelaine, you were nearly attacked."

"He was vandalising my wall, that's very different to being attacked. I'm not suddenly incompetent. I feel fine to work, so I'm going to. Plus, we've got these really demanding clients who won't tolerate late drawings for their clubs."

He opens his mouth to argue more, but Atlas interrupts him.

"Quinn, it's Madelaine's decision. We'll be here with the team, anyway."

"Okay, fine, but I'm staying in here with you." I roll my eyes at his stubbornness. Maxton and Atlas go to my office to do whatever it is scary gang men do at crime scenes, and I spend the afternoon completing some plans and trying not to stare at Quincy. I'm not massively productive and spend a lot of time replaying our Sunday by the pool, but he doesn't need to know that. All three Titans in swim shorts is something I will be remembering for a while.

It turns out Quincy also has tattoos, but he has a sleeve that looks like it's been sketched. Also gorgeous, of course. He's leaner than the other two, really leaning into the surfer vibe he has going for him. I google the man holding the Earth and it's Atlas, one of the Titans. Quincy's and Maxton's tattoos were also Titans, but that was as far as my research went. I didn't want to look like a fangirl now, did I?

Quincy jumps up dead on five o'clock, ready to go. The others aren't ready yet, but I am certainly done for the day.

"How about I take you to the cinema?" Quincy asks me with a grin. "These two can get a lift home with Jeremy. I drove us over."

"That actually sounds great," I admit.

"We'll go to the one with the recliners and the menu. It's a longer drive but way more comfortable and we can have your edible apology. They bring your food to your chair mid-movie." I get caught up in his excitement and can't wait. Atlas doesn't mind even though it's his birthday, saying he's got a lot of work to sort out. I feel guilty that my problems have caused him and Maxton stress but there's not much I could've done about it.

We didn't check the movie times before we left and end up seeing the only thing on, a horror, which is not my usual idea of a good time. Quincy spends the whole time whispering dirty and hilarious things in my ear though, and it improves the experience immensely. We have mountains of food. Nachos, pic 'n' mix (one of my favourite things), and salty popcorn mixed with M&Ms.

All washed down with multiple Slurpees. Perfect. Edible apology accepted.

When we get home I join Atlas in his bed to make up for his boring birthday evening.

It's Friday so I'm driving in with Quincy, but they have a joint meeting, so Maxton and Atlas have jumped in with us.

"I've got a half-day at work today so Jeremy is going to come and get me," I explain to the car. Quincy already knows this as I'm leaving to set up for the party we've been planning. I love that he's been so into it and hasn't even minded running around town for supplies. Much. He's arranged a dinner with them both and some friends so they get back at the perfect time.

"More top-secret prison visits?" he asks me, humour in his tone. I think we're mainly good, especially after yesterday, and that he's just testing the waters. Risky Quincy. I poke my tongue out at him in the rear-view mirror and his shoulders relax, knowing I've taken it as the joke it's meant to be.

"I only go twice a year," I say, surprising them with the information. I don't know if I'm feeling vulnerable after yesterday or if I've gotten to the point where I want them to know. They're all quiet for a while, gauging my reaction.

"Why?" Atlas eventually asks.

"That's when my sister lets me visit." There's a loaded silence while they all absorb the new information. I haven't told them much about my family, except that my dad had died, and I only mentioned it in passing to Maxton, really. "Birthday and Christmas."

"Whose?" Quincy asks in a small voice, and I start to regret telling them.

"Ours," I reply simply. His face falls and I worry our light atmosphere is going down the drain.

"What's up, Quincy? Not giving yourself extra points for ruining my birthday without even knowing?" but even my joking tone doesn't seem to soften the blow he feels.

"Shit, Lai. I'm so, so sorry."

"I'm kidding, it's fine. I actually had a great morning and evening so it was alright if we forget the middle."

"That's what you went out with Lia for?" Maxton asks her. "Why didn't you tell us?"

"More importantly," Atlas interrupts, "how did you not get that information from her background check?"

"I didn't even think to look for it!" Quincy insists.

I shrug, regretting bringing it up. "It's really not a big deal."

"But you clearly love birthdays," he says, not letting it drop.

"I love other people's birthdays. Lia makes a fuss for mine and has for the last few years. What else do I need?" And I mean it. No plans would make up for not celebrating it with my twin, so I visit her and spend the rest with Lia. We pull up outside my office and I hop out. "Can we forget I even mentioned it?"

"Sure," Quincy says with a weak smile, and I return it, shutting the door behind me and heading into work.

SEVENTEEN

THE STRANGER

Father isn't happy I'm still going after her. He thinks that now Warren is dead, she's worthless. But we're meant to be. He used to tell me that all the time but he's forgotten. He thinks if Gia finds out that Madelaine is seeing a Viper, then she'll spill everything. It's been three years and she's kept her mouth shut. I'm sure she knows nothing.

Father isn't willing to bet on that, but I am. Madelaine is worth it. He doesn't understand that Madelaine was never just a means to an end for me. She is my end. The second I saw her, I knew it. She's mine. If

Father thinks he has me under control, he needs to think again. My warnings aren't working and I've had enough of waiting. I just need some time alone to explain everything to her. Somewhere no one can take her away. Where she'll have no choice but to listen. Then she'll understand. It was always supposed to be me and her.

EIGHTEEN

MAXTON

"That's weird, Madelaine didn't say she was going out," Atlas remarks and I'm instantly tense. I was sadly excited to see Madelaine, but when we pulled up to our house it was completely dark. Quince rolls his eyes as we get out of the car and head to the front door.

"It's fine, everyone. Chill." He opens the door and steps back to let us in. Coloured lights flash around us with a yell of "*Surprise!*" and everyone rushes us, clapping me and Atlas on the back.

When I manage to extract myself from the crush of people, I see Madelaine in Atlas's arms with her tanned legs wrapped around his waist. She catches my eye and wriggles from Atlas's hold, jumping into my arms next. I'm still stunned I actually get to touch her, so I hold on a little too long and she pulls away, grinning.

"Happy Birthday, Maxton."

She's wearing high-waisted loose shorts with a baggy cami tucked in. It's all black and highlights all the golden skin left on display. She looks incredible, and her hair is loose and wild around her shoulders. She looks so carefree and relaxed.

"Did you do all this for us?" I ask, looking around at the open area that's been transformed.

"Any excuse for a good balloon, eh?" she laughs.

We wander towards everyone else who has moved back towards the party. There's a huge balloon arch over the patio doors leading to the pool that's covered in floating decorations reading 'Atlas' and 'Maxton'. Inside, there's catering and more decorations, and there's a bar set up on the terrace outside next to a DJ. There must be at least 100 people here. I spend some time wandering around as people grab at me to wish me a happy birthday and chat. I'm at the bar to grab a refill on my 'Maxton' cocktail when

I spot Madelaine through the crowd. Before I can head over to her, someone sidles up in front of me.

"Should one of the birthday boys be on his own?" A girl drawls, stroking my chest. "Fancy a dance? I'm sure I can cheer you up."

Before I can answer I'm shoved from the side, my drink spilling all over my shirt. I turn, ready to rip someone a new one and see Madelaine with an innocent expression on her face.

"Oops, sorry," she says lightly, sounding anything but. "I'm Madelaine." She extends her hand to the girl who regards it suspiciously but shakes it in hers.

"Kate," she replies. News to me.

"Nice to meet you, thanks for coming." Madelaine continues. "How do you know Maxton?"

"We hooked up at a club before."

We did?! Oops, I definitely didn't recognise her. I keep my face straight and don't show the surprise but notice the slight tightening of Madelaine's expression.

"Oh, cool," she says easily. "Well, have a great time!" With that, she wanders off into the crowd.

"Excuse me," I tell the girl. Kim? I head after Madelaine but lose her in a sea of heads on the makeshift dance floor as I'm caught up by some more friends.

A little while later I spot her with Atlas, chatting with the guys we went for dinner with.

"Lorenzo was our partner in crime," Madelaine is explaining. "We couldn't have done it without him." She mock-salutes, which gets a laugh out of him.

"Anything to put a smile on these grumpy bastard's faces," he replies, nodding his head towards me. "Plus Quince didn't give me a choice."

Madelaine doesn't turn as I come up behind her. "Speaking of the devil, I should make sure he's enjoying the spoils of our labour." She gives everyone a smile and wanders off.

Atlas gives me a confused look. "What did you do?"

"I have no idea," I say, watching her walk around the pool into the house.

"Well, go and apologise, dude," Lorenzo instructs. "She threw you both an epic party."

"Thanks for the advice," I tell him sarcastically, following Madelaine into the house.

"Are you okay?" I ask when she stops to peruse the food table and I catch up to her.

"I'm fine. Where's Kate?"

"How would I know?" I ask, pulling her away from the table for a bit of privacy.

"She looked like she wasn't planning to leave you alone," she says when we're in a quieter corner.

"Are you mad at me for that?"

"I'm not mad," she says and I believe her. There's hurt in her eyes rather than anger.

"Did I do something?" I ask, cupping her cheek in my hand and tilting her head so she has to meet my gaze.

"I don't enjoy watching other women paw at you."

"I don't care what other women do, you're my girl."

"Didn't look like she knew that."

Realisation dawns on me, and I know I'm an idiot. "Shit, I should've made it clear to her as soon as she tried anything."

"Yeah, you should've."

"In case there's any doubt, you are the only one whose hands I want all over me. You can put them anywhere on my body, any time you want." I smile down at her, leaning into her mouth. She smiles back at me as I press her into the wall, kissing her with everything I have. I try to convey the depth of feeling I have for her in that kiss, and it soon heats as I press my thigh between her legs and she arches her body into me. I've forgotten there's anyone else in the room, let alone an entire party, as I snake my hands around her waist.

"For fuck's sake, this is my karma," Quince interrupts us. I pull away from Madelaine reluctantly and turn my head to look at him.

"You don't have to watch."

"As if I could look away. Me, and half the party." He gestures behind him as people avoid my gaze. Good idea. "Anyway, it's cake time."

"Yay!" Madelaine squeals, clearly not caring how many people saw us making out in the corner like teenagers. She grabs my hand and leads me back outside to stand with Atlas where everyone sings Happy Birthday to us, and the biggest cake I've ever seen is wheeled out. Yes, wheeled out. Madelaine looks so happy that I just go with it, losing myself to the fun of the evening.

The party is winding down and I'm looking for Madelaine, more than ready to take her to bed for the night. We've spent the night dancing and laughing with everyone, and I swear she's been teasing me on purpose, rubbing up against me any chance she gets. Quince sees me searching and puts me out of my misery. "She went to her bedroom," he tells me with a sigh. I clap him on the shoulder and head that way.

"It's Max," I call, knocking on her door. She shouts for me to come in but I'm not ready for what I walk into. She's standing with her hand leaning on the wardrobe doorway and I scan her slowly from head to toe. Her hair is still loose, but she's freshly washed her face, her natural beauty more than enough to make her glow. She's wearing a simple red satin bra that showcases her breasts to perfection. I groan, already so hard it's getting painful. A matching suspender belt sits around her waist, just above those red satin panties. It's attached to sheer stockings that cover her endless legs down to stilettos. Fucking hell. I'm actually speechless. A Titan, taken down by one spectacular woman.

"Jesus Christ," I say out loud when I find my words.

"You like?" she asks, spinning to reveal the criss-cross of ribbon over her ass cheeks.

"I love," I say, trying in all honesty not to drool. She walks over to me and I meet her halfway, gripping her nape in one hand and her ass in the other, pulling her into me. Just as our lips are about to meet, she whispers, "We should wait for Atlas."

"We really fucking shouldn't," I mutter.

She laughs, not making any genuine effort to stop me. "This is technically his birthday present."

"Fine." I'm a rational man, I can control myself. I lead her over to the bed, standing her to face it and bending her over at the waist. This is definitely a position we will be revisiting. I snap a photo of the top of her ass, cheeks wrapped in ribbon with that bow sitting at the top, and send it to Atlas as Madelaine straightens up and spins to face me.

"He's got two minutes."

"How about I distract you until then?" she asks, as she drops to her knees in front of me.

"Madelaine..." I lose my train of thought as she undoes my trousers and pulls my hardness out into her soft palm. She doesn't reply as she licks the bead of pre-cum from the head of my cock. It feels like it's pulsing, I'm so turned on. She licks again, this time along the underside, and wraps her lips around the tip. I run a hand into her hair as she gives me a few tentative pumps with her mouth, then sucks and pops off the end.

"I want you to do it," she says. I can't piece one thought together, seeing her on her knees like this.

"Huh?" I ask her.

"I want you to fuck my mouth."

"Holy shit, *belle*," I groan, tightening the grip in her hair. I tilt her head back slightly with my hold and she opens her mouth, taking my cock as I slide it in slowly. She holds onto my thighs as I push in, testing how far she can take me. I pick up speed just as Atlas comes to stand next to me. I didn't even notice him coming in. She looks up at us both, desire in her eyes, and I have to pull out so as not to end the party early. I crouch down and kiss Madelaine passionately, her hands coming up to grip my biceps.

"You are perfect."

I help her back up to her feet and Atlas wastes no time in claiming her once she's upright, grabbing her waist right over the suspender belt and kissing her.

"Happy Birthday to us," he says as he steps back, twirling his finger to encourage Madelaine to spin. "Fuck, baby, you're incredible."

She grins bashfully and reaches her arms behind her to undo her bra clasp. It falls away and her breasts sit perky, nipples hard. Next goes the suspender belt and Atlas and I stand statue-still, more than content to watch the show. Madelaine steps out of her heels, sitting on the edge of the bed to roll each stocking down, torturously slow until they're both off. She stands again and shimmies out of her panties, letting them fall to her feet before stepping out of them. We're both enthralled, taking in every inch of her bare skin. She starts fidgeting now that she's fully nude, and Atlas grips her chin in his fingers.

"You don't even know how stunning you are." He trails his fingers up her stomach and runs them lightly over the curve of her breast, grazing over her nipples, making her breath hitch. "What do you want to do?"

She looks confused at the question. "I'm not sure." Atlas's fingers continue trailing a soft path over both breasts and Madelaine rubs her thighs together slightly.

"Did you like Max fucking your mouth? Taking what he wanted?" he asks and her lips part as she nods.

"You need to tell us if you don't like something, okay?" She nods again. "With words, Madelaine. What's your favourite colour?"

"Black," she replies, a frown appearing between her brows.

"You say black if it's too much, okay?" His fingers continue skating over her skin and she releases a breathy yes. He releases her, stepping back to undress himself. I've already gotten rid of my trousers and reach over my shoulder to remove my shirt. Madelaine turns to me slightly and I take the opportunity to kiss her, running my hands over her bare back.

"We mean it, we're only happy when you're enjoying yourself," I reiterate.

"Okay," she replies, pupils blown with lust. I release her to search the bedside table, hoping for lube. Bingo. Atlas sits himself on the edge of the bed and pulls her back so she's stood between his thighs, facing me.

"Take Max in your mouth again," he instructs as I stand in front of her. He holds onto her hips so she bends at the waist, taking me in without preamble. Atlas leans forward and buries his face in her pussy, causing her to moan around me. I groan at the sensation and thrust myself into her mouth, in and out, fucking it like she wanted. Atlas continues his work from behind until she's panting and moaning all over my cock.

"On your knees," I say, pulling myself from between her lips.

"Facing me," Atlas adds. Madelaine does as we ask, and I kneel behind her. Atlas pulls her hair into a ponytail, holding it in one hand, and as she takes him into her mouth, he hisses through his teeth. "Fuck, baby."

I squeeze the lube onto the top of her ass and watch it run down between her cheeks, holding myself in my fist and following the trail with my cock.

"Is this okay, *belle*?"

She releases At and nods but he cups her cheek. "Words, baby."

"Yes."

Grabbing a cheek with my other hand, I line myself up with her slick entrance and my thumb with her backside, slowly pushing both in at the same time. She arches back with a moan and Atlas uses her ponytail to direct her back into his lap.

I pull myself nearly all the way out and slam back in, taking long, hard thrusts into her as I circle my thumb.

Her orgasm comes out of nowhere and she tightens around me, pulling away from Atlas to scream. We wait for her to ride it out and then I pull out completely, swapping my cock to her back entrance and my fingers to the front.

"Push back when I push in, Madelaine," I tell her, slowly pushing my cock in just past her ring of muscle and two fingers into her slick opening. I still halfway, wanting to check on her. "Are you okay?" She doesn't answer, and I panic. "Madelaine?"

"Yes! Move, Maxton!" she demands, so I push the rest of the way in as she moans her pleasure. Atlas grabs her hair again and ups the ante, pushing himself further into her mouth as I thrust into her over and over, mirroring my actions with my fingers. I'm not going to last much longer, so I move my hand from her hip, snaking it round to pinch her clit, and she explodes around my fingers. She moans around Atlas deep in her mouth and he groans, finishing down her throat. She clenches around me and it sends me over the edge, coming with a growl and pouring myself into her. I pick Madelaine up as I stand and collapse onto the bed next to Atlas with her in my arms, where I would happily stay for the rest of my life.

NINETEEN

QUINCY

We all get up feeling a little delicate on Saturday morning and since the weather is supposed to stay awful all weekend, decide on a movie day. This is a major change we've made since Lai came into our lives, actually taking time off to relax, and I don't even remember doing it consciously. Before we were always in work mode, wandering in and out of the office at all times of the day. Now we have weekends because Lai has weekends and we all want to spend as much time with her as possible.

Lai looks ridiculously pleased when Max picks movies from her gift and crosses them off as we go. She's cuddled up between Max and Atlas, looking adorably dressed down and relaxed. I love her like this. She looks hot as sin dressed up to the nines going out, and the sexy secretary look she has going for her at work is killer, but she's so pure and beautiful when she's natural and chill.

We watch a couple of films before starting to get a bit antsy from sitting around for too long. With the rain not letting up we swap movies for cards, introducing Lai to her first Titans poker night, albeit scaled back slightly. It starts out light by betting little things like who orders dinner, that we then eat as we play. Who makes the next round, who gets out of our super early meeting tomorrow morning. A good one for me to win, especially as they were going to Atlas's weekly lunch with his family after. I could do without his mom wiping my face after every bite, as lovely as she was.

"What about strip poker?" Atlas suggests, leering at Lai, who rolls her eyes at him.

I groan at the thought of Lai sitting there in her underwear or less. "Does it have to be so torturous?"

Max laughs and takes pity on me. "Or the winner gets to take Lai to bed."

Lai raises her eyebrows at that. "What if Lai wins?" After a few fortunate hands at the beginning, her streak had fully gone down the drain by this point. The only reason she hadn't made every drink so far is that she was playing with three guys she had fully whipped.

"Beginner's luck, baby," Atlas tells her. "You're mine tonight."

"Wouldn't count on it," Max replies, proceeding to decimate every one of us.

"Where did that come from?!" Atlas demands.

"Just had the right motivation." Max downs his drink and lifts Lai over his shoulder as she laughs from upside down. "Night, guys."

I turn to Atlas. "Joining me with blue balls tonight, dude?"

"I've just been hustled," he complains into his drink.

I gather the cards from across the table and shuffle. "Preference?" There's no way I'm going to bed just yet, not with my room sharing a wall with Maxton's.

"Slapjack," he replies. We haven't played that in years. "How's it going with Madelaine?" Atlas asks.

"Okay, I think. What do you think?" I deal the cards out between us, but we're distracted and don't start playing just yet.

"You know I think you were an idiot from the very beginning."

"Not massively helpful now," I say. "I'm trying to take it slow and gain her trust properly. I don't want her to think I'm saying I believe her just because you two are getting some and I want to join in."

"But you do."

"Of course I do, but that's because of her, not my massive FOMO."

"Well, I'm not going to tell you anything she's said to me, but I'd say you were heading in the right direction."

"Oh, hoes before bros now, is it?" I joke.

"More like Madelaine before anything these days," he says with a slightly confused expression on his face, as if he's not quite sure how that happened.

"I can't blame you for that."

I'm laying in bed the next morning, revelling in my lie-in after my win last night and wondering if Lai would be up yet when a scream comes from next door. *Max's room.* I burst in and scan the room for anything amiss. There's nothing immediately obvious, so I turn my focus on Lai in the middle of the vast bed. She's breathing heavily and looks on the verge of panic.

"Shit, Lai, are you okay?" I sit down hesitantly on the edge

She whips her head around to face me as if she's come out of a trance. "Yeah, sorry," she chokes out, "just a bad dream, I guess."

She starts to shake and I get up next to her, taking her in my arms.

"I hate this," she says as she continues to tremble.

"It's been an extreme time," I say, trying to console her.

"No one else is cracking."

"We've been through worse than the past few weeks, so it's not shocking to us. It's a good thing it is to you. Do you want to go back to sleep?"

"Where's Max?" she asks, belatedly looking around the room as she registers where she still is.

"He had that early meeting with Atlas this morning and probably didn't want to wake you. They've got lunch with Atlas's mom after, so they'll be there for a while."

She stiffens and I hate that it could be at the thought of being left here alone with me.

"Can I come to your room?" she practically whispers.

"I can lie with you here, I won't leave," I answer truthfully. I'd lay next to her all day if it brought her comfort.

"Do you have a balcony?"

I suddenly get the link between this room and her unexpected nightmare.

"I do," I admit. My room is next to Max's along the back of the house, so we both open up onto balconies and the back view.

"Oh, okay. Ignore me, I'm being stupid."

"You're not. Why don't we go to your room?"

She nods, and I let her go so she can wrap the bed sheet around her, padding to her own room.

The next time she wakes is a lot more peaceful. I've been awake for about an hour, having woken to her wrapped around me and happily enjoying the feeling. She slowly opens her eyes and registers her face nestled into my neck, an arm and a leg thrown over me. She pulls back gently, flicking her gaze up and finding me awake, unable to hide the smile she gives me.

"Sorry, it took me a while to wake up. I feel like I've been in a coma," she explains, rolling onto her back and rubbing her eyes fervently.

My smile turns into a chuckle. "That's what happens when you nap for six hours."

She gapes at me, then turns to look out the window. "Jesus, how do I still feel drained?"

She sits up too fast and wobbles slightly. I place my hand on her back to steady her and she puts both hands out to stabilize herself, one straight down onto my very solid cock.

"Shit, sorry," she says, pulling her hand back like it's been burnt, which makes me laugh.

"It's okay, I don't know any man who could lay here with you draped all over them and not have this result."

"Quincy..." she starts, spinning to face me. She put a T-shirt on when we got into her room for some modesty. I can't wait to see her in one of mine, nothing underneath. Thoughts like that are not helping with the erection situation.

"Lai, it's fine. I know I don't deserve to have you yet, but I will."

She smiles. "You still want that?"

"You? Absolutely. Why wouldn't I?"

"I don't know," she shrugs. "I've spoken to Max and Atlas about being both of theirs and I guess I've never heard it from you."

"Then let me be very clear," I say, sitting up and gripping her face in my hands. "I want you more than any other woman I've ever met. Not because those lucky fuckers already have you, and not because I think I'm missing out with the group. I want you because you are fucking incredible and I can't wait to call you my girl."

Her face splits into a grin as I speak, causing her cheeks to chipmunk in my hands.

"I can't wait for that either," Lai admits. "I swear I'm not dragging it out to punish you."

"I'd deserve it if you were, but I know you're not that type of person. As soon as you're ready, I'm ready."

She turns her head and places a kiss on my palm. I pull her face towards me and give her a simple peck on the corner of her mouth, then release her. I'm fighting against every instinct in my body to lay her out underneath me and kiss every inch of her, but I meant every word I said. This needs to be on her terms.

"That was pretty intense, wasn't it?" she smiles mischievously.

"How about we start from the beginning?"

"Like a fresh start?"

"Like a first date," I offer.

"I'd love that," she replies, beaming at me. Fuck, she's gorgeous. Her whole face lights up when she smiles.

Max and Atlas interrupt that conversation from going any further by barging into her room, the frowns on their faces replaced with surprise when they take us in.

"Did we miss all the fun?" Atlas asks with a smirk.

"Fuck off, At," I say lightly, hopping off the bed and heading back to my room to get ready. I'll leave Lai to fill them in on everything that happened, however much she wants to tell them.

Later in the evening, I join them at the dining table.

"This smells amazing, Lucy," I admit. She smiles warmly at me as I sit in front of a huge plate loaded with roast dinner. "Where's Lai?" I ask the others, noting only our places with food.

"She went for dinner with Lia," Atlas tells me. "Apparently her boyfriend took her away for the weekend last-minute, which is why she missed our party."

"How she's going to eat anything after all of those tacos she had when she got up, I'm not sure," Max laughs.

"She slept for ages, I bet she was starving." I chuckle along with him.

"That nightmare must've taken it out of her. We need to get this creep sorted already before it affects her even more. She's strong, but it's a lot to have going on for anyone."

"I know," Max agrees with Atlas. "He's definitely escalating, both in what he's doing and how often he does it."

"We have nothing on them whatsoever. Nothing to tie him to the Vipers or anyone else. As soon as we do, whoever it is will be annihilated, mutual destruction or not," Atlas promises.

"Agreed. In the meantime, Lai goes nowhere alone," Max adds. "Jeremy's going into work with her instead of just dropping her off. The security they have is useless, they shut those balcony doors with a catch, not even a lock."

"Which has changed now, surely," I say, and he gives me a straight stare. Of course it has. I wouldn't be surprised if that place was tighter than Fort Knox by now. "What about the event tomorrow?" It was some fundraiser used to raise money for the city but really turned into a peacocking contest between the powerful and elite of Ironhaven. Realistically, we have to go. It will be our first one since moving into town.

"We'll still go," Atlas decides. "Even just to show our faces. Whoever it is can't think we're rattled and we can't afford to lose any ground."

"We'll give Madelaine the choice but we're not hiding her away either. Sounds like your plan's going in the right direction," Max adds.

"Hopefully," I say happily. "Slow and steady wins the race."

"I'm sure she's due to make decisions about what to do with the insurers this week." Atlas and I slow our eating and look up at Max.

"What's she said?" I ask him.

"Doesn't matter," Atlas declares. "She's not going anywhere, not while it's so unsafe."

"So once this is all over, you'll let her move out, then?"

"Fuck, no. She's our girl, and she's staying here with us."

"We all want that, At," Max agrees. "But don't get carried away with your stubbornness. At least pretend to let her decide," he half jokes.

Atlas shrugs. "No promises."

TWENTY

MADELAINE

"I can't believe I go away for a week and you gain two boyfriends!"

I laugh at Lia's blunt appraisal of my last seven days.

"I want to hear all the details. Who's the biggest? Who's better with their hands? Who's better with their tongue?"

I roll my eyes at her. "I'm a bit too busy to be ranking their skills."

"I just bet you are," she says with a wink. "So could your life get any better, or are you now permanently the envy of all women everywhere?"

"Well, this creep could fuck off, then I think I might be on the way."

"Oh, yeah. What's happening with that?"

I haven't caught her up on anything yet, not wanting to have her worrying about me through her surprise weekend away, so I quickly give her the abbreviated version. "I walked into my office last Thursday and there was some guy trying to spray a message onto my wall."

"What the fuck?" she exclaims, mouth hanging open.

"I know, it was the creepiest shit. He came through the balcony doors."

"Do you think it was the person responsible for the fire or someone doing their dirty work?" The same question the guys had been mulling over.

"I can't be sure, but I think it was him. He had these soulless, dead eyes, like a psychopath. I can't even explain it." I shuddered, recalling them.

"Someone you turned down at Encore?"

"No," I reply, and I'm pretty certain. "I'm sure I would recognise those eyes anywhere."

"How are you handling it?"

"I thought I was okay, then I fully freaked out this morning. We slept in Maxton's room that has a balcony and it gave me a nightmare."

"Oh God, Lai," she says, covering my hands with hers on the table between us. We'd only come to a cheap and cheerful place halfway between our place and hers for a quick dinner, but I had a feeling we'd be here for a while.

"I know, it was horrible. I dreamt he walked in through the doors and I couldn't move when he came towards me. When I could, I ran for the balcony, but the doors were suddenly locked. I woke up screaming." Explaining it again reminded me of the pure terror I felt as the man crept towards me and I shudder.

"*Eurgh*, it sounds awful," Lia agrees, shaking her head.

"Yeah. I'm trying to carry on as if nothing's wrong, but I think it's taking its toll on me a bit."

"Of course it would be. Are the guys supporting you?"

"Yeah, they're pretty amazing, to be fair," I admit. "Quincy laid with me so I could sleep again."

"How's that going? Ready to turn your threesome into a fully-fledged reverse harem yet, or what?" she asks, lightening the mood.

"Is that what it's called?" I'd never heard that term before in my life, and I wouldn't put it past Lia to be winding me up.

She nods though, and I shake my head disbelievingly at the whole idea.

"It's going well. He's so sweet and is giving me the space I need to get over what's happened between us."

"Yeah, yeah, super sweet. Probably helps that he's hot as fuck. They all are!"

"Don't let Coze hear you say that," I joke.

Her face drops slightly. "I don't think he'd mind too much, to be honest."

"Oh no, what's up?" The server comes over for a third time trying to take our orders but we still haven't looked at the menu, so we wave her off apologetically.

"Nothing, exactly. He just seems preoccupied all the time. You know how I love to have all the attention on me most of the time," she says, trying to brush off the seriousness of her words.

"Is he busier with work at the moment?" Caus has always been busy, but it's never seemed to affect their relationship before.

"Yeah, so he says. I don't see how project management can be so interesting that you spend half a romantic weekend with *me*, on the phone. Especially when he was so insistent on us going. I would've been happy chilling out and going to your party. How did it turn out?"

"Yeah, it was great fun," I say, knowing she's changing the subject. "You know I'm always here for you, right? Whatever you need, anything." I would hate for her to not come to me if she was down.

"I know, and I love you for it. Same for me. Next time that creep strikes, you tell me straight away, okay?" I nod to agree but worry I've neglected our friendship, and she obviously reads the guilt on my face like an open book. "Don't start berating yourself, you haven't abandoned me! I love that you're engrossed in your love life. I just need to know everything, especially when it comes to your safety."

"Okay." I smile at her. "And if you ever need to talk, I'm here for you. Even if I have to climb out from under a pile of Titans."

That makes her laugh and I hope she feels better and knows that I mean every word.

"Deal. Can I order my dinner now?" She winks, definitely cheerier, and all is okay again.

The next couple of days are relatively normal considering everything that's been going on, and it's bliss. I wake up between Atlas and Maxton for the second morning in a row and have to drag myself out of bed, against much persuasion to stay. Work is going well and we should be able to pass all the Titans projects over to the next team in about a week. I've also decided with the insurers. I don't want my old house back, I wouldn't feel comfortable there. I'm going to take the rebuild money, sell the land, and start afresh. I might still ask Atlas about the car, though.

Jeremy and I have just gotten home for the day, and I'm still trying to decide whether to go with the guys to their event tonight. I'm always up for a decent dinner but I'm close to bailing for a chill evening with a long, pampering bath. But then maybe it'll be fun to get dressed up? I'm so indecisive. It's a formal event and I don't think I picked anything fancy enough when we went shopping, but Lia might have. She seems to think of every occasion. If not, I'm sure I could fancy up something I already have.

I head straight to my room to raid my wardrobe, planning to let the outfit options decide whether or not I go. I walk in and halt in my tracks, staring at the most beautiful dress hanging from the back of the bathroom door. It's a floor-length ivory gown, with the top consisting of two thick straps over the shoulders that follow to the waist, giving it a plunging neckline that would also show off a lot of my back. Another thick band runs around the waist, and then the skirt falls from there like a waterfall of cream silk. It's gorgeous, with a definite Greek vibe. *Guess I'm going out.*

I grin at the dress as I rush to the shower to get ready, scrubbing every inch of my body and using a moisturiser with a sheen. I redo my makeup with bronzed, highlighted skin and golden eyes, complete with false eyelashes. If there's ever an event for long, fluttery lashes, it's a black-tie fundraiser. My hair sits in a side part with sleek waves pinned behind one ear, playing up the Grecian vibes. The dress is the perfect shape to match my birthday bodysuit from Lia, so I put that on underneath, as well as adding golden strappy heels. They show when I walk thanks to the thigh high slit that appears every time I take a step and I feel amazing. I'm excited to see what the guys think of the dress, wondering whose choice it was.

"Fucking hell, you look incredible."

That was the kind of reaction a girl could get used to. I wander over to Quincy on the other side of the open area.

"Thanks," I grin. "You don't look too bad yourself." And he really didn't. I've seen him in swim shorts, I've seen him in a shirt and trousers, and I've seen him casual. None of those outfits prepare me for seeing him in a tuxedo. He seriously belongs in a magazine.

Atlas, who comes round the corner with Maxton, interrupts his reply and stuns me just as badly. They're both in black and white too, but Atlas has opted for a three-piece suit and Maxton is in a dinner jacket and cumberbund.

"Jesus, Madelaine, you look stunning," Atlas gapes. "Maybe we don't have to go to this thing after all."

I laugh at him as he approaches me, but take a step back as he gets close. "You can't kiss me."

He slips a hand under my waves, around the nape of my neck, and angles my face up to his. "I can do what I like."

I roll my eyes at him even as my skin heats, loving when he goes bossy on me.

"If you ruin my makeup I'm going to be even more nervous about this whole thing." I was absolutely fine meeting new people, but this event seemed like a big deal and is our first official outing as a group.

His eyes soften. "We'll make up for it later."

"How about we have some fun that doesn't involve your mouth?" Maxton asks from behind him. He pulls something from his pocket and holds it up for me to see as Atlas steps around me, standing at my back. It looks like two balls in a kind of silicone sack, with a loop of string on one end. I must look as confused as I feel because Maxton slips his hand inside the slit on my dress and runs a finger up my leg and along my seam. I suck in a breath at the sudden contact, and his pupils widen. "It goes in here."

I gulp as I register what he means, his finger still stroking me. "What do you think?" he asks. What do I think? I think I'm intrigued, and it's certainly distracted me from worrying about the event.

"Okay," I say breathily, and he beams back at me. He crouches down and lifts one of my legs over his shoulder, sucking the toy before moving my bodysuit to the side and pushing the thing up inside me. As I place my leg back on the floor I can feel the weight of it settle, and it sets my nerves on edge. Jesus, am I going to be able to do this? Only one way to find out, I guess.

Everyone is definitely staring at us. Clearly, the Titans are still fresh news and normally the gazes would agitate me, but Atlas's fingers trailing along my bare thigh have my mind fixed on other things. The fullness inside of me has become more prominent as the night has gone on and I'm feeling flushed and slightly strung out.

"I'm going to get a drink," I mutter, pushing away from our table.

"I'll go," Atlas offers, but I shake my head.

"I think I need a breather."

I've just ordered my drink when a guy comes up to the bar next to me.

“Hey,” he offers.

“Hi,” I reply with a tight smile.

“Can I get you a drink?”

Before I can let him know I’m here with someone, the toy inside me vibrates, and I nearly jump out of my skin. I whip my head around to look at our table and see Atlas and Maxton staring over at me.

“Actually, I’ve got to go,” I stutter, just as my drink arrives. I push it over to the guy. “Here, have this.”

“What the fuck was that?” I hiss at them both when I return.

Both of them look at me with smug, very turned on faces as Quincy comes up behind me. I didn’t even notice he’d left the table.

“Can I have this dance?”

The tension eases from my shoulders as he holds out his hand for me. I place mine in his and let him lead me onto the packed dance floor, finding a space in the middle. I go happily into his arms and let him sway us around, the skin on my bare back feeling like it’s electrified everywhere he touches me. Suddenly, I twitch into him as the vibrating starts up again, going for a few seconds before stopping.

"Are you okay?" he asks. I can only hear him over the noise in here because we're so close, so our conversation should be private.

"Yeah," I say, trying to look for the guys, but we're surrounded by people. He cranes his neck to follow my gaze, but looks perplexed. I spasm again and groan, the vibrating making everything in me clench and my knees go weak.

"What's going on, Lai?" he asks, looking down at me, worried.

I hesitate in answering, but then wonder why. This is Quincy. I look up, meeting his gaze, our lips millimetres from each other.

"It vibrates," I whisper.

"What does?"

"Maxton's toy." Shocked understanding dawns on his face while heat radiates off mine, a mixture of being so close to him and everything happening between my legs.

"Fuck," he mumbles, and I feel his breath on my lips. "Is that okay?"

It was. I loved how reckless they all made me and how free I was to be sexual with them. I've never done anything close to as hot as this in my life.

"Yes," I say, keeping eye contact.

"Shit, Lai, you're going to kill me." He presses his crotch into my stomach and I feel how this is affecting him.

"You probably deserve it, but Atlas and Maxton first." I gasp as the vibrating sets at a constant pace, trembling in his arms and whispering unintelligible sounds into his mouth.

"Quincy..." He feels my stomach tense and his eyes widen as he realises how close I am to the edge. If the vibrating stops now, I will personally hunt Atlas and Maxton down and make them pay. He grabs my face with one hand, his other pulling me closer, and kisses me. That pushes me over and I grab onto Quincy's biceps, my whole body quivering as I orgasm, light flashing behind my closed eyes and the feel of Quincy's tongue breaching my mouth lengthening my release. The fact that we're surrounded by people is not bringing me back to reality as I'd thought it would, but rather heightening the pleasure. Quincy doesn't stop kissing me until my legs have regained some form of stability and I can breathe normally again. Neither of us say anything, content to share the afterglow between us, with our gazes locked and his hand caressing my cheek. I lay my head against his chest and he sways gently with me in his arms as we take some time to enjoy being together like this.

As I'm coming out of the bathroom, suitably cooled down and refreshed, a server rushes up to me.

"Your man, he wants you," he insists in a stern tone.

"Pardon?" I ask, my brain not ready for this unexpected change so soon after the dance floor.

"Your man, this way."

Confused but not thinking straight, I walk with him along the corridor, feeling the constant pressure of his hand on the small of my back. We head out of a side entrance right by the front of the hotel the event is being held in. Up ahead, idling on the road that runs along the front of the hotel, is a limousine. Have the guys rented this as a surprise? I couldn't piece the details together. Can too many frequent orgasms actually give you brain damage?

As we reach the rear car door, it swings wide open and I find myself looking straight into those eyes. Soulless, dead. I scream, my preservation instincts working a lot quicker than my brain. The guy in the car reaches forward to grab for me at the same time the server shoves me from behind. I twist and push on my feet, hitting the side of the car with a thud rather than going straight into the open door. My arm throbs but I keep screaming. *Madelaine, you cannot get in this car. That will be it for you. Scream, and scream some more!*

It's quiet out being so late on a Tuesday, but hopefully my noise is drawing attention. The server certainly thinks so, running off down the street as soon as he realises this won't be as easy as he thought. The guy in the car makes a wild grab from inside again, but my momentum has me spinning away from the open door and down the trunk. I stumble backwards and someone catches me before I hit the ground, the car already screeching away from the curb.

"Miss Lai, are you okay?!" Jeremy. Thank God!

I turn in Jeremy's arms and hug him tightly, so thankful that he's here. He fiddles with his phone one handed for a second and then returns my hug, comforting me when I need it most. "How are you here?"

"They parked me right across the street. I didn't notice anything until you screamed and then I ran straight over." It must've only been a few seconds since we got outside, but it felt like it was in slow motion. Less than a minute later one of my guys pulls me out of Jeremy's arms and envelops me in his. Then they're all there, surrounding me, and I know I'll be okay.

TWENTY ONE

MAXTON

We're on the way home from the event, all of us piled into the Hummer with Jeremy driving and Madelaine squashed in the back seat between Atlas and I. She seems to have settled okay now that we're moving away from the hotel and may be ready to discuss it.

"Can you run us through it?" Atlas asks her, but she's distracted by her phone.

"I don't know much, it all happened so quickly. The server walked me out the back and I stupidly went with him."

"Hey," Quince says, twisting in the passenger seat as Madelaine looks up. "None of this is your fault."

"I know, I just wish I hadn't made it so easy for them."

"You didn't," Jeremy insists. "That twist was great quick thinking, Miss Lai."

She hums noncommittally and returns to her phone.

"And what about the guys?" Atlas prods.

"Sorry," she says, putting her phone down. "I was just updating Lia. She made me promise I kept her up to date with anything involving my safety."

I take over the questioning. "The server doesn't matter, as he'll be on CCTV. What can you tell us about the guy in the car?"

"It was the same guy from my office, definitely. Those eyes are now seared into my brain. Apart from that, he looks like an average guy, medium build with short brown hair. I couldn't see much as he was sitting in the shadows."

"That's fine. Anything you can tell us is helpful," I reassure her.

"I got the licence plate, but the guys have already found it dumped and burning," Jeremy explains.

"Jesus, it's definitely someone with help and resources. They must've had a second-"

"Wait!" Madelaine interrupts me. "He had tattoos." We all turn and stare at her intently, hoping this means something. "I couldn't tell what was on his neck, but when he reached out to grab me there was a snake's head coming out of his cuff."

"The fucking Vipers!" Atlas growls, simmering with anger.

"Are you sure?" Quince asks her, knowing what Atlas will set in motion with this information.

"I'm sure that he had a snake tattoo. That doesn't mean he has to be a Viper, does it?"

"In this town it does," I tell her.

We get home and head straight for the office, having spent the last part of our journey calling everyone in.

"Do you want someone to stay with you?" I ask Madelaine.

"Where are you going?"

"We've got a meeting in the office, then we'll be going out to see if we can track down some information on who may have attacked you. Jeremy will be in the house at all times, plus the guys posted outside. You're safe here." She doesn't need more details than that, not because she can't handle them, but because she shouldn't have to.

"I'll be okay."

"I'll stay," Quince offers. "You can fill me in later."

Atlas and I nod, both taking a turn to kiss Madelaine, and then head to the office. We walk straight through the wood-paneled room to a door set in the back, pushing it open and revealing our conference space. The room is already half full of our guys and filling up fast from the entrance to the other side, separate from the house. We wait for the rest to arrive before we start, needing everyone fully briefed and on their game. Before that can happen, my mobile rings.

"Yeah?" I answer, wondering why Quince is calling so soon after we left him.

"You need to get back out here," he says, his tone like steel. I tap Atlas on the shoulder and gesture back towards the main living quarters, retracing our steps.

Stepping out of the office we see Quince straight ahead, gun pointed towards the front door.

“What the fuck is going on?” Atlas asks as we walk into the lobby. Madelaine stands between Quince and the door looking shell-shocked, but she’s not the object of his gaze. That honour is reserved for the Latino guy standing behind her, looking very relaxed considering he has a loaded gun aimed at his face.

“What the fuck are you doing in our house?” I spit out, danger coating my voice.

“Nice to officially meet you,” he replies lightly.

Madelaine whips her head between us all, surely getting dizzy.

“You know each other?”

“You know him?” Atlas echoes.

“This is Coze.” Of course it fucking is. What the fuck has she gotten herself into?

“Coze is *Causus Jiles*?” Quince clarifies.

“Yes,” Madelaine confirms. “It’s an inside joke.”

“Sounds hilarious,” Atlas deadpans. “Say goodbye to him.” Surely we couldn’t actually kill him in front of Madelaine. “Now get the fuck out of my house,” he directs at Causus, obviously realising the same thing.

"I came here for a reason," he says, not making any move to leave.

"That reason is redundant, and the only reason you're still alive is because Lai is here," Quince spells it out for him.

"Wait!" Madelaine squeaks, moving to stand in front of Causus, making everyone tense up. "What the fuck is going on?"

"Do you even know who he is?" I ask her.

"Of course I do, I've known him for years! He's Lia's boyfriend, for God's sake."

"Oh, so you know he's the second in line to the Vipers, then?" Atlas grits out sarcastically. "The gang that has dreams of running this city."

"Like you can talk," Causus spits back at him. Madelaine whips round to face him, leaving us all behind her back.

"Is that true?"

He nods at her, his eyes like night and day from when he was glaring at us.

"Does Lia know?"

"No," he says simply.

"What are you doing here?" I ask him, bringing the conversation back to the most pressing issue. Quince hasn't lowered his gun and his shot is stellar, but we all relax minutely when Madelaine moves backwards so she can see all of us again.

"I know you're probably planning an attack on us right now," he says, not sounding worried about that at all. No one says anything in response, so he continues. "It's what I'd do if I found out a Titan was harassing my girl."

"Lia told you?"

"About tonight, yeah. I've been keeping track of the other things."

"You know who it is," Atlas accuses. "Why haven't you done anything?"

"And what exactly am I supposed to do?" Causus asks. "You know I can't be seen defending the Titans' girl over one of our blooded members."

"And yet you're here."

"Unofficially." Which meant secretly.

"Do you know why?" Madelaine asks him.

"I think it's about your dad and Gia," he mumbles. Her entire body tenses, and confusion floods her face. "Can we have a minute?" she asks us.

"No fucking way," Quince commands.

"You better start telling us everything you know because you're not walking out that door until we've heard it," Atlas tells Causus.

"Already begging me to stay, Atlas? Shall we get friendship bracelets?"

"You don't seem too tense considering you've just waltzed into enemy territory," I tell him.

"Because I know we need each other. A war is the last thing either of us wants right now, so I'll deal with my guy subtly, and you call your army off."

"You want some kind of peace treaty?" Atlas asks disbelievingly.

"If that's what you want to call it," Causus shrugs.

"Are you even able to make these kinds of deals?"

"There's a lot you don't know about the Vipers. Change is coming. Just know I'm more than capable of making these decisions," he tells us seriously.

"Are you expecting us to actually trust a Viper?" Quinn laughs.

"I do." We all turn to face Madelaine, who has been quiet since the revelation. "I do, I trust him. If Coze says we're safe to call them off, then call them off."

There's a long silence during which we all gaze around at this unexpected set-up. I have no idea what the best move is and I'm happy to defer to Atlas.

"Fine," Atlas agrees, shocking me. "But you know what a huge deal this is. We're not ending up with very much information."

"No," Causus agrees. "Just know that Madelaine is like a sister to me, I'd never knowingly let harm come to her," he offers.

"Connor Jones makes sense now, you didn't want the house found. If one hair on her head is touched, I will hold you personally responsible," I promise him.

"I can handle that."

"Good. Now fuck off before I change my mind and put a bullet in your head," Quince says.

Causus mock salutes the three of us before angling his body towards Madelaine.

"I know this is a huge ask, but can you let me tell Lia?"

She looks conflicted, but eventually gives a slight nod. "You've got until I see her at the weekend. Only because it's better coming from you."

He gives her a small smile in thanks. "I'm glad you're okay."

"Thanks, Coze," she says, still using his nickname and giving him a hug. We all tense in fury.

"You're pushing your luck," Atlas informs him.

He chuckles and leaves through the front door.

Madelaine deflates with an enormous sigh. "At least Coze knows who it is now."

"Why does it feel like our troubles have only just begun?" Quince asks, finally lowering his weapon.

"I'll go and let the guys know," Atlas says, turning for the office.

"Hang on, I'll come with you," I offer. "I want to know how the fuck he strolled up to our front door. Do you want to wait up?" I ask Madelaine.

"Not really," she replies. "I'm sure Quincy will tuck me in."

He holds his hand out to her and she takes it with a small smile, her face suddenly looking drained.

"You probably all figured this out already," she says, stopping us in our tracks, "but Gia is my sister. I genuinely do not know how she's connected to all of this, though."

"What's she in prison for?" I ask, sure she won't mind me asking now of all times and hoping it gives us a lead.

"Murdering our dad." With that bombshell, she turns and lets Quincy lead her down the corridor.

It's hours before Atlas and I finish up and I can't wait to feel Madelaine's soft curves in my arms. I climb into bed behind her and pull her off Quince's chest and back into me, covering her with my arm and breathing her in. I get a glare from Quince, but he's had her for hours so I ignore him. Madelaine stirs, wriggling further into my hold.

"Goodnight," I whisper, kissing her hair, inhaling her familiar scent.

"Maxton," she murmurs on a contented sigh, and her entire body relaxes into me. My chest swells at her reaction, and I follow her quickly into sleep as Atlas climbs onto the bed next to Quince.

What feels like minutes later, I'm peeling my eyes open to a blaring phone alarm. Madelaine mumbles something incoherent and buries further into the duvet.

"Someone turn it off," Quince grumbles. Madelaine sits up slowly and reaches over me for her phone on the nightstand, silencing it. She rubs her eyes, then looks around at the men surrounding her.

"I need a bigger bed," she says as she crawls over the duvet towards the foot to extract herself.

"You definitely do," Atlas replies as he leans forward and smacks her ass, so very tempting in that position.

"There are many others in this house." She gives us each an amused look as she stands.

"Not with you in them," I say. "Are you going to work today?"

"Yeah, why wouldn't I?"

Quince shifts, more awake now. "Oh, I don't know. How about you almost getting kidnapped last night and then finding out your friend is the leader of a rival gang. Ring any bells?"

"If I stayed home every time something inconvenient happened, I'd have lost my job by now." I scoff at her use of the word 'inconvenient' but don't comment on it.

"Jeremy's going to be stuck to you like glue, Madelaine. Any meetings, any lunch runs, any bathroom breaks." She opens her mouth to argue, but I interrupt her. "Not up for negotiation. This guy is clearly getting braver. Even if Causus says he has it handled, we're not lowering our guard until we have proof."

"Fine," she concedes. "Can I get ready now?"

"Need a hand in the shower?" Atlas asks, sitting up.

"I think I can manage," she says, rolling her eyes with a smile and heading into the bathroom.

"Are we really letting her go to work?" Quince asks.

"You try to tell her no," I say. "See where that gets you."

"I don't like it either but Max is right," Atlas adds. "Jeremy will follow her and we've put guys at all the entrances. That creep isn't getting anywhere near Madelaine."

Quince reluctantly accepts and pushes Atlas out of the way so he can get up. "I can't believe you crashed my first night with Lai."

We both laugh at him. "Get used to it."

TWENTY TWO

QUINCY

"What are your plans for this evening, Lai?" I ask as we're all finishing up breakfast at the island.

"I've got to meet the insurers and then I'm hoping to face-plant my bed," she replies. "Why, what's up?"

"Nothing, just thinking about our date."

She smiles at me. "We can definitely do that tonight."

"No, it's cool. I think we're all running on steam. What about tomorrow?"

"Deal," she says, smile widening.

She stands and takes her dish over to the sink to rinse. Atlas follows up behind her and winds his arms around her waist. "I'm starting to feel left out. Max got his evening and now Quinn gets a date?"

"Hey, I won that fair and square," Max protests, taking his dish up and standing next to them both, leaning on the side. "Were the weeks when you were the only one who had her not enough?" he jokes.

"It'll never be enough," Atlas says, spinning Madelaine in his arms and kissing her.

"Are you done marking your territory?" she asks with a laugh as he releases her. "I've got to go, Jeremy will be waiting outside." She tries to walk away, but Max grabs her hand and twirls her into his chest, gripping her chin and claiming a kiss. She shakes her head with a grin as he lets her go and she walks over to me, still at the island, with a quirk of her brow.

"Third time's a charm," she teases and I don't need anymore encouragement. I pull her between my thighs and cradle the back of her head as I kiss her. It starts off gentle and when it heats I pull away, knowing I could easily get carried away. She looks at me for a second before dipping forward and taking another kiss, just a soft touching of lips, and I know she's appreciating me not pushing her. She steps back and smooths her skirt, heading to the door and waving at us over her shoulder.

"We're all so screwed," Max says as we watch her leave.

There's no denial coming from me.

The next evening, I'm leaving my bedroom ready for our date just as Madelaine comes out of hers, looking sensational in wide-leg black trousers and a red bustier top. She has on red lipstick to match and her hair is poker-straight down her back.

"You look incredible," I tell her, walking over to where she's standing in the doorway.

"Thanks, so do you." I'm in a black shirt and trousers, nothing special. "Are you ready?"

"Yep." I grab my wallet and car keys and we head out, driving to a tiny Italian place about twenty minutes away.

"Why did you choose here?" Madelaine asks when we're settled into a corner booth, away from prying eyes.

"I like how small and private it is. Plus, the food is amazing."

"You've been here before?"

"Yeah, but not on a date or anything," I reply quickly.

"Quincy, it's fine. It's not like I think you're a virgin." I pull a face at her, hoping she never finds out quite how laughable that idea is. "What's good, then?"

"What are you in the mood for?" Her gaze heats as I ask her that, and I'm thankful for the booth hiding the way my cock springs up under the table. No one has ever had an effect on me the way Madelaine does.

"Surprise me," she says, reminding me of the first time we met. Even then, I was desperate to impress her. The server comes to take our order and I pick a few dishes, knowing we can share or swap.

"This is actually my first date, you know," I tell her once we're alone again. She looks surprised by that. "I never wanted to make the effort before."

"Because no one's made you wait before?"

"Because they weren't you. But they were completely different situations, you were kind of thrown into this blind."

"I think I'm done with the waiting, though."

"Really?!" Cue more springing under the table.

"Yeah. I think one reason I've been so hesitant, other than the fact you were a huge asshole and had some grovelling to do," she says with a grin, "is that I know once it's all three of you, that's it." I say nothing, letting her carry on as she clearly wants to explain, even just for her own benefit. "Obviously it is with the other two, but when you aren't there, I know you're not all complete. It would be the same if one of them were missing. It's like I still have an out."

"You want an out?" The idea terrifies me. Not that any of us would let her go by now.

"No, but it scares me a bit."

"We won't let you lose yourself," I promise her, remembering what she said to Atlas. "We think you're perfect exactly as you are."

"Smooth talker," she says with a laugh, obviously feeling lighter.

We sit in comfortable silence for a beat, and I hope she's got everything she wanted to off her chest. "So, how are the plans coming along?"

"You don't follow along with the refurbs?"

"Not the ideas, I'm the numbers, so they'll reach me later."

"Does that mean you're super smart?"

I chuckle. "Not that you'd ever know. I have zero qualifications. I kind of fell into it when we started and found a knack for the figures."

"How did you start? Or is that a tell me, kill me situation?" She takes a sip of her drink and leaves red lipstick on the glass. I picture red lipstick left elsewhere and clear my throat, having to refocus myself on the question.

"The guys haven't told you?"

"I guess I never thought to ask before."

"They'd tell you anything you wanted to know, you know. But we all grew up super poor. I won't go into their stories but I was in the system, abandoned at birth, tragic cliché. I never really found a family I fit into, until I found the guys." Her face falls. "Don't give me the pity look. I did fine, and I think I've ended up okay. I'm not that damaged..." I trail off jokingly.

That gets a small laugh and I don't think I've ruined the mood totally. "And you're happy now?"

"Yep, all that matters I have, or hope to have soon."

"I'm quite sure I don't know what you mean," she says, but slides her hand up my thigh so her fingertips brush my cock. Just then our food arrives and she tries to snatch her hand away, but I saw that coming and clasp mine over the top, keeping it there. She's soon distracted by all the food being laid out on our table.

"You were supposed to surprise me, not order the entire menu!"

"We'll take anything leftover home. The guys will be pleased, it's Lucy's day off."

We dig in, trying a little of everything and even managing to squeeze in a tiny taste of dessert that Lai feeds me. She gets cream on the corner of my mouth and when I'm about to wipe it off, she leans in and licks me clean.

"Okay, time for the bill," I say, wildly waving in the air.

Once it's all paid up and we have our doggy bag, I drag her out of the restaurant, swinging her around and pressing her to the side of the car. I drop the takeaway bag, holding her waist in both of my hands and staring at her. She must have heels on as she's not that much shorter than me tonight. I wait for her to lead, but as soon as she leans forward to press her lips to mine my resolve snaps, and I kiss her back with gusto. She wraps her arms around my neck and arches her body into mine, giving as good as she gets. I pull back reluctantly.

"I don't think either of us wants to be arrested tonight, and that's the way this is heading. Plus, I've waited long enough to have you in my bed, I'm not wasting my chance." She laughs and stands upright, her smudged lipstick turning me on even more. I run my thumb under her bottom lip, trying to help her clear the smear. We head home and I take my girl to bed, finally.

I wake up to Lai's bare ass fidgeting against my rapidly hardening cock.

"If that's how you're waking me up, you'd better be well-rested, gorgeous," I say, pressing into her ass. She jumps at my gravelly voice and stops her wriggling, spinning round to face me with a grin. Without my glasses on everything is slightly hazy, like I'm still dreaming. Best dream ever.

I roll her over quickly, pulling the sheets around us and holding my weight over her on my arms, eliciting a squeal. As soon as she makes the noise she shoots a glance at Atlas and Maxton, who are sleeping on her other side. They must've joined us last night once we were asleep, clearly not managing to stay away from her. I raise an eyebrow at her, silently offering the chance to stop, but she holds my stare with playful eyes and runs her hands down my torso, taking me in her palm and lazily pumping my solid length. Lai in vixen mode gets me harder than steel and I want to see how far I can take it, so I lower myself onto a forearm, lifting her leg around my waist with my free hand and lining myself up with her entrance. I can feel how slick she is from our silent play and she gasps as I push slowly in, her mouth falling open and her eyelids fluttering shut. I take my time, savouring the feel of her tight pussy taking me in. When my full length is seated inside of her, I feel her clench around me.

"Fucking hell, Lai," I groan before capturing her lips with mine and kissing her until we're both panting as she rocks her hips beneath me, digging her fingernails into my biceps. I pull nearly all the way out and plunge back in again slowly, trying not to rock the bed too much. She wraps both legs around my waist and trails her hand around the back of my neck, gripping the hair at the nape and tugging in a silent plea. I keep going, torturing us both with the languid pace until I feel her tightening around me. I push all the way in, grinding my pelvis into her clit, and she screams nearly noiselessly into my mouth as she rides her climax out. That finishes me off and I pull away, burying my face in her neck as I come with a groan. As I lay over her, both of us catching our breath, I feel the bed dip to our side and turn to see Atlas waking slowly. He registers what's going on next to him as I pull out of Lai and flop to her side.

"You fucker," he aims at me. "You couldn't wake me up?"

"We didn't invite you," Lai jokes, leaning over to peck him on the lips and then jumping out of bed and heading for the shower before he can catch her.

TWENTY THREE

MADELAINE

I walk through the lobby with Jeremy on the way to get lunch when I spot all three Titans hanging by the doors. Everyone is giving them a wide berth with looks filled with either envy or lust. Seeing them all here makes me instantly worry that something is wrong, but they've all got peaceful expressions on their faces. Atlas steps towards me, but I take the same step back, looking around at everyone milling about and giving him an arch of my brow. Atlas clearly takes that as a challenge as he continues forward, grabbing my face and kissing me deeply. *Asshole. Super hot, amazing kisser asshole.*

“Didn’t we talk about your work outfits?” he says as he pulls away.

I ignore that completely. “What’s up?” I ask them all, hoping it’s nothing bad.

“I came to take you to lunch, but then these bastards caught wind and tagged along,” Quincy complains.

“Oh, okay. Great!” Beats taking a sandwich back to eat at my desk.

We head around the corner to my usual lunch spot at a little cafe. I normally take my lunch to go, but we find a table near the back and settle in. We’re halfway through our sandwiches when the guys’ phones seem to go off all at once.

Atlas glances from his phone back to me, then answers. “Yeah?”

The general hubbub of the cafe muffles the sound from the other end, but the call doesn’t last long, anyway. “Okay.”

“What are your plans this afternoon, baby?” he asks, putting the phone down.

“I’m just in the office.”

“Great, don’t leave with anyone except Jeremy.”

"What's going on?" I ask him, worry setting in.

"Just work, but we've got to go."

I wasn't sure I ever wanted details of the darker side of their world. "Am I safe?"

"Do you think we'd leave you if you weren't?" Maxton asks, which is a fair point.

Atlas leans across the table to kiss me goodbye, quickly followed by Maxton, who then trails after him out of the cafe. My cheeks heat at the looks we're getting from the other patrons, and Quincy scoots round to sit on the seat next to me that Maxton just left.

"You'd better get used to it. None of us have any intention of not showing everyone that you're ours," he says before kissing me on the corner of my mouth and following the guys out. Jeremy comes in as he leaves and hovers by the door. I beckon him over.

"Come on, Jeremy, you don't have to be a doorman. Don't make me finish my lunch alone?"

He smiles warmly at me. "Never, Miss Lai."

Jeremy and I get home a few hours later and the guys' cars are all there, but no one seems to be around.

Figuring the office is the best place to start, I dump my stuff on the dining table and give the door a knock, but there's no answer. Having not been dismissed, I push open the door but find it empty. I'm about to pull the door closed again and search elsewhere when I notice another door in the corner. It's been panelled, and I'd never noticed it before, only standing out now because it was ajar. I shouldn't snoop. It's a secret hidden door in a gang leader's office. So, obviously, I go through it.

It opens to a huge conference area, a gigantic table able to seat at least 40 in the middle with more chairs stacked either side. Someone's entirely covered one wall in images and text. Everything to do with the creep is there: photos of the fire, photos of me that must've been sent in, photos of my office. I wander along, reliving the timeline so far. As I get to the end, I freeze in place. There's a note pinned to the wall. Not a photo, but the real thing. The handwriting matches the messages scrawled before and it reads *'If you won't come to me, maybe you'll come for Amelia'*. My blood runs cold and I stare at it, transfixed. I need to find out what's going on.

There are more doors at the end of this room. Jeremy comes in as I head towards them. "Miss Lai, maybe you should wait for Max, Atlas or Quince?" I ignore him and push mystery door number one open to reveal a massive garage, completely empty. I guess the sports cars being here doesn't mean the guys are, after all. I didn't even know there was another exit to this place. I step back into the main room and try the next door. It leads to a set of stone steps with another door at the bottom. Even without the huge lock on it, you couldn't have paid me to go down there.

I run back through the room and the office to the living area, picking up my phone.

"What's wrong, Madelaine?" Maxton asks when he answers.

"Please tell me she's not actually involved. Please, Maxton," I beg, pacing the open area.

Long pause. "*Shit.* I can't."

Silence comes from both ends of the line.

"*Belle,* please," Maxton says softly, but it's not enough.

"Is she okay?" I practically whisper the question, dreading the possibility of not getting a yes.

"We don't know yet."

"I can't believe you kept this from me, she's my best friend! If anything happens to her, I'll never forgive any of you for not involving me in this." Anger simmers in my veins.

I hang up and he immediately tries to call back, but I ignore it. I can't bring myself to answer. The longer I hear nothing, the longer I can pretend she's absolutely fine.

I sit at the table for hours, tears slowly falling until my eyes run dry and my throat aches. Then I just stare into space for a little while longer. I can't lose Lia, it's not an option. After losing Dad and G, she's my person. When my mind clears slightly of the fog, I decide to call Caus, wondering if the guys have already told him what's happening.

"Hey, Lie," he greets sunnily.

"Coze, he's got Lia."

He obviously knows exactly who I mean. "Where?"

"I don't know, the guys have gone."

"Where are you?"

"At the house."

"Give me five minutes," he says, hanging up.

True to his word, five minutes later Caus walks through the front door on his phone.

"I don't care. He's got my girl, now find the fucker," he says, ending the call as he walks over, sitting in the chair next to me.

"What do you know, Lie?"

"Not much." I don't tell him about the conference room. I trust him, but it's not mine to share, and I'm painfully aware that he is a rival gang leader to the guys. "He sent a note, he took Lia to draw me out."

"Where?"

Before I can answer, the front door opens and Maxton walks in. He's wearing a tight black long-sleeved top with a bulletproof vest over the top and black cargo pants. He looks amazing and the sight of Atlas and Quincy walking in behind him in the same gear causes my mind to go blank. *Your best friend was just kidnapped, Madelaine, have some decorum.*

Lia walks in right behind them followed by another guard, and I jump up and throw myself at her, causing us to stumble. Thankfully the guard catches us both as she hugs me back, just as tightly.

"Oh my God, Lia, are you okay?" I ask, pulling back and searching her face.

"Yeah, Lai. I'm fine, I promise."

As I let her go, Caus is there to pull her into his arms.

"Why are you in my house again?" Atlas asks him.

"Why the fuck didnt you guys call me?"

"There are three of us plus our additional security, and one of you. We followed the trail as soon as the note was delivered. We had it covered."

"She's my girlfriend and under my protection, you should have told me! I should've been there. Where is he?" Caus growls at them over Lia's head.

"We don't know," Maxton admits with anger in his eyes.

Lia pulls back from Caus's hold. "He knew they were coming. He got really angry, then left about half an hour before they got there."

"How did he get you?" he asks, cupping her face in his hands.

"I was getting into my car to head to a meeting, and the next thing I knew I was waking up in some derelict room," she shrugs.

"Did he hurt you?"

"No, he just ranted at me the whole time. He was clearly just waiting for Lai."

"How did this happen? I thought you had an eye on him," Atlas asks Caus.

"I did. He was supposed to be on a job. I guess seeing as he was grabbing my girlfriend, he thought it wouldn't matter if he did it or not."

"Well, fuck knows where he's gone now. We've got everyone on alert."

"The Vipers, too," Caus offers. "You've got a rat."

"It looks that way," Maxton concedes, "but I'll figure it out."

"He won't stop, he thinks you belong to him, Lai," Lia says.

"What?!"

"That's what he kept saying. You were meant to be his."

This doesn't make any sense. "I've never met him before in my life," I tell everyone.

"Why don't we sit down?" Quincy suggests as I sway slightly, feeling lightheaded. We all move over to the table and take seats, the guys on one side and Caus and Lia on the other. I take the seat next to Lia, gripping her hand in mine.

"What the fuck is going on, Causus? It's time to put it all on the table," Atlas demands.

He looks at me before deciding to answer. "Lai's dad is Warren Nobes."

They look at me like I just grew three heads.

"But you're a Noxx," Maxton says, disbelief in his tone.

"Yeah, my mum's surname. Why does my dad matter?" I ask, thoroughly confused.

"He was the Vipers' unofficial VP. He was due to take over that position before he died," Caus explains.

"My dad wasn't a Viper." Impossible.

"He most definitely was. Now it makes sense why your background check was half empty," Quincy says.

My head is swimming. Could Dad have hidden this from us for 20 years?

"You and Gia were hot commodities. With your dad about to be so important, everyone wanted you for themselves, or their sons. Leighton's got his head full of shit about you being meant for him," Caus tells us all, but it feels as real as a fairytale.

"But I didn't even know who any of you were. Are!"

"Your dad never wanted either of you involved, but he wouldn't have had much choice when he got to VP. Then everything happened with Gia and they cut you off, but Leighton obviously didn't get the memo."

"Why does Lai's dad dying mean she's exiled?" Maxton asks exactly what I was just thinking.

"Something I'm trying to figure out," Caus says cryptically.

"That doesn't matter." I couldn't fit many more unanswered questions into my head without it exploding. "What matters is this freak coming after me."

"As soon as he pops up, we'll find him," Caus tries to reassure me.

"Because you did so well looking after him in the first place," Atlas responds sarcastically.

"Says the guy with the leak who let him get away."

They both glare at each other, and that's the productive conversation officially over with.

"Come on, Lia, I'll take you home," Caus offers.

"Actually, I think I'll stay with Lai tonight. That's okay, right?" she asks me.

"Of course, we'll eat Taco Bell in bed," I tell her, mustering up a small smile.

That's exactly what we're doing an hour later, having both showered and Lia changed into borrowed pyjamas.

"How are you feeling?" I ask her.

"Stunned, I guess. I can't tell if I'm in shock or what, there's so much to take in."

"I'm so sorry this happened to you, Lia."

"It's not your fault."

"I would've come for you in a second."

"I know, and he did, too. Your big heart would've gotten you into serious trouble."

"What do you mean?"

"He sent that note to your office, thinking you'd slip away from the guys. How do you think they knew where I was so easily? He left a trail to make it clear, not bothering to hide it, knowing you'd just run to me."

"It doesn't change my answer. Coze would've as well, if he'd known."

"I know," she says simply.

"What are you thinking?"

"I don't even know. Would I have wanted to know about him if this hadn't all blown up? I was happy just being a part of his personal life. I never would've wanted to enter the gang side. But then, that's not a relationship, is it? Only knowing half of your partner's life? He didn't even tell me there was another side."

"I guess so."

"I feel mad that he let me fall for him without letting me decide that first."

"That's fair. What are you going to do?"

"I think I need some time. I might go home for a bit."

Home was where her parents lived. They moved out of town a little while ago, so Lia hadn't actually grown up where they were now, but they had the most beautiful country house an hour away.

"If that's what you want. You know you can stay here for as long as you need, though," I offer.

"I know, and I love you for it, but I think you've got enough to deal with."

I don't answer and we finish our tacos in silence, falling asleep to something rubbish on the TV.

The next morning, we lounge in bed until our stomachs growl. Jeremy takes us to the same diner Quincy took me to for breakfast but we decide to share a special instead of having one each. Two cars follow us, one from the Titans and one from the Vipers.

"How long will you be gone?" I ask her once we've filled up on all the food.

"I'm not sure. You're not getting rid of me that easily, though. I'll text and call regularly, like the needy friend I am."

"You'd better!"

We hug goodbye and I watch her drive away with the Vipers. They're taking her home to grab some bits and then driving her to her parents' place. I tried to convince her to let me or Jeremy go, but she's happy to let Caus provide security.

We head home and my mood deteriorates, like a black cloud is descending. When we get back, all three guys are in the kitchen area. I go to walk past and Quincy steps out into the way.

"Lai, come on. You would've wanted to trade."

"Of course I would have, and that's my decision to make." My anger bubbles to the surface. "I'm a fully grown adult with a functioning brain, having a vagina doesn't mean I lose all mental capacity. You had no right to take that choice away from me."

"We would never and will never let you sacrifice yourself," Maxton says calmly, and I turn my head to narrow my eyes at him.

"So who's next? A colleague? Lucy? One of you? You expect me to just let people pay the price for me?"

"None of this is your fault," he insists.

"It doesn't matter." And it doesn't. I couldn't live with myself if anything happened to someone else in place of me.

"The whole world can fucking burn for all I care," Atlas says, coming to stand next to Quincy. I'm done with the conversation and try to walk past them, but Atlas reaches out to grab my arm and stop me. "Madelaine, I mean it. You won't be at risk for even a second, whether you want that or not." We stare each other down, stubbornly butting against each other.

"*Yes, sir,*" I say sarcastically and shrug my arm out of his hold, walking to my room.

I spend the rest of the day curled up in bed, trying to process everything that's happened. The guilt I feel for Lia being put through this is immense, it's eating me up.

The frustration at being cut out of the decisions by the guys stings, especially as they did it because they knew they wouldn't like my choices. I thought we were equals in this relationship; I know they're possessive and protective, but can I handle them making decisions for me? I at least want to know what's happening. Then I try to think of the situation the other way around, and the thought of having one of them walk into danger makes my heart hurt. But it was Lia, my Lia.

My mind whirls and flips back and forth. As the evening draws in I feel drained, even though I've done nothing all day. I get up to take a shower and end up standing under the spray, motionless. I hear the door go and feel someone come in behind me, wrapping their arms around my middle and resting their chin on my head. Atlas.

"Please, baby," he whispers. "Come back to us."

He says nothing else but washes me, starting with my body, gently taking care of me. He moves onto my hair and when he finishes washing the conditioner out of my hair, presses a kiss to my head before silently leaving me to my thoughts again. I'm always comforted in his hold and as soon as he leaves I find myself missing being in his arms.

I dry my hair, then dress casually in some leggings and an oversized sweater before heading to the kitchen. Maxton's eating at the island, but stops and spins on his stool when he sees me. I step between his thighs and hug him, letting him surround me with his body.

"Are you still mad?" he asks, breath tickling my hair.

"I wasn't mad," I clarify. "Sad, maybe. Overwhelmed, frustrated."

"About what part?"

I let out a huge sigh.

"What Lia had to go through. That she's gone. You guys taking my choices from me. That you don't trust I'm strong enough to know what's happening."

"That's not it at all. We know how strong you are, that's why we didn't tell you. We knew you'd want to be there, front and centre." He lifts my chin and wipes a few stray tears away. "We can't lose you, *belle*, we only just found you."

I tuck my face back into his chest and breathe him in. I can't think any more.

We stay like that for a while and I feel another set of arms come from behind and one more from the side. All three scents mingle together and I feel like my whole body relaxes, melting into their holds. Everything melts away as I stand there, safe and comforted by my Titans.

TWENTY FOUR

ATLAS

I wake up late on Sunday morning and try to extract myself from the tangle of limbs, leaving a space next to Madelaine that Max quickly moves into.

"What's up?" she asks, having been woken by the jostling.

"Nothing, baby. I have to get going for lunch," I tell her, stopping at the end of the bed.

"Oh my God, how did we sleep so late?"

"I guess we all needed the rest. What are your plans for today?"

"Don't think I have any," she says, sitting up and rubbing at her face.

"Do you want to come with me?"

Her eyes widen slightly, but she tries to hide it.

"They're not scary, I promise."

"I don't know, it seems like a big step."

"Step towards what? You're definitely stuck with us anyway, whether you come to lunch or not."

She rolls her eyes at that. "How long do I have to get ready?"

"I can give you half an hour, tops, but it's only casual."

She thinks about it, a small frown appearing on her brow.

"If you come, I'll tell you our surprise," I taunt her.

"Hey," Quinn mumbles sleepily, "that's not fair."

Her eyes light up though, and she jumps up to the end of the bed, giving me a quick peck. Walking over to the bathroom, she stops in the doorway and looks back at us. "Anyone want to give me a hand?"

Quinn is suddenly way more awake than he was thirty seconds ago and leaps out of bed, running for the door. He's on the same side as the bathroom so he beats

Max, slamming the door shut in his face. Madelaine laughs and then squeals from behind the door.

"I'm blaming you for that," Max grumbles, flopping back into bed.

Madelaine surprises me by meeting me in the open area exactly half an hour later. She looks stunning, even dressed down in an olive green T-shirt and black cropped jeans. A pair of Vans leaves her way shorter than me, with her hair loose and a fresh face.

"You look amazing," I tell her and she smiles her thanks.

"You look pretty great, too. I never get to see you dressed casual."

"You don't like the suits?"

"Oh, I love the suits, but I love the casual too. Pretty much anything you wear. I'm kind of pissed I didn't get to really appreciate the tactical gear," she says, her serious expression making me grin.

"You ready to go?"

"Do I get to know the surprise now?" she asks, practically bouncing on the spot.

I laugh at her excitement. "Is that the only reason you're coming?"

"No, I can't wait to grill your mum about baby Atlas," she teases. She stands on tiptoes and gives me a soft kiss. "I'm ready."

I take her hand and we walk to the car, like an average couple going home to meet the parents.

The whole journey we chat and laugh and I'm so glad we get time to enjoy this. The guys and I spent a long time yesterday discussing everything going on and we decided we can't let Madelaine live her life waiting for the shit to hit the fan. Leighton has gone to ground, but we have the entire team as well as the Vipers looking for him. We couldn't drag Madelaine into that, so we're moving on as best we can. Yes, she'll still have a shitload of security at work and Jeremy will take her everywhere, but she needs some normalcy. We want to enjoy our time with Madelaine, and enjoy being happy. That's why we came up with our surprise.

A few minutes out from my parents' house, I decide to let Madelaine in on it.

"So, your surprise..."

She whips her head around to face me with glittering eyes.

"We thought we'd take you away for a break."

"Just us four?" she asks eagerly. My chest swells at how easily she includes all of us. It doesn't cross her mind that we would go away without the other two, and yet she gives us all couple alone-time, effortlessly. I nod, and she grins widely. "When do we go? I'll have to book it off work."

"It's already sorted, we go tomorrow," I tell her. "Quinn spoke to Jason, you've just handed over all of our plans early so it seemed a good time for a break. He was absolutely fine with it." I thought she might give us grief for sorting her time off without consulting her, but she seems pleased.

"Where are we going?"

"To the beach."

"I love the beach!" she exclaims, jigging in her seat.

I chuckle at her childlike excitement. "We go tomorrow and come back Friday. Five days of sun, sea and us." Hopefully sun, anyway. The weather is so temperamental here, but it's supposed to be good this week.

"Oh my God, I'm so excited!" she says through a huge grin. This is the Madelaine we wanted to get back, carefree and full of happiness. We pull up and she leans over, kissing me passionately.

"I definitely should've told you this while we were still in bed," I murmur against her lips.

She laughs and pulls away, letting herself out of the car. I adjust myself and follow her out, leading her through the front door. I can see her taking in the house as we enter. It's quaint and double-fronted, the same place we grew up in. It has a small farmhouse vibe, natural wood furniture everywhere that's older than me but well cared for. My parents have always refused to move, even if we can afford for them to live anywhere now.

"Hey, Mum," I call through to the kitchen as we walk down the hall.

"Hey, darling," she replies, not turning from the stove. "Your dad's in the garden."

"Okay. Mum, this is Madelaine."

My mum drops her spoon into the sauce she's stirring and whips around, shock clear on her face. She stares open-mouthed for a few seconds, and Madelaine looks up at me with a hesitant look on her face.

"Don't mind her, she'll come to in a second. She's not used to me bringing girls back," I explain.

"Not used to?! You've never, ever done it, and when you finally do I don't even get any notice?" she chides, whipping me with the tea towel that sits over her shoulder.

Madelaine chuckles as I dodge out of the way of my mum's assault.

"And she's so gorgeous, too. Wow!"

"Thank you," Madelaine says, shuffling slightly.

"Madelaine, this is my mum, Emily."

"Lovely to meet you." She offers her hand, which my mum promptly ignores, crushing her to her chest in a hug.

"You too, dear, you too." She gives me an arched brow over Madelaine's shoulder and I just shrug. I know what a big deal this is, but I didn't want to scare Madelaine out of coming.

"Can I have her back now? We're going to say hi to Dad."

She lets her go, and I lead Madelaine out the back door into their garden. "Hey, Dad."

"Hi, son," he says, turning from his rose bushes to shake my hand.

"This is Madelaine."

He does a double-take as he sees her standing next to me but recovers well. "What a beauty you are, Madelaine!"

"Thank you, sir. It's nice to meet you." I'm sure her cheeks are flaming under her tan complexion. Madelaine doesn't take compliments well, she always thinks people are overreacting to be nice.

"Please, it's Cole."

She smiles in return.

"Have you given her the tour?"

"Not yet, we only just got here."

"Well, get it done before Wade gets here. He's bringing the whole brood."

I mock-salute him and we turn back to the house. I'm sure Madelaine would survive without knowing every inch of my parents' house, but I won't hear the end of it if I don't show her around.

"Who's Wade?" she asks as we go back through the kitchen and down the hallway to the front door.

"My brother."

"What?! Do I know anything about you?" she jokes.

"You know what counts," I reply, and I mean it. "But he's 15 years older than me, he moved away for his job when I was 6. We're not really that close. I only see him occasionally, and it's normally here at Sunday lunch."

"Who's the brood?"

"His wife and two kids."

She doesn't say much more as I show her around the dining room to the left of the front door and the living room to the right. We head up the stairs straight opposite that lead to three bedrooms and a bathroom.

"Have they kept it as some kind of shrine?" she asks in awe as we go into a bedroom decorated for a little boy.

"No," I laugh, "this is where Wade's kids stay."

"Oh, obviously." She sounds distracted.

"You okay?"

"Yeah, I'm good. Just preparing myself to meet your entire family in one sitting," she tells me with a pointed look. "I'm not great with kids."

"Baptism of fire? Plus, I know they'll all love you. How could they not? The kids' opinions have no gravitas with us," I joke.

She rolls her eyes but the corners of her lips lift, albeit reluctantly.

"I'll make it up to you," I promise.

"Yeah?"

"Yeah." I grasp her head, running my hands through her hair. "And I don't offer that a lot."

She puts her hands over my wrists and I pull her into a kiss full of heat and promise. She rises on her tiptoes and I loop one arm around her waist, pulling her into me. Just as I'm genuinely considering spreading her out on a child's bed, the front door opens downstairs to a cacophony of noise and she pulls away from me, lips plump and eyes sparkling.

"What do you do to me?" she asks, and I ask myself the same thing about her, having to adjust myself for the second time in half an hour.

We head downstairs and I introduce her to everyone else before we sit down for lunch. As soon as everyone is seated and served, Mum starts up with the questions.

"So, Madelaine, how did you two meet?"

"We were at a club, and I offered to buy him a drink."

"Wow, ballsy lady! I like it," Dad says, approval shining from him.

I roll my eyes at my ego going down the drain but say nothing. I may run a gang, but good luck to me trying to rein my parents in. Madelaine doesn't seem bothered, either.

"What is it you do?" Mum continues.

"I'm an architect."

"So, brains, too! How long have you been together?"

Madelaine shifts in her seat as she thinks of how to answer.

"Not long, Mum, only a couple of weeks," I jump in.

"Have you met the other two yet? Like three peas in a pod they are."

Madelaine shoots me a look, but Mum launching into her story saves her from having to answer. "They've been best friends since they were little, you know. Couldn't keep them away from each other. I think Quincy stayed here every weekend for about six months at one point, and after Max's mum passed, he was here all the time, too. Never any trouble, any of them. Polite as you like, always helping around the house. Sometimes I feel like they're all my sons. We're so proud of how well they're doing now with their businesses. You must bring them round again soon," she directs at me.

"Max was here last weekend, Mum. I didn't bring them today because the house would've been overrun."

When my mum is happy we've eaten our own body weight in food, we manage to make our escape. Madelaine is grinning at me while I get behind the wheel, settled into her own seat already.

"What?"

"You're a mummy's boy," she says, full of glee.

"I am not," I protest, trying hard to hold on to my fierce Titan image. It's hopeless though. This woman has me wrapped around her little finger.

"You so are," she insists.

I reach over and tickle her ribs. "Oh, you think that's funny, do you?" She tries to wriggle away from me but is confined in the small space, laughing and spluttering.

"Okay, okay," she says, calling a ceasefire.

"Did you enjoy yourself?" I ask her when I've pulled away from the house and we're on our way home.

"Yeah. It was so interesting to find out about your childhood."

"It was pretty great, to be fair."

"How do you go from angelic blonde-haired boy to leader of the Titans?" she asks, sounding genuinely curious.

I shrug as I think it through. "It was never a conscious thing. Max and Quinn had completely different upbringings to me and dealt with way more shit than I ever had to. Things escalate when you're trying to survive, and where they go, I go."

She seems satisfied with that answer and we drive in quiet for a bit as she ponders everything she's learnt this afternoon, gazing out the window.

"Have you got to rush back?" she asks after a while. I shake my head at her. "Can we pop into the city? We should have time before the shops shut, I need to grab a few things."

"Sure."

We spend the last hour of the shops' opening hours grabbing bits for our week away. Madelaine didn't take her cards to lunch so I take the very rare opportunity to treat her and also throw in some extras that I'm dying to see her in, most of the silk and lace variety.

When we get back, the guys are in the living room about to start a movie.

"How was lunch?" Quinn asks.

"Great, everyone is lovely. Emily said next week you both have to go, no excuses."

They laugh at her message delivery and Max reaches out, grabbing her hand and dragging her down to sit in his lap.

"This is a movie from the list, so the rule is you have to sit with me."

"Oh, really?" she chuckles.

"But the sequel isn't on there, so that's my turn," Quinn adds.

She grins over at him and settles down with Max. I throw myself on the couch with them all, where we stay all evening.

TWENTY FIVE

QUINCY

Lai is up at the crack of dawn, buzzing for our trip. She stayed up late to pack so we could leave early this morning and I don't know how she has any energy left. We go to our favourite breakfast diner and eat way too much food before setting off for the drive. The beachhouse is only about an hour outside of the city, but Lai falls asleep five minutes into the journey with her head in At's lap. He shakes her awake when we pull up outside the house and she pushes herself up sleepily. She gasps as she looks out at the house, while Max collects her from the back seat and walks her in.

"Oh my God, this is gorgeous!" she says as they enter. The ground floor is one big open space with cosy couches, a small kitchen, and a dining table. This place was meant for us to relax away from Ironhaven, not as an entertaining space, so it's small and comforting.

"There are two bedrooms and a bathroom on the basement level, and the master suite upstairs," I tell her. She heads straight over to the all-glass back wall and stares out at the view.

"This doesn't even look real," she says.

"That makes two of you," I reply as I walk up behind her, wrapping my arms around her waist. "Are you going to get some more sleep?"

"No way, I want to go swimming," she says, spinning in my hold.

"Swimming?! That water's going to be freezing," Max tells her.

"It'll be fine once we're in," she says, smiling over my shoulder at him, but I'm pretty sure none of us have any intention of getting in that water.

"I'll start grabbing the bags," Atlas calls, heading back out the front door.

"This place is so cosy," Madelaine says, escaping my arms and wandering around the ground floor. "I love it."

We haven't been here since we bought it just before we moved to Ironhaven, but seeing the way Madelaine's eyes light up as she explores makes it worth every penny. The house isn't linked to any of us, so we thought it was a perfect safe house for our break.

Atlas comes back in carrying Madelaine's bags, gesturing up the stairs.

"I'll put these upstairs, do you want to see?"

She nods and follows him up to the room inside the pitched roof. The entire back wall is glass up there as well, giving views over the beach for miles. It's got an enormous bed and its own ensuite. A couple of minutes later Lai comes running back down the stairs in a tiny string bikini, and I know instantly that we're all going into that damn water. I don't think I'd be able to say no to Lai under any circumstance, let alone when she's looking like a Swimsuit Illustrated model.

We end up swimming for ages, and yes, it is freezing. When all of our lungs are burning, we lounge on the sand in front of the beach house deck.

"I haven't been to the beach in forever," Lai says when we're all drying in the sun. "It used to be our thing." She says nothing for a while, staring out to sea.

"You don't have to tell us," I tell her, not wanting to dampen her mood.

"I know, but you and Atlas shared, and I want to, too. My dad was perfect. That's why it's so hard to reconcile him being a Viper."

"'Cause all gang leaders are evil?" I joke.

She rolls her eyes with a small smile. "No, because he was always there. He attended everything, every event. Never once was he not there exactly when I needed him. How did he hide that from me?"

The guys and I swap looks. We got it. It's exactly how we planned to be for her.

"G and I were inseparable," she continues. "I couldn't even comprehend she would do anything like that. She never would."

"What do you think happened?" Atlas asked gently. We'd read about the death in the papers like everyone else, but there weren't many details. They didn't even confirm he was a Viper.

"I have no idea. I didn't attend the trial, G didn't want me to and to be honest, I barely even believed it was really happening. I didn't read anything, it hurt too much. She just kept telling me to lean on Lia and it would all be okay."

"And now you don't see her?" Atlas prompts.

"That's her choice, and I'll do whatever she needs to make her time in prison easier for her. When it happened, I felt like I'd lost everyone. Lia saved me, I'll always owe her. It's why I'd never let her take my place, ever."

I understand exactly how she feels, but we would still never let her give herself up to danger. Lai shivers now the sun is going down but makes no move to go inside. Max pulls her back into his chest, sharing their body warmth.

"Sometimes I still forget that neither of them are here. Something great will happen at work, or I'll meet three amazing guys and the first people I'll want to tell are Dad and G. I mean, Dad would've definitely hated you," she laughs, "but we didn't hide things from each other. At least, I thought we didn't. Turns out that was just me."

"I can't even imagine what it feels like, Lai," I say, not knowing what else to do.

"You lost your parents too."

"Not like you did, I never knew mine. Max is the only one of us who probably knows how you feel."

She tips her head back and looks hesitantly at him.

"It's okay, *belle*, I'll tell you anything. My mum fled her abusive husband in Togo when she was pregnant. She had an aunt here, but she was elderly and passed shortly after my mum arrived. She got really ill when I was a teenager, I was already friends with these guys by then. The way you feel about Lia is how I feel about Atlas and Quinn."

She sits back and presses a kiss to his bicep, and we all mull quietly.

"Well, you know all of my secrets now," Lai declares after a while. "Nothing left to hide."

Her stomach rumbles as if to punctuate her point, and it breaks the serious atmosphere.

"What do you want to do for dinner?" Atlas directs to her.

"I don't mind," she says offhandedly.

"Choices!" Max calls out, and Atlas and I gape at him. I can't remember the last time he was so lively and carefree. Lai is pure magic.

Lai chuckles at our expressions. "I don't know what's around here," she says with a huge yawn.

"Let's order in tonight, then we can think about going into town tomorrow and exploring," I offer.

"Okay. Indian or Taco Bell?"

"I don't think your beloved Taco Bell stretches this far out, so Indian it is. What do you fancy?"

"Anything, surprise me. I'm going to take a shower."

We all head in after her and by the time I've finished placing our order, Lai's back downstairs in what looks like just one of Atlas's henleys. *Control yourself, Quince.*

I use the basement-level bathroom to have a shower myself and hear the front door just as I'm putting on some sweats. Max is laying out enough containers to feed ten, and my stomach grumbles as the smells waft over. I grab plates and cutlery on my way over and sit myself down, ready to dig in.

"This smells incredible, thank you!" Lai says as she joins us.

"You're welcome. I got a bit of everything."

"We can see that," Atlas says, amused and handing out drinks.

We say nothing else as we all pile huge mounds of food onto plates, apparently determined to try everything and work our way through every last bit.

"I don't think I can move," Lai moans as she leans back, looking very full and very satisfied. "That was amazing."

We clear up and then settle on the sofas to watch another of Max's films. I pull Lai's feet into my lap, Max having stolen her using the stupid list rule, and she's asleep within minutes. Once the film ends, he carries her up to bed and we all climb in around her, happy to make do with less space if we get to wake up to Lai.

I wake up the next morning to Lai's naked back as she's sitting up.

"You okay?" I ask quietly.

"Yeah, just enjoying the view."

"Me too," I say, sitting up and kissing her shoulder. The sun is just up over the sea. "What do you want to do today?"

"Did you say there was a town?"

"Yeah, a proper little seaside one. The boardwalk starts just down the beach."

"Can we go there?" she asks. "I need all the rocks and all the tacky fridge magnets."

"Oh, no. You have a collection, don't you? I knew there had to be something wrong with you."

She laughs at my mocking. "I do, actually. Well, did, so your penance for making fun of the poor homeless girl is having to display said tacky magnets on your fridge until I have one of my own."

"I'll take my punishment like a man," I promise.

"What punishment?" Atlas asks, skating his fingers over Lai's bare back.

She shudders as she turns her head to answer him. "Quincy's letting me cover your fridge in souvenirs."

He looks perplexed and we both laugh.

"What's so funny, so early?" Max asks from my other side.

Lai lays back down so she can see him behind me. "Sorry, did we wake you?"

"Yeah, but I'll take an apology kiss." She spins onto her forearms and leans over to kiss him.

As soon as they break apart, Atlas pulls her back into his chest and she giggles.

"I didn't get that kind of treatment," he says against her ear.

"You didn't ask," she replies as she spins to face him.

"I don't ask, baby." He grips her chin between his thumb and forefinger and kisses her until she's moaning and pressing herself into him. She pulls away and looks over her shoulder at me, and I arch a brow. She grins as she sits back up next to me and I grab her thigh, pulling her over so she's straddling my lap.

"Last, am I?" I ask when we're face to face.

"Never," she promises, holding my face in her hands and kissing me. The way Lai kisses is so uniquely her. A perfect mix between soft and exploring, fierce and bold. We break apart and I lay back down so she's sitting on my lap, looking down at all of us.

"Is this okay?" Max asks. We haven't been with her yet, not all three of us at once, and we don't want to push her too far too fast, but she nods.

Gripping her hips, I pull her down to grind on my hard length. Her mouth pops open and her eyes hood. She looks fucking magnificent sat up there like a bronze goddess. Her skin has deepened from the sun yesterday and her hair cascades around her shoulders.

"Touch yourself," I tell her, and her eyes widen slightly as I put my hands behind my head to give me a better angle. Atlas pulls his cock out into his hand and leisurely pumps it, giving her the confidence she needs as she places her hand between her legs. She looks over to Max, who is in the same position as Atlas and she slowly swirls her fingers. Rocking slightly, she drags her core against my cock that is throbbing underneath her. *Fuck, that's hot.* She picks up speed, rubbing her fingers over her clit and torturing me with her swaying hips. Her breath gets shallower, and she lets out a quiet gasp, signalling that she's close.

"Wait," I say, and she jolts to a stop with a little whimper. "Ride me."

"Fuck," Atlas mutters next to me, enjoying the show.

Madelaine is staring at us all, and I sit up and give her a gentle peck on the lips. "Ride me, Lai," I murmur into her mouth, my eyes locked on hers. She lifts herself up with her thighs and lines the head of my cock up with her entrance. I lay back down as she slowly sinks down my length, taking me inside her fully. I groan as I'm fully seated in her tight core, and she rolls her hips, making me jerk inside her.

"Shit, you need to move, gorgeous." The torture of her grinding on me while she played with herself has put me right on the edge. The teasing has also affected Lai, and as she lifts up and down slowly, I feel her quivering. Max and Atlas have picked up their pace on either side of us, gazes fixed on Lai's face radiating pleasure. As she returns her fingers to her clit with a sensual moan, we all seem to explode as one. Lai clenches around me and I grab her hips, thrusting a couple of times and emptying myself into her with another groan. She collapses onto my chest, breathing hard. After a minute, I stand with her in my arms, heading to the bathroom. We clean up and then she curls into my chest. Max and Atlas clean themselves up and get back in on either side of us, all of us promptly falling back asleep.

TWENTY SIX

MADELAINE

Later that morning, we wake up for the second time and decide to head straight to town and find food there. The weather is amazing. We spend the entire afternoon browsing in all the little gift shops along the boardwalk and eating all the seaside snacks. We go past a funfair that stretches out on a pier but decide to save that for another day. When we reach the end of the boardwalk, we find a gorgeous beachside restaurant that we promise to come back to when we're dressed more appropriately. I fall asleep on the couch for the second evening in a row, nestled between my guys and tired out by all the sea air.

Wednesday morning I wake in bed with that spectacular view, but alone. I take a leisurely shower and dress casually again, not sure what our plans are for the day. I head downstairs expecting to find my guys but instead, I find Lia chilling on the back deck. Screeching in a volume that likely sets all the local dogs to barking, I throw myself at her, hoping the wicker chair can hold us both.

"What are you doing here?!"

When I've eased my hugging so it's not at boa-constrictor levels, she tells me.

"Your Titans convinced me to surprise you. Although I would've come for this view alone, honestly," she teases, and I wouldn't blame her. I make us fresh drinks as we catch up under the sun. She's staying until tomorrow afternoon and I am so excited.

"They've made themselves scarce for the day so we can do whatever you want," Lia explains.

"What do you want to do? You're the one who's visiting."

"What have you done already?"

I talk her through our two days so far and as soon as I mention the funfair she sits up straight with excitement, so funfair it is. We walk down, trailed by one

Viper and one Jeremy, and stop for some breakfast at a cute cafe overlooking the sea.

"How are you doing?" I ask her.

"I'm good," she says, and she does look good. "Work is letting me work remotely, so I'm just taking whatever time I need. Caus is being really understanding."

"Why are you saying that like it's not a good thing?"

"No, it is. I just wonder if it's a sign we're not in this for the long haul. I thought I'd be dying to see him by now and kind of hoped he'd be banging my door down, but we both seem fine with some space."

"Maybe that's just what you need right now, don't write anything off."

"I won't. Anyway, enough of my boring solo boyfriend. How are the triplets?"

I can't help but laugh at her question. "I think we're great, actually. It's weird, it just feels right. All that shit I was worrying about before, I just don't think about now. We all fit together perfectly and everything is so easy. That's not to say they don't piss me off regularly and make me want to strangle them when we butt heads, but I know they have my back throughout it all. We're a team, and they like me exactly how I am. None of them ever try to diminish me or dampen my flame. Sorry, huge monologue over, I'll stop gushing now."

"No, never! Seeing you so happy makes me so happy," Lia says, and I know it's true. It's the same for me and I can't wait for her to figure out what's going to make her happy.

We spend the afternoon getting on and off rides and eating all the funfair treats. I very nearly throw up doughnuts and I'm sure my skin is 50% cotton candy by this point, but my face hurts from smiling, so that's a win for me. We even convince Jeremy to try the rollercoaster with us, although he stays a fetching shade of green for an hour afterwards.

It's dark by the time we walk back to the house along the sand and I spot the guys lighting a bonfire as we approach. It seems like it's going to be the perfect end to a perfect day.

Lia and I get up early the next morning to maximise her beach time. We used to have one dedicated tanning day at the beginning of every summer, and we would take it very seriously. It's more of a joke now, especially as we're both already several shades darker than when we arrived, but we still gather our supplies and set ourselves up on the beach. We sunbathe and swim and relax, and the guys bring us cold drink refills regularly, like the hottest shirtless servers you've ever seen. They join Lia and me for the last part of the afternoon before she leaves to head back to her parents' place. Because we have company, I realise how much they all touch me constantly. It doesn't even seem conscious but if I'm within reaching distance I'm either in someone's lap, held in someone's arms, or touched in some way by them.

As soon as I've seen Lia off, I realise they must have some plan because they're definitely ganging up on me. All afternoon they grab me for kisses, trace their fingers over my bare skin, or tug me from one another's arms. Well, four can play at that game.

We decide to go to the restaurant we saw on Tuesday for our last full night here. I put makeup on for the first time since we arrived, but keep everything golden and glowy to highlight my tan. Fluttery lashes and lip balm gives me the perfect sun-kissed look. The salt from the sea has given my hair great beachy waves, so I skip styling it before we go, loving the vibe it gives. My dress is another Lia find and is perfect for tonight. It's an oversized sleeveless shift dress with curved hems that cut to the top of my thighs and a racerback, showing a hint of side boob. The material is flowy and loose and I love that it's sexy but also comfortable, and it has pockets. Very handy! I can't wear a bra with it and decide against underwear, settling on Atlas's torture for the night. I slip on some flat sandals and give myself a once-over before heading downstairs to meet the guys.

"Jesus, you look incredible," Quincy says as soon as he sees me descending. The other two spin and stare, watching me until I'm in front of them. They all look hot enough to eat and for a minute I can't believe I get all three of them for myself. Max is in cream trousers and a white shirt tight over his chest and biceps, the pale colours looking incredible against his deep skin. Quincy is also in a white shirt but has teamed his with navy shorts, the nerdy-surfer vibe really benefiting him right now. He looks like he belongs in a porno set right here at the beach. Atlas is wearing a khaki shirt with the sleeves rolled up, showing his tattooed forearms and black trousers, hair pulled back into a bun. I can't think straight for a second. How am I going to go through with my dastardly plan when I can barely make my brain function when I look at them?

"Thanks." I grin at Quincy as he dips and kisses the corner of my mouth. I love it when he does that. He's normally so fun and casual, but that kiss is a promise of what's coming. "You three look pretty great yourselves."

"As long as our girl is happy," Atlas says, taking Quincy's place as he steps away and kisses me lightly.

"I think every girl within looking distance of you is going to be happy," I joke. The guys always get plenty of attention when we go out and I'm sure it'll be the same here, even if the Titans aren't as well known in this area.

"We wouldn't even notice," Atlas says, trying to reassure me, but I'm not worried at all. The guys have never given me any reason to feel anything but totally secure in this relationship. I move my hand from my pocket to his, slipping my underwear inside.

"Good," I grin. He feels the lacy material, then groans.

"You're going to be the death of me."

Maxton tugs me over by my hand to where he's sitting at the table, so I'm standing between his thighs. The height difference is unusual this way around for us, and he has to tip his head up to look at me. I rest my forearms on his shoulders, running my fingernails over the nape of his neck. "Are you behaving?" he asks, trailing his hands up the backs of my thighs. I shrug as he reaches my bare ass and I lean forward to kiss him softly on the lips as his eyes widen.

"Are we ready?" I ask as I step away, letting Maxton's hands fall back to his lap.

"Yeah," Quincy says, with a knowing smirk. "Let's go."

We drive over to the other end of the boardwalk and settle in at our table by the window. The sun is just setting, and it looks stunning. Maxton holds my chair out for me, and I make sure to grind my ass against his crotch as I move past to take my seat. He tenses as I do, and I know I've hit my target.

The sun completely sets while we're waiting for our starters and the restaurant gets a warm, romantic atmosphere with low lighting from all the candles dotted everywhere. Our food arrives and we tuck in, chatting easily about our trip. I lift my foot and slide it up Atlas's leg as I talk and his gaze heats. Quincy looks down into Atlas's lap, noticing the movement, and snaps his eyes back up to mine, but I ignore his looks. The food keeps on coming and I'm sure I'm going to have to roll back to Ironhaven at this point.

When we arrive back at the beach house, I kick off my shoes and head to the kitchen, where I pour a glass of water. The guys all stand together, watching me as I drink and rinse my glass.

"Well, I'm off to bed," I say casually, walking towards the stairs.

I know they're all horny as shit after my games at dinner and to be honest, so am I. They wait me out, though, and I stop at the bottom of the stairs, spinning to face them. Pushing the hem of my dress up the tops of my thighs, I bite my lip before gripping the fabric and slowly lifting my arms up over my head, revealing my naked body to them. The dress hasn't even hit the floor before I'm over Maxton's shoulder with a squeal and he runs up the stairs, throwing me on my back on the bed.

"Did you have fun teasing us?" he asks as he crawls over me.

"I don't know what you mean," I protest.

"No?"

He runs his knuckle along my jaw and down my neck, over the mound of my breast. My nipples peak as his knuckle continues down my stomach and between my legs. The other two stand like sentries at the end of the bed, and I realise I may have bitten off more than I can chew.

"Open your legs, Lai," Quincy demands. There must be something wrong with me because his alpha tone has everything inside me tightening, so I do as he says. How can the chill, carefree surfer turn so dominating in the bedroom?

Maxton settles himself on his knees, looking down at me.

"Hands above your head." I follow Quincy's next command and he holds his hand out to Atlas, who places something in it. Quincy crawls onto the bed by my head and ties my wrists together using the scrap of lace I'd put in Atlas's pocket earlier. It wasn't too tight and I could rip through them if I wanted to, but I really don't want to. Quincy leans over so his face is upside down in front of mine and gives me another of those kisses to the edge of my mouth. He gets back up and resumes his position at the end of the bed, Atlas sitting where he just vacated.

“Do you remember what I said about these breasts?”

My brain is cloudy as he lightly traces patterns over my chest, grazing my nipples as he goes. I arch my back to press into his hand, but he doesn’t give me any extra pressure, just keeps up his relentless caressing until I’m trying to pull my thighs together for some friction. This, of course, is when he stops, laying back against the headboard.

“Breathe, Lai.” I had definitely forgotten to do that, so I focus on my breathing and feel my orgasm receding.

Maxton settles himself on his front and suddenly blows on my core. My whole body reacts, tensing as he slowly licks my seam. He circles my clit and then moves down slowly towards my entrance, where he slowly penetrates me with just his tongue and fucks me with it at a leisurely pace. I try to grind on his face, but his hands hold my hips and I can’t get any friction. I let out a groan of frustration. He circles my clit again, and when I’m right on the edge, he stops.

I moan, and they both stand up next to Quincy, stripping down and watching me writhe.

"Don't close your legs," Quincy orders as I was about to do just that. "What do you want, Lai?"

"I want you," I gasp.

"Who?"

"All of you."

"Almost, gorgeous. Do you remember your word?"

"Black."

He squeezes lube he got from God knows where into his hand and rubs it softly over me. He wipes his hands on his discarded shirt and then undoes my wrist restraints before kissing me. "You're so fucking perfect."

Maxton leans over next, kissing me, and I can taste myself on his tongue. *Why is that so hot?* He helps me sit up with a gentle tug on my hand.

Atlas lies on the bed with his legs off the edge as Maxton pulls away. "Come here, baby."

I sit up and climb over him, straddling his waist as he pulls me close to his chest, kissing me with awe and barely contained restraint.

Maxton stands behind me and massages my ass cheeks, spreading the lube and stretching me with his thumb.

I try to grind against Atlas, but Maxton pulls my hips back up. "It'll be worth the wait, *belle*, I promise." He presses his tip against my hole, and I remember to push back and breathe out as he slides into me. I feel an aching relief after all the teasing and moan, resting my forehead on Atlas's chest.

"You okay, Madelaine?" he asks, tipping my chin up with his finger.

"Yeah," I barely whisper. "Move," I plead. This tension is too much. I need some friction.

"Hang on, baby," Atlas says as he pulls my hips down and I expect Maxton to pull out, but he rests one knee on the bed instead, so he lowers with me.

Atlas lines his tip up with my entrance and slowly slides in. *Fuck, that feels incredible.* He doesn't stop until he's completely inside me and I've never felt so full and so loved in my life. I could explode just from this feeling. I curl my fingernails into Atlas's chest.

"Quincy?" I ask, not really knowing where my brain is going but needing to have all my guys present.

"I'm here, gorgeous. They're going to move now, okay?"

"Yes," I murmur on a breath.

Maxton moves first, halfway out and in again, and I can't believe how close I am already.

As he finds a rhythm, Atlas lifts my hips, controlling me on top of him and dragging me back down his length. I detonate, my orgasm exploding after all the lead up.

They both pick up the speed as I ride it out and Atlas joins me soon after, thrusting up into me as he releases and Maxton stills. Atlas pulls out and Maxton sits with me in his lap, laying us both down so my back is to his front, with him still inside me.

Quincy steps up between Maxton's legs and pushes into me, filling me straight back up again. He holds my legs up to his chest and ploughs into me forcefully, Maxton matching his pace. I'm strung so high that it doesn't take long for me to climax again, pleasure shooting through my whole body, and both guys follow me soon after.

Quincy collapses to the side and I lay on Maxton's chest, my limbs like jelly. I don't think I could move if my life depended on it. Eventually, Maxton lifts me up, carrying me to the bathroom to clean me up before he carries me back to bed again. I could get used to this. Atlas pulls me into his arms and as soon as my head hits the pillow, I'm out for the count.

TWENTY SEVEN

LEIGHTON

They ruin everything. She definitely would have come for Lia if she'd known. I didn't know they had someone intercepting her mail. I would've made the clues more obscure. When I heard them planning their assault, I left. Lia was nothing to me anyway. I practically forgot she was there, the anticipation buzzing in my veins, waiting for Madelaine to arrive. She fought me off well last time, I was proud of her. My fighter. But that's okay, these have just been dress rehearsals.

I'll need to preoccupy the Titans for the big finale and give her a reason to stay. Maybe if she hears my explanation, she'll understand. I'm just waiting for the perfect opportunity. Even with both gangs now on my tail. It was a necessary evil, involving Causus's girl, but other people aren't relevant. Madelaine is the sun, and everyone else revolves around her.

TWENTY EIGHT

MAXTON

"You're back in my house and you've got nothing?"

Causus sits opposite us in the office looking thoroughly bored. We got back from the beach house earlier this afternoon and Atlas had wanted an update as soon as possible.

"I didn't ask to be here. Don't you think if I knew something I'd have reached out?"

"Not really, no."

"Have you found your rat yet?" he asks pointedly.

"No." I was reluctant to admit it, but we had no inkling of who our rat might be. We couldn't think of anyone who was the least bit suspicious. Our guys had been hand-picked over the last few years and we knew and trusted every one.

“Are you still covering Lia?” I ask him.

“Yeah. My guy was a bit surprised when he trailed her straight over to the Titans, that’s for sure.”

“Who did you send? That place is supposed to be secure.”

“Don’t worry, my brother went. He couldn’t care less about gang politics, his only loyalty is to me.”

“Don’t you think it’s about time we made this truce official?” Quince asks us. We all turn and look at him like he’s crazy. “What? The whole mutual destruction shit is working for both sides right now. Why not roll that out further?”

“It would mean I don’t risk getting killed every time I sneak into here,” Causus agrees. “I’ll think about it. If my grilling is over now, I’d like to get out of here.”

He walks over to the panelled door and pushes it open, leaving through the conference room and garage. He’s not in danger of being spotted that way as all the guys are out on the hunt. The hunt that is turning up absolutely fuck-all at the moment.

"Quinn, what are you thinking?" Atlas asks him once Causus has gone.

"Exactly what I just said."

"It makes sense," I say. "We'd have one less thing hanging over our heads. We'd probably have to come to some agreements with our businesses, but we could work it out. We never wanted to rule the world, our slice of Ironhaven will do just fine."

Atlas shrugs. "It's your call, but on your head be it. What's Madelaine up to?"

The weather had turned, so we decided to cut our last day at the beach short and we'd come straight back to the office to get caught up.

"She was getting in the shower when Causus arrived," I tell him.

"Do we know what her plans for the weekend are? I've got a ton of meetings in the city in the morning to make up for our week off," Quince explains.

"I'll come in with you. I've got some things to do before our afternoon ones. Madelaine's car shopping tomorrow."

"Yeah, I was supposed to go with her to Audi, but I don't think I can now," Atlas says. "I've got some calls to make from home, then I'll meet you both in the city in the afternoon."

"Alright, Jeremy will go with her. I'll brief him after."

"I don't even know why she needs a car. Jeremy can drive her anywhere if we're busy."

I roll my eyes at Atlas; he asked the same question he's already asked Madelaine a thousand times.

"You know she wants more independence. You can't stifle her, it never works out well. We'll put her in a convoy if need be, but she wants her own car."

"Whatever, I'm going to go and find her. I can be very persuasive when I put my mind to it," he says, standing.

"Somehow I don't think it's your brain you're going to use to persuade her," Quince jokes. "Bets on Lai doing exactly what she's wanted this whole time, anyway?"

"I'd never bet against that," I say with a laugh.

I walk into the kitchen the next morning and greet Madelaine with a kiss.

"You sure you don't mind going by yourself, *belle*?" Atlas's persuasion had gone as well as Quince and I had thought.

"You do know I got by in life perfectly fine before you three showed up?" she asks with an arch of her brow. "I'll be fine. And we both know I'm never actually alone, Jeremy will be with me."

"Okay, are you test driving?"

"Not sure, I want to see my top three picks in real-life first. I'm not massively fussed, as long as it gets me from A to B."

"Do you want me to make you some breakfast?" I offer. Lucy was off for the whole week, seeing as we were away Monday to Friday, anyway.

"What exactly can you make?" Madelaine asks suspiciously, having never seen me cook before.

"Cereal is probably pushing it."

"I'm good, thanks," she says with a laugh. "Quincy brought me something earlier."

Speak of the devil and he appears.

"I think that means I'm currently winning," he gloats, and Madelaine rolls her eyes at his competitiveness. "Are you ready to go?"

“Yeah, sure.”

We both give Madelaine a kiss and head into the city.

The morning speeds by with meeting after meeting. We’re getting ready to open three places within the next month, so we’re kept plenty busy with all of the business decisions that need to be made. Our last morning meeting finishes a little early and Quince and I have some time before we’re due to meet Atlas. We’re further out than Madelaine is at the dealership but decide to see if she’s still out and wants to grab lunch with us. Quince tries her phone, but there’s no answer.

“She might still be in there, I’ll call Jeremy.”

“Hey, Max. Everything okay?”

“Yeah, just trying to get hold of Madelaine.”

“She left her phone in this car, she’s driving hers home now.”

“She picked one already?”

“Yeah, and they had it in stock.”

“Okay, can you have her call us when you’re back?”

A beep of the horn and some choice words from Jeremy stop him from replying.

"What happened?" I ask him.

"Some wanker just cut me up at the crossways."

There's more beeping as Jeremy presumably goes around the other driver.

"You've got eyes on Madelaine though, right?"

"Her car's right in front of me."

"Where are you?"

"Milver Way."

"That's not on the way home."

"Guess she's enjoying the new ride."

I remind him to get Madelaine to call when they're home and hang up.

"Atlas is just leaving, said he'd meet us here," Quince says, looking up from his phone.

I fill in the gaps of the conversation with Jeremy and then attempt to focus back on work, trying to be productive, seeing as our girl isn't around for a break. I've successfully stared at the same page for fifteen minutes when Jeremy calls back.

"What's going on?" I answer, putting him on speaker so I don't have to repeat everything to Quince again.

"Nothing really, but we're on the I50 and Madelaine's definitely not heading home."

"What's out that way?" I ask, mainly to myself.

"Not a lot for quite a while," Quince supplies.

"Do you want me to pull her over?"

"No, I don't want you to surprise her at that speed, just keep your eyes on her."

Jeremy hangs up with an affirmative.

"I just got the weirdest text from Atlas," Quince says, showing me the phone. I read the text and run through the first phone call with Jeremy in my head.

"Something's not right. Can you ring him?" He doesn't answer. Quince and I are both tense, everything feels off. Madelaine was in no way under our control but she wouldn't take Jeremy on a wild goose chase without letting him know, she was way too fond of him for that. I call Jeremy back.

"Try to get in line with her without alarming her," I instruct. We wait in stressed silence while he does what I've asked.

"She's speeding up," he replies in a confused tone. "She won't let me get in line with her."

"Put your foot down, Jeremy."

"But-"

"Just do it."

We hear the roar of his engine as he speeds up.

"Shit, it's not her." All the blood in my head roars in my ears. "Miss Lai isn't driving the car," he confirms.

Quince asks what I'm thinking. "Then where the fuck is she?"

TWENTY NINE

ATLAS

I wake up slowly, my thoughts like they're wading through treacle. What the fuck happened to me? I feel like a truck has hit me. A splash of cold hits my face and I jerk my eyes open, pain instantly searing through my brain.

"Fucking finally. How long does it take?"

I don't recognise the voice, but it echoes slightly, wherever we are. I pry my eyes back open, absorbing the pain and taking in the face from the photos plastered all over our conference room wall.

"Who are you?" I ask, trying to buy some time to collect my scattered mind. No such luck.

"Don't try me with that shit, I know you know exactly who I am."

He chuckles manically in my face, then shoots out a fist, connecting straight with my jaw at lightning speed. My mouth fills with blood, but I feel nothing else.

I can't feel my body at all, so it's only the fact the room stays upright that I know I haven't been floored. It feels like cement has replaced the blood in my veins. My limbs have no sensation other than heaviness.

"What the fuck did you give me?"

"It's all about you, isn't it, Atlas? Don't you want to know why I'm here?"

"Not really," I reply, disdain dripping from my words. At least the cloud over my brain is clearing. My lack of interest causes his face to scrunch in fury, but a ding from his phone distracts him and it disappears instantly. This guy is fucking creepy.

"God, these besties of yours sure are needy, aren't they?" he asks, grinning. It isn't his phone, it's mine. While he's sidetracked with that, I take the chance to look around and realise exactly where we are. The basement, in my own fucking home. "Shall we go with engine trouble delaying you or someone keeping you? What's the maid's name again? Lucy!"

I don't answer him, but he doesn't seem to need any encouragement. How the fuck he knows that information or how he got in here in the first place are questions I'll ask once I'm out of here. He stands right in front of me, knowing full well he won't receive any retaliation from my frozen body. My phone rings and he lets it ring out, watching the screen until another text comes through.

"Wow, they'll really believe anything. Where were we? Oh yeah, why I'm here."

"I don't give a fuck," I hiss at him.

His fist shoots out again and gets me right on the nose. A crunch of bone makes me cringe, and I definitely felt that one, which is a good sign. Whatever I'm under seems to be wearing off pretty quickly now that I'm awake.

"You're really fucking rude, do you know that?"

"Okay," I relent. "Why are you here?" If I can keep him talking, I might be able to gain some mobility back. He must've tied my wrists because my arms are behind my back and there's no way I'm capable of holding them there right now.

A huge grin eats up his face again. The manic smile and dead eyes belong in a horror movie, not in my basement.

"Yes! I'm here for Madelaine," he says as if he's made a huge reveal, like he hasn't been stalking *my* fucking girl for weeks.

"Madelaine's not here," I spit.

"But she will be soon. See, you really should be more interested in what I have to say. I could've told you everything about the car swap. I think it would've impressed you, honestly."

"What car swap?" I have no idea of the time but if Madelaine is due back soon, it must be no later than early afternoon. The last thing I remember is being on a morning call, so I've either lost a few hours of time or the drugs have impaired my memory. Did someone hit me? How am I down here?

"In fact, she should be here any minute so let me just top this up, can't have you ruining my surprise."

He gags me and then pulls out a syringe from his pocket, uncapping the needle. I'm completely powerless to stop him and as soon as he steps back I feel the minute sensations that were returning to my body disappearing again. My mind stays alert, though, so it can't be the same thing he gave me last time.

"Atlas?"

Madelaine! I hear her calling me but I can't reply. I thought my mind was clear but it sounds like her voice is coming from right in this room. Leighton jogs up the stairs and disappears. Is this it? He's going to take my girl and disappear. The guys will eventually find me down here but Madelaine will be gone. I will search my whole life for her if that's what it takes to get her back. Nothing happens for the longest few minutes of my life, but then the door opens at the top of the stairs.

"Atlas!" Madelaine calls my name in relief as soon as she's low enough on the stairs to see me. "Atlas?" she calls again as she reaches the bottom, heading for me.

"Stay the fuck away from him!" Leighton calls, stopping her in her tracks. "Over against the wall. Go near him and I'll have to shoot him, which will be really fucking irritating because I waited for him to come round for ages."

Madelaine sits about 10 feet away from me, arms wrapped around her legs in front of her, pure fear in her eyes as Leighton walks over and removes my gag.

"It's okay, baby." The words are clear in my mind but they come out slurred. God, I wish I could go to her, hold her in my arms. Preferably after I've crushed this fucker's head under my boot. She sags with relief when she hears my voice.

"Are you okay?" she asks me.

"I'm good. Are you okay?" I want to reassure her, but my words still come out slower and more slurred than I'd like. I don't want her wasting any energy worrying about me. She needs to be focused on getting herself out of here, since I'm in no position to do so. Madelaine is my priority here and I would die a thousand times to keep her safe.

"Didn't I say I was going to die in this house?" she asks with a watery half-smile.

"You're not dying," I say fiercely, but her expression shows me she doesn't believe me.

"I would never hurt you, Madelaine," Leighton says. "Can I tell my story now so *he* can die and we can go?" He obviously has a lot to get off his chest, but I can't give him any of my attention. This beautiful, brave, captivating woman in front of me demands it all. She isn't paying him any mind either, our gazes unwavering, tears swimming in her eyes.

"I love you," she says, one tear slipping free and rolling down her cheek.

"Madelaine-" I start but can't finish, my chest cracking at her expression and my frustration growing.

"Enough of this shit!" Leighton roars at her. "You'll love *me* soon. It was always meant to be me and you. Just let me explain!"

"Okay," she concedes, tearing her gaze from mine. "But what did you do to Jeremy?"

"Nothing, your precious Jeremy is fine. It was actually so slick, another one of my great ideas. You got separated when he was cut off at some traffic lights, now he's busy following another car down the I50 while my guy followed you in an identical car so you didn't figure it out." His chest puffs out as he regales Madelaine with the tale. A text alert followed by a static crackling catches his attention and I see him walk towards the bannister, but I keep my eyes on my girl.

"For fuck's sake! Can't catch a break around here," he mutters. "Guess that's your time up."

Madelaine's eyes shoot back to mine with horror, and suddenly she's launching herself at me. I hear a pop and her weight collides with me. All I can feel is Madelaine's warmth and the feeling of falling. If I have to go, I'll go with Madelaine pressed to my chest. My head cracking against the floor puts me out for the second time that day.

THIRTY

QUINCY

Fuck, there's so much blood.

"Someone call two ambulances!" Max roars behind me. Guys are swarming the place now that we've called them all back.

"Lai, gorgeous, can you hear me? At?" I check both of them for a pulse and my hands come away red.

We saw both of their cars here and searched the house, but we wouldn't have even checked the basement if the door in the conference room hadn't been open. What we saw as we came down the stairs will haunt me forever. Atlas in an upturned chair with Lai splayed across his chest at an unnatural angle. Neither of them seemed conscious, and they were laying in a pool of blood. An enormous pool of blood.

"Quincy, you're ruining the scene."

I whirl on the guy behind me and grab him by the scruff of his shirt, coating him in the blood from my hands. "I don't give a fuck if I'm causing the sky to come down. If you try to tell me to leave them there bleeding, you can dig your own grave."

"Understood," he stutters as I throw him away from me.

I turn back to Lai and Atlas, and two guys have taken my place, pulling Lai off of him and searching them both. They cut through the rope tying Atlas's hands and then through their tops, and when it becomes apparent the blood is Lai's, my heart almost stops in my chest. There's a hole in her shoulder, pulsating with blood. The guy working on her rips his shirt off and balls it up, stemming the flow, but it's everywhere already. It doesn't look as if Atlas has any serious injuries other than his busted nose, but he's non-responsive and we don't know how long he's been down here.

The paramedics arrive and wisely don't ask questions, getting to work as quickly as possible. One takes over the pressure on Lai's shoulder as they attach oxygen to her and Atlas, strapping them both onto stretchers. They're carried up the stairs and I follow them up, finding Max upstairs barking orders at the guys. We've got about two-thirds here in front of us but some, including Jeremy, are still on their way back.

"How do they look?" Max asks once he's dismissed everyone. He's a calculated weapon when he needs to be, but since his mum passed away, loved ones being hurt really gets to him. I sugarcoat nothing, though; I have way too much respect for him to think for a second he can't handle it all.

"Atlas has a pulse, but they're worried about how long he's been unconscious. Lai has lost a lot of blood and her pulse was way weaker. Are we following them to the hospital?"

"Yeah, of course. You shower and we'll go."

I look down at myself, having forgotten that I look like I bathed in blood. "Okay, give me two minutes."

We get to the hospital twenty minutes later and they direct us to Atlas's room. Lai hasn't been assigned one yet. As we head down the corridor, we hear shouting from that way and up our pace.

"I don't give a fuck, I need some answers!" Atlas bellows as we push into the room. There's a terrified looking doctor standing at the end of Atlas's bed. Atlas is still coated in sticky red and looks outwardly furious, but I can see the worry pulling at his eyes.

"What's going on?" I ask them both.

"I want an update on Madelaine."

"I was just explaining to Mr Grayson that she's in surgery, so I know nothing else at this stage, and he can't move at the moment," the doctor offers. "It looks as if he's been drugged with something that causes paralysis, we've taken blood for analysis. We think movement should come back pretty quickly now that he's alert but it's not returned just yet. That's probably a good thing, considering the state of your hands."

"What's wrong with your hands?" I direct at Atlas.

He shrugs like it's not a big deal, but the doctor informs us. "They're both severely bruised from the fall. It seems as if they were tied behind his back when he and

Miss Noxx fell, causing their combined weight to crush them under the chair-back. It's a miracle nothing's broken, but they should heal fine with some rest and time."

"Jesus." I shake my head, not believing any of this shit has actually happened. "And Lai?"

"Miss Noxx is in surgery. She has a gunshot wound just below her shoulder and the bullet remained inside."

"How's she doing?" Max asks, though I'm sure we know everything we can at the moment.

"Her pulse was extremely weak when she went in and she had lost an extensive amount of blood, but she's pulling through so far."

"And she will pull through," Atlas growls.

"Yes, sir, I'm sure she will."

"How long until I can get out of here?"

"We'd like you to stay at least 24 hours for observation."

"That's not happening."

"Atlas, come on," Max entreats. "We'll be staying with Madelaine, anyway." They share a look, and I know Atlas only gives in for Max's peace of mind.

"We'll share a room," he concedes.

“That’s not-” Glares from all three of us stop the doctor from finishing his sentence. “I’ll see what I can do. If you’ll excuse me.” He shuffles quickly out the door, relieved to get out of the crushing tension in this room. Max and I pull up chairs on either side of Atlas’s bed, prepping for the long haul.

“Do you know what happened?” I ask him.

“I know that fucker got one over on me. I woke up in the basement not able to move.”

“Jeremy’s sending over the CCTV footage as soon as he’s collated it. There’s obviously no footage in the basement, but we should be able to see before and after,” Max explains.

“He spouted a load of shit, then Madelaine came home and he brought her down.”

“Why didn’t he just leave with her?” Nothing he did today made any sense.

“He wanted me to hear his explanation, thinks we’ll all understand that she belongs to him once we’ve heard the truth.” He must not know we’ve heard his ridiculous reasoning from Causus already.

“But why did he hurt her, then?” Max asks, equally perplexed.

“I don’t think he did, I think she put herself in front of me.”

“What?!”

“It’s all really fuzzy, but something distracted him and then the next thing I know, she’s running at me. We got knocked over and it put me out again.”

“So, what? Something makes him point a gun at you and she throws herself in front of the bullet?” I ask, shocked at that.

“I don’t know! I can’t fucking remember shit. I think so.” Atlas’s frustration is boiling over and I get it, he’s going to blame himself for not being able to protect Lai.

“Okay, everyone, just relax. Jeremy will send the footage over soon and hopefully it’ll answer at least some questions.” Max was always the voice of reason between us. Any further discussion is interjected by Causus storming through the door.

“What the fuck happened?” he asks when he spots Atlas covered head-to-toe in red.

“What are you doing here?”

“I got one of the guys to call him to meet us here,” Max explains.

"Your fucking lunatic of a Viper happened," Atlas snarls.

"You got him?"

"No, he got me and our girl."

Causus looks confused, so we recap what we know so far. "Fucking hell," he says, rubbing a hand down his face.

"Tell me about it," I reply with a gigantic sigh, just as Max's phone dings.

"It's the footage from Jeremy." He only has his phone screen to watch it on so we all crowd round the head of Atlas's bed and prop it on his tray.

We watch silently as Leighton strolls through the garage into the conference room like he fucking owns the place. He inspects the wall and when Atlas wraps up a call and walks out of the office, Leighton walks in, standing behind the door to the rest of the house. Atlas walks back in and is stuck by a needle. Simple as that. Even as he spins, he falls, hitting the floor with a bang. Leighton then drags him through the office and the conference room, through the door to the basement where we lose him. The video then skips to Madelaine walking into the office, calling Atlas's name. Leighton appears again and follows her out to the kitchen area where she's at the sink. She spins and drops her glass of water when she sees Leighton there, holding his gun at her. For an excruciating moment, the only sound was the smash of the glass.

"Hi, Madelaine," he says cheerily. "I'm so glad to finally officially meet you." Madelaine says nothing in response, standing statue-still. "I know you're probably scared right now, but this is just for protection," he explains, waving the gun around. "If you'll come with me, I can explain everything." Madelaine still doesn't move or speak, clearly testing Leighton's patience. "Come on!" he shouts and Madelaine jumps out of her trance. "Sorry, love, but we don't have time to waste. I want Atlas to hear what I have to say before we go."

"Atlas?" she squeaks, the first we hear from her since she called his name the first time.

"Yeah, unless you'd rather I just kill him now and we can get going?"

She slowly walks towards Leighton. "Great. Through the office, love, and don't run. Surely you know by now I can always find you."

She doesn't try to run and doesn't speak again, following Leighton's instructions silently until they both disappear into the basement. The video skips again to Max and me entering the house, checking the office quickly before retreating. We then see Leighton come rushing out of the basement door and through the garage before the guys check the conference room a minute later, spotting the open door.

"Well, that's pretty self-explanatory," Causus says. "So your rat told him it would be empty."

"He definitely has help," Atlas adds. "Someone followed Madelaine in Jeremy's place and was keeping him informed by text."

"But how did he know when to go?"

"Maybe they told him you'd ordered everyone home?"

"The timing's too close to be a coincidence. We ordered them home when we left the city, he would've had plenty of time to take Madelaine and run. I doubt his help stuck around outside and risked being spotted."

"How did he know Atlas had left the office in the beginning? It's soundproof."

"He's got it bugged," Atlas declares.

"What?"

"The office. That's how I heard Madelaine so clearly down there. How he knew you were back when you checked the office. He can hear everything we say in there."

"Fucking hell," Max says, grabbing his phone off the tray. "I'll call Jeremy."

"Wait," Causus says. "Whatever is said in there now, Leighton will hear."

"So? He's going to be alerted when we cut it off anyway, whether or not he hears Jeremy finding out."

"But then we're still waiting for him to come to us again," Atlas adds.

"So what's the plan?" I ask.

"We use it to our advantage."

"Exactly," Causus agrees. "Lure him out."

"We're listening."

THIRTY ONE

ATLAS

By the time we've gone through the logistics of our plan and Causus has left, I've got full mobility again. Max and Quinn brought me some spare clothes so I shower haphazardly with my bruised hands, watching the red water run down the drain. We're all staying here tonight. Madelaine should be out of surgery imminently, but I'm not sure how long it'll be before she can be in our room. Washed and changed, I rejoin the guys. We aren't putting anything into motion until tomorrow and this place is swarming with our guys, so we're pretty safe here tonight.

We were all relieved that it didn't look like we had a rat after all.

The doctor swings by to let us know Madelaine's surgery went well and we'll be able to see her as soon as she's conscious. We all sit around silently, lost in our own minds for the next hour.

"It's not your fault, you know," Quinn says out of nowhere.

I look up at him, dragging my thoughts back to now. "Yeah," I say, very unconvincingly.

"That could've been any of us," he adds.

I know logically he's right, but that doesn't mean much at the moment. I went on about how she could never sacrifice herself for someone else and then let her be in a position to do it for me.

"We know what you're thinking, because we'd be thinking the same," Max says.

They probably would. We're so similar with things like this. Probably why our trust for each other is so high. Over the years we've proved we'd do whatever it takes to save each other.

"This time it was us on the other side, but we all know you've been the one saving before and will be again. It's why we work so well."

He was right, they both were. You couldn't do everything alone and you couldn't be successful every time, it's one reason we need each other.

My self-pity stops when the doctor calls back in to tell us we can see Madelaine now. We all shoot up and follow him closely until he points out a room at the end of the hall. We rush through the door and there's Madelaine, our girl. She has a nurse checking wires and screens, who jumps at our sudden entrance.

"Ahh, here they are," she says to Madelaine. "You're all set, I'll be back for your walk-around in half an hour."

"Thank you!" Madelaine replies with a genuine smile to the lady.

She squeezes past us and leaves us alone. We all hurry over to Madelaine's bedside.

"Hey," she says, looking thrilled despite being in a hospital bed hooked up to a million wires on her left side.

"Hey baby," I say, cupping her cheek gently.

"You look like shit," Quinn jokes with a half smile, but his eyes are pinched.

She laughs gently. "Gee, thanks Quincy."

"I don't even know what to do with you," I admit. "Spank your ass raw for being so stupid or kiss you until you can't breathe."

"How about both?"

Her flippant reply, dismissive of the sacrifice she made, makes my chest ache.

"Thank you," I say seriously, bending down to peck her on the lips. "I need you to know that we'll get you out of any situation. Whenever you need us, we'll make it. Even if I'm not good enough for you alone, that's why you have all three of us. You deserve all three of us."

"Atlas, you are more than good enough for me," she says with a pained expression on her face.

"Do you need anything?" Max offers, breaking the moment.

"Actually, I'd love a Slurpee. I can already feel the sugar rush."

"I'll check with the nurse on what you can have," Max offers. She frowns slightly at him leaving, with that being the only thing he's said so far.

"Don't mind him, this sort of thing is a lot for him."

Quinn strokes the other side of her face with his knuckles, distracting her. "I can't believe you did that for him," he says, gesturing to me with a nod.

"I know, it aches like a bitch but I guess he is really pretty."

We both smirk at her, so glad to have her back.

"A girl gets shot and can't even get a kiss around here?"

Quinn leans in and kisses her softly. "We missed you."

Max comes back in from his intel mission with water and crackers. "The doctor said you can eat and drink, but simple things, to make sure you don't vomit."

Madelaine pulls a face. "So, no Slurpees and Taco Bell? That's the worst thing to happen to me today."

Max's face shuts down at her joke. She registers the look on his face and holds her hand out to him. He steps forward to take it and she shuffles her legs over so he can sit on the edge.

"I don't want to make you uncomfortable," he insists, remaining standing.

"My legs are absolutely fine. I'm going to have a walk around in a minute, anyway." She pats the spot she's left and Max reluctantly sits and takes her hand in his again.

“Maxton, I’m fine, I swear.”

“I can’t believe you did that.”

“Okay, it’s clearly a group decision to never save Atlas again. This is a democracy. Sorry, Atlas!”

“It’s not a joke, *belle*.”

“Why not? It’s over, we’re both fine. Why do we need to be all serious about it?”

“Stop saying you’re fine, you’re not fine! You’re laid up in hospital with a hole in your shoulder.”

“Yeah, and the alternative was Atlas laid in a grave with a hole in his head, so I don’t regret it for a second,” she rants, getting agitated. “I’m serious, seeing as that’s apparently what you would rather have happened.”

“Okay, let’s calm it all down,” Quinn tries.

“No, this wasn’t some superfluous decision that I came to. He was firing his gun at Atlas’s skull, and my other option was to watch him die and be taken from all of you. Even with time to think, I would do it again.”

“But-”

"Ready for your walk?" the nurse asks as she comes into the room. "Do you need a minute?" she asks, sensing the strain.

"No, I'm ready."

"*Belle-*"

"If you keep everything down and walk around okay, you'll be alright to eat and drink other things when you fancy," the nurse offers as she helps Madelaine stand.

"Great, thank you."

They leave, and Quinn immediately turns on Max.

"What the fuck, dude? She's supposed to be recovering, not getting stressed justifying her actions to you."

"I know," Max says, wiping his hand down his face. "But she's not fine! How does she not realise what a huge thing it was for her to do?"

"Okay, judging her decisions is normally my repertoire," I joke. "You know this isn't the same as your mum, right?"

He whips his head up to stare into my eyes with a heartbreakingly vulnerable look on his face.

"Max, that was completely different."

"I know, I just hate feeling so out of control when it comes to someone I love."

"But Madelaine is over the worst now, it's only recovery from here."

He releases a sigh, slumping back onto the bed.

"You're right. I should apologise."

"To me, I hope?" Madelaine asks as she walks back through the door with the nurse right behind her.

Max sits upright again, helping her back into her bed.

"They'll come and move you to another room in a little while, try to get some rest." The nurse finishes reattaching Madelaine's tubes, and leaves with a smile.

"Yes, to you," Max picks up the conversation again. "I went a bit over the top, I'm sorry. What you did was ridiculously brave and I am so grateful you're the reason my brother is still alive."

"Great apology." She grins, but it turns into a yawn halfway through.

"Get some rest and we'll eat properly when you're awake."

She nods as she lays back and closes her eyes. We all grab seats around her bed. I'm sure Max's eyes don't move from the steady rise and fall of her chest. She looks so peaceful, you'd never guess the day she's had.

"Someone you love?" Quinn asks Max when Madelaine's breathing gets heavier.

"Someone I love," he replies, not taking his eyes off our girl.

THIRTY TWO

LEIGHTON

It only goes wrong when people don't follow my plans. I had to leave Madelaine there with them. She needed a hospital. If I took her there, they'd have tracked me down in seconds. Not that they're taking great care of her now. Why would they leave her so unprotected here? Would they? It's risky, but I was so close last time. I can feel it in my bones. We're nearly there, together. Soon, my love. So soon.

THIRTY THREE

MADELAINE

I wake up the next morning feeling like a new woman. A new woman with a hole in her shoulder, but a new woman all the same. I'm in a new room which is a lot bigger than the first one. It's bright, with the outside wall covered in windows that start about knee height and run to the ceiling. It also contains a second bed, currently occupied by Lia, with Maxton, Atlas and Quincy slumped in chairs around the room. I try to sit up but twinge my shoulder and gasp at the stab of pain that runs down my arm. Quincy opens his eyes and jumps when he sees me awake.

"Are you okay?"

"Yeah, just trying to get up. I need the bathroom."

He helps me get off the bed and I make quick work of relieving and refreshing myself before Quincy helps me back into the bed.

"Sit with me?"

"Anything, gorgeous."

He moves the top half of the bed so it's more upright and leans against it, pulling me back so I'm under his arm, resting my head on his shoulder.

"I must've been out for ages."

"You clearly needed it. They gave you some more pain meds while you were asleep, too, which might have helped. It's late Sunday morning now."

"Is Max okay?"

"Yeah, I'm sure he'll explain it to you," he says, not expanding any further than that.

"When did Lia get here?"

"Last night. Causus is around here somewhere, too. No one wanted to wake you."

I wince slightly as my shoulder throbs again.

"Should I call for the nurse?"

"No, let everyone sleep." Before he can argue with me, Caus comes through the door holding a big white bag that I can smell immediately.

I sit up, careful to use my other arm. "You bought Carlo's?!"

"Of course, only the best for the best," Caus grins.

Lia stirs next to us and sniffs as she wakes up.

"Carlo's?!" I can't help but laugh at her bloodhound nose. "Lai, you're awake! How are you feeling?" she asks, hopping off her bed and coming over to stand next to mine.

"Not too bad, thanks for coming."

"Of course! And now the pastries have made it all worth it." No wondering who I get my nonchalance from.

Quincy reaches over me and pushes the call button, not looking at all repentant when I narrow my eyes at him.

"What? Now it's only those two lazy fuckers still asleep."

Caus is ripping into the bag and hands Lia an almond croissant and me a Pain au Chocolat.

"When can you get out of here?" Lia asks me before taking a big bite.

"Yeah, about that," Caus starts, but Quincy shoots him a look.

"We'll discuss it when the others are awake," he says to my questioning gaze.

Caus walks over to their chairs and waves pastries under their noses, both of them rousing in seconds, which makes me laugh.

"Problem solved," he announces.

"What's going on?" Atlas asks sleepily, stretching out his back.

"I'm waiting for one of you to tell me that. Apparently when I leave needs discussing between all of us, and not me and my doctors."

They both exchange glances with Quincy and Caus before Maxton speaks. "Do you trust us?"

"Absolutely." I didn't even need to think about it. There was no question.

"We have a plan," Atlas starts.

"Well, technically, we started a plan already," Caus jumps in.

"My God, dude. Shut up!" Quincy groans.

Caus shrugs and shoves a third turnover into his mouth.

"We haven't talked with you that much about what happened after you got shot, but Leighton obviously got away," Atlas carries on and worry seeps into my brain. "We realised before you got out of surgery that he must've had somewhere bugged, most likely the office. Jeremy swept the house, and it turns out it was the office, the conference room, and the second garage."

"So..."

"So, we thought we could draw him out sooner rather than later and deal with him once and for all."

I nod slightly, it all making sense so far.

"We left the listening devices in and made sure he heard us saying what we wanted him to hear," Max explains.

"Which was what?"

"First, arguing with Causus and severing our new treaty."

"Why? He wouldn't go back to Caus after taking Lia," I say.

"No, but it takes away another level of security that he won't be expecting," Caus explains.

"What else?"

"Our plans for security in the hospital, with fabricated gaps."

"You're drawing him *here*?"

"Yes, but you'll never be alone, I swear," Quincy assures me.

"So why would he come?"

"He doesn't know that."

"So you're expecting him to stroll in thinking there's no one here to protect me and you'll grab him when he surfaces?"

"Pretty much, yeah," Quincy shrugs.

"How long do I have to stay?"

"He thinks you're leaving tomorrow morning and his best chance is tonight, so not too long. I doubt they'd release you before then, anyway," Maxton explains.

"Okay." I nod slowly, absorbing everything. "Lia, you can't be here," I insist.

"I wasn't planning to be. The further I am from that creep, the better."

"We haven't even told him the right room, Lai," Caus tells me. "You'll be fine."

The nurse ends their explanation by coming in to administer some more pain medication. My shoulder is pounding and my head has joined in the party, so I'm very grateful.

"I'll leave you to it," Lia says. "I really just wanted to see for myself that you're okay."

"Always," I promise. "Thanks so much for coming."

"I'll see you out," Caus offers, grabbing a fourth pastry before following her out of the room.

I eat three pastries myself before my eyes droop again.

"Do you want some space?" Quincy asks as I relax back against him.

"Never."

I wake up to Quincy shuffling out from under me.

"Sorry, gorgeous," he says when he sees me awake. "It's go time."

Confusion washes over my face, I'm still groggy from my nap. "What time is it?"

"3 p.m., earlier than we thought. He must be keen."

"He's here?"

"They're following someone who fits his description on the other side of the hospital, headed towards your fake room," Maxton explains as Jeremy enters the room. "Jeremy will stay with you."

"Good afternoon, Miss Lai. I'm so glad you're recovering."

"Thanks, Jeremy," I reply with a smile. "I'm good. I'm glad you're okay, too."

Maxton, Atlas, and Quincy all kiss me before leaving together.

"I'm so-"

"Please don't apologise, Jeremy. None of what happened was your fault."

He smiles tightly at my refusal. What was it with alpha men and taking the blame for everything?

"Would you mind helping me up so I can use the bathroom?"

"Of course," he says, reaching over to bring me to sitting. The door goes, but Jeremy is blocking my view. "Did you forget something?"

Jeremy jerks forward and then slumps to the floor.

"Only you, love."

"Leighton," I breathe in terror.

"You remembered! How could you forget? We're soulmates," he says as he waves a gun between us, that must be what he hit Jeremy with. I look down, trying to find a sign he's okay, but he's motionless on the ground.

"What are you doing?"

"I've come to get you. Are you ready?"

"Leighton, I need to recover. Here, in the hospital. I was shot, remember?" I don't make any move to get off the bed, continuing to stare at him dressed in scrubs with a mask and tinted glasses.

"Yeah, that was careless of you," he mumbles as he pulls at my uninjured arm.

"I can't go anywhere with you."

"You can and you will," he breathes in my face. I cringe back in shock and my bad shoulder twinges, making me hiss through my teeth.

Leighton doesn't notice my pain as Jeremy's phone rings, down near the floor. He bends to fish it out of Jeremy's pocket and I think about hitting him but it seems futile at the moment. I can't exactly fight him. Leighton answers the phone and listens to someone on the other end before hanging up without replying.

"Fuck's sake, they really ruin everything, don't they?"

He grabs me by the upper arm below my injured shoulder and I cry out at the torrent of pain, but he ignores me. Jerking me over to the window wall, we stand with our backs to the glass. He yanks me in front of him, one hand gripping my injured arm and the other pointing his gun under my chin. This is how Atlas, Maxton, Quincy and Caus find me when they return.

THIRTY FOUR

MAXTON

"This is the second time you're pointing a gun at *my* girl, and you're sure as fuck going to regret it," I murmur, my voice deathly quiet. He hears it, though. You could hear a pin drop as we all take in what's happening. Madelaine looks stoic, but her arm can't be comfortable so soon after her surgery, and she's avoiding looking at any of us directly.

"Nice of you guys to join us," Leighton spits sarcastically.

"You must know you have nowhere to go from here," Atlas tells him.

"I know, but it's nice to finally have an audience, if nothing else. Please, come in. Shut the door."

All four of us move towards them into the room, noticing Jeremy on the floor next to the bed.

"That's far enough," Leighton calls when we reach it. I crouch down to check Jeremy over, but I'm denied by Leighton, and we'll all happily follow his instructions while he has hold of Madelaine.

"What are you doing?" Causus asks him disbelievingly.

"Oh, Caus, looks like the treaty is working out just fine in the end."

"Seems that way, doesn't it?"

Leighton laughs manically at Causus's casual tone. "I did almost fall for your bullshit. But then I thought, how can they possibly think they deserve Madelaine when they leave her so available? Which is when I realised, you wouldn't."

We all have our guns concealed, but his head is only a foot above Madelaine's and we can't risk anything with his finger on the trigger and the gun under her chin.

"Who was the guy?" Quincy asks, referencing the man we'd all headed over to see who was just taking a stroll.

"Some random I paid to walk the halls dressed suspiciously. Worked, huh? I really am not appreciated enough in this life."

"What are you here for?" Atlas asks, getting impatient with the stalemate.

"I came to get Madelaine, obviously, but I guess we all keep underestimating each other, don't we?"

"Madelaine doesn't belong to you," I hiss, my anger simmering under the surface.

"But she does," he replies simply. "Her father promised mine that I would have her. Now I've come to collect."

"He would never do that," Madelaine insists, the first time she's spoken since we entered. Her eyes flick up to us all, her gaze unwavering. Her voice is quiet but adamant.

"He must've known we were meant to be," Leighton replies, pulling her back to his chest and making her wince as he yanks on her arm.

"Stop pulling at her fucking arm, you're hurting her."

"I wouldn't hurt her, she's mine."

"You left her dying in the basement," Quince tells him, coldness seeping into his voice.

"An accident that was partly her fault. Anyway, I left the door open for you. Even you lot couldn't miss that."

Jeremy stirs but appears to be hidden from Leighton's view by the bed.

"Why would Madelaine be yours?" Causus asks.

"I deserve her. My father said everyone could see that I was destined for big things in the Vipers and Madelaine would help me get there."

"Who's your father?" Causus asks but Leighton is mid-diatribe and ignores him completely.

"The Nobes twins were to be introduced to the Vipers when they turned 21, but stupid fucking Mackie couldn't wait that long."

"Mackie died," Causus says with resentment.

"Who the fuck is Mackie?" Quince asks but Causus remains staring at Leighton, who answers for him.

"He was the son of our VP. Caus's best friend."

"He's not *our* anything. Don't you fucking dare think you're anything to do with the Vipers anymore," Causus snaps.

"What has he got to do with Lai?"

"It's all got everything to do with everything. Madelaine, Mackie, Gia, Warren; the Vipers hierarchy."

"Leighton, we need some fucking answers," Causus roars, tolerance running thin.

"It's irrelevant now." He brushes it off, oblivious to the fury smouldering around the room. "If everyone had stuck to the plan for once, none of this would've happened. We'd be happy right now," he directs at Madelaine. "Your dad would be here to give us his blessing."

"He wouldn't do that," she repeats, voice weaker, and I notice red spotting through the bandage on her shoulder.

"My father wouldn't lie," Leighton bellows, jostling Madelaine, who sways.

The guys all stiffen as they notice her lightheaded state and the fresh blood.

Jeremy is awake now and shuffles onto his stomach, gun poised, but I shake my head minutely. I don't know why; I trust Jeremy with our lives, but it's hard to relinquish control in a high-pressure situation like this.

"What happened?" Quince asks Leighton, trying to distract him from seeing Jeremy too. Quince's body stiffens taut like a bow, and I know he's ready to snap into action.

"Now you all want to listen when it concerns you?"

"Gia found out their dad was promising them off and snapped?" Causus guesses, reeling Leighton back in. He rolls his eyes and sighs like we're all so stupid, though.

"Gia would never do that," Madelaine whispers.

"Who knew her well enough to know that?" Leighton asks cryptically.

"So they set her up," Atlas declares.

"We wouldn't," Causus insists. "My dad was in charge even back then, he and Warren were thick as thieves."

"How much do you actually know from three years ago?" Atlas asks Caus.

"It's only fully involved me the last couple of years. Dad took a step back in private when Warren died. As I told you, he was practically his second."

"This is supposed to be my show!" Leighton calls to us all, waving the gun around Madelaine's head erratically to regain attention. She's going more slack by the minute and he's practically holding her up by her injured arm, putting a lot of pressure on her wound.

"You're not surviving this, Leighton," I promise him.

He directs his answer at Madelaine, as if we're not even there anymore. He's clearly done with the audience now that he's left riddles for us all. "If we can't be together in life, love, then we'll be together in death."

He's still swinging his gun around and his mistake is moving the barrel away from Madelaine's head for a split second. In that instance, Jeremy shoots his elbow from under the bed. Leighton's gun goes off and glass showers down over him and Madelaine.

Everything moves in slow motion. Leighton's grip remains around Madelaine's arm as he looks down in horror at his elbow and her legs give out. Quince whips his gun from his waistband, getting a clean shot straight through Leighton's temple. The force of the bullet tips Leighton backwards, his calves catching on the wall and his body falling backwards into thin air. Madelaine sways wildly but Causus and Atlas are there, grabbing her away from the open window as Leighton's body thuds to the ground outside.

THIRTY FIVE

QUINCY

The aftermath is pure chaos. The gunshots have our guys swarming the room, and Atlas carries Lai over to the bed. Her eyes are closed, her face scrunched in pain.

"Hold on, gorgeous, the nurse will be here any second." I ring the bell repeatedly next to the bed.

Max and Causus are busy directing the guys to clean up and intervene with the police. I don't even bother to tune in, I know they have it covered. Jeremy is in the crowd and ready to do what's needed, but Max gets him to stay for medical attention too. The nurse runs in and steps up to Lai, looking at her shoulder.

"She needs pain relief," I tell her.

"I think she's going to need more than that. What happened?!"

Lai is laying back, groaning and breathing heavily. "She got pulled around by this arm. Has it done any more damage?"

"It could've. Can we clear the room out? I'll get a doctor in here."

The guys finish funnelling out to complete Max and Causus's orders, and we all gather around Lai on the bed.

"Hang on, baby. It'll be over soon."

She nods her head but doesn't open her eyes. A doctor rushes in and after a quick inspection decides Lai needs surgery again. The three of us kiss her and Causus wishes her luck before she's wheeled out. The nurse notices the blood on the back of Jeremy's head and leads him to his own room. As some guys return to board the window, we follow the nurse to the empty room. She fixes Jeremy's wound as we all remain silent, the nurse talking to him about concussion and what to look out for. He nods along, but we all know nothing will slow him down. The nurse is eventually satisfied and leaves.

“Fucking hell,” Atlas breathes on a sigh, scrubbing a hand over his head.

“What now?” I ask the room.

“Our lawyer should be here any minute. He’ll work on keeping the police away, but we’ll have to speak to them at some point. Even if we are the Titans, a dead man just fell six floors from our room.” Atlas raises some good points. We all know they’ll take what we tell them but it doesn’t stop the rigmarole of giving statements.

Causus stands up. “Let me know what the story is, I’ll be back by the time Lai wakes up.”

“Where are you going?”

“It seems I’ve got some mistakes to correct.” He leaves us there with his cryptic exit.

A couple of hours later, when everything is calming down and it’s getting late, the doctor lets us know we can see Lai. We walk into her room and see double. Sat next to her are Lia and who can only be Gia, their resemblance uncanny. They’re not identical but you can clearly tell they’re related. Lai looks drained, but happy.

"Guys, this is Gia, my sister! Gia, this is Maxton, Quincy, and Atlas," she says, pointing us out with her good arm.

Gia stands with the expression of a deer in headlights. "Hi," she says softly, offering her hand, which we all shake.

"I'm going to go, Lai. I'll come back first thing tomorrow, okay?"

"I'll walk out with you," Lia offers.

Lai nods and hugs them both, even as she winces.

"Bye, everyone," Lia says, Gia awkwardly giving a mini-wave as she leaves.

Atlas walks closer to Lai, cupping her face. "How are you feeling, baby?"

"A bit overwhelmed, to be honest. I don't really understand what's happened."

"Gia's release has nothing to do with us, that was all Causus's doing," Max admits. "What did Gia say?"

"She doesn't really know anything either, someone came to get her an hour ago and suddenly, she's free." There's awe in Lai's voice and her eyes are shining, even if they are tired. They shoot to the door as Causus walks in. "Thank you so much, Coze."

He shrugs, nonchalant as usual. "She shouldn't have been in there."

"How did you manage to get someone convicted of murder out of jail in five hours?" I ask him.

"How did you manage to get away with shooting someone out of a six-story window in a busy hospital?"

"Touche, dude. Touche."

A smile touches his lips. "I just wanted to check in on you, Lie. How are you doing?"

"I'm good. I don't think it's sunk in yet that it's over."

"Well, it is. Just focus on recovering now, okay?"

"Okay, Coze. Thank you."

"Stop thanking me, I'm blushing."

Lai laughs and gives a wave as he turns and leaves. Atlas, Max and I start dragging chairs around her bed, but she shuffles over awkwardly.

"Sit with me?"

"Who?"

"All of you."

None of us can turn that down after the last 48 hours. Atlas and Max sit side by side against her headboard and she snuggles back between them, while I sit against the end rubbing her feet, which are propped in my lap.

"Mmm, that feels amazing," she says, her body relaxing now it's just us.

Atlas turns his head to press a kiss against her hair. "Get some rest."

"I feel like I've been resting forever. I want to spend some time with you three."

"Baby, we have forever for that."

And we did. Lai was safe, and our lives stretched ahead of us. I couldn't wait to see what it brought us all. Together.

EPILOGUE

MADELAINE

"Wake up, *belle*." My body is jostled lightly and I force my eyes open.

"What's going on?" I ask as I slowly sit up. All three of my guys are standing at the end of my bed. It's now significantly bigger than my previous one and was waiting for me when I got back from the hospital 11 months ago. How they had time to organise it between catching a stalker, avoiding a murder charge, and sorting out my sister, I'll never know.

"Get up!" Quincy insists, a huge grin on his face. In fact, they all have matching grins on their faces and are all dressed.

"What time is it?" I ask, trying to spot any sunlight through the thick curtains, but not succeeding.

"5 a.m., come on!" Atlas pulls at my arms, pulling me forward onto my knees.

"There better be a fantastic reason I'm getting up at the crack of dawn," I tell them.

"There is, promise," he answers, giving me a light kiss.

I shower and get dressed, opting for casual seeing as I have no idea what we're doing.

I head out into the kitchen following the scent of pastries. My favourite white bag is set on the counter.

"Carlo's isn't open this early."

"They are for you."

They're all practically bouncing and their enthusiasm and the promise of a Pain au Chocolat has me getting excited too.

"Can I know where we're going now?"

"Nope," Quincy says. "Let's go, we'll eat these in the car."

I follow them out to the Hummer, where Jeremy's waiting for us. "Good morning, Miss Lai."

"Good morning, Jeremy. I don't suppose you'd like to tell me where you're taking us?"

He mimes a zip over his lips, and the playful motion makes me laugh.

I stuff myself full of pastries while we drive before arriving at an airstrip.

"Are we getting on that?" I ask in shock, staring at the jet in front of us. No one answers me as they all get out and fetch bags from the trunk.

"Come on." Maxton offers me his hand, keeping hold of it across the tarmac before gesturing for me to head up the steps.

"Good morning, Miss," a flight attendant greets me when I step inside. "Welcome aboard, the others are already here." She slides open a door and a shout of surprise comes from inside. I spot Lia first and stumble over to her, shellshocked.

"What is happening?" I ask as she stands and hugs me.

"Just wait and see," she grins. I say 'hi' to everyone else as the guys follow me on, greeting everyone too. Just as I'm about to find a seat, another 'surprise' goes up and I spin to see Gia looking just as shocked as me in the little doorway. I laugh at her expression and happiness floods through me. I hug her and shrug my shoulders at the questioning look she gives me.

"Just wait and see, apparently."

We move out of the way for the others and the attendants come in to help store bags, the plane slowly filling with guests and security. We go nowhere without them now. I walk over to my guys, where they've found a set of four seats, but opt to sit in Atlas's lap instead of my own chair.

"Are you going to explain now?" I ask them all, running my fingers through the hair at the nape of his neck. They exchange looks, very pleased with themselves indeed. Quinn is the one who finally answers.

"Well, we... I... fucked your last birthday up so badly, we needed to recover pretty spectacularly, so we thought we'd make a treat week of it. Of course, it's your first birthday in a while with Gia on the outside and we'd never have forgotten Lia, so we're all going," Quincy explains.

Lia had actually cancelled her birthday dinner the other day saying she had a stomach bug, but now I bet it was because she's awful at keeping secrets.

I can't wipe the smile off my face as I stare at them all. "Where are we going?"

"Bali."

My mouth falls open in shock.

"No sassy remark? We might've broken her, guys."

I elbow Atlas in the ribs to a satisfying "*oof*" but can't keep the grin from splitting my face. I don't even worry about time off or packing or anything, knowing my guys would have it handled.

"We're going to take off, so could you please take your seats?" a flight attendant calls out. I settle into my own seat, still stunned at our destination. Catching Gia's eye down the aisle, we beam at each other. I can't believe the last year. The difference between that birthday and this one couldn't be starker. My life has flipped 180 degrees in all the best ways, all thanks to the people on this plane.

My recovery after my second surgery was slower than I'd have liked. Some internal tissue tore when Leighton was dragging me around, but the guys were amazing. They had a lot of work to do with keeping the police off their backs and also establishing their link with the Vipers in the beginning. They're still separate groups but the treaty is going well, and they even started some businesses together to solidify their connection. Not that Coze was really at any risk from the Titans. I owe him more than I could ever repay.

"You okay, *belle*?" Maxton asks, catching my eye from opposite me.

"I'm great," I say, with a big smile that shows no sign of dimming.

The plane lands in Bali late in the evening, and it is stunning. We're in a vast villa set within the hilltop with an infinity pool and the most incredible view. We all decide to get some sleep and meet up in the morning for breakfast.

I wake up sometime in the night, my body clock officially screwed by the time difference. Not wanting to disturb the guys after all the travel, I head out to sit on the balcony. This place is seriously breathtaking. Over the edge of the pool, you can see right down into the valley and the jungle covering the cliff on the other side. It's like we're in our own little bubble, our perfect paradise.

The doors slide open behind me, pulling me from the views to one that rivals it, in all honesty. I would never look away from Atlas in his underwear again.

"Happy Birthday, baby," he says, leaning down to kiss me.

"Thank you."

"What are you doing up?" he asks, leaning against the railings.

"I couldn't sleep," I say, standing up in front of him. "I need to be tired out."

His gaze heats as I drop my robe and he wastes no time in picking me up, spinning and sitting me on the edge of the railing. "Mission accepted," he says as he steps between my legs. I wrap my arms around his neck and kiss him deeply, pressing my body against his, loving the feel of his skin against mine.

"Fucking hell, Madelaine. I will never get enough of you."

"Good."

He carries me back inside and throws me on the bed, jostling the others who wake up pretty quickly when they see me naked and wanting.

"Jesus," Quincy says, rubbing his eyes.

I crawl over to him and he grabs my face, kissing me forcefully. He winds his hand in the hair at the back of my head and pulls me away from him, angling me towards Maxton.

Maxton kisses me as Atlas comes up behind and caresses my ass. I'm still on all fours so he has access to play, and as Quincy pulls me back from Maxton, Atlas spears me with one finger, making me gasp into Quincy's mouth.

"On your back," he whispers into mine. I spin, always happy to follow Quincy's orders in the bedroom. He stands and pats the edge of the bed. "Put your shoulders here." This leaves my head hanging over the edge, and Quincy crouches down, stroking my throat. "Happy Birthday, gorgeous."

He cups my cheek upside down and slides his thumb against my lips. I open my mouth and suck it in, biting down lightly when his eyes hood. "You want to play?" He reaches onto the chair behind him and grabs a t-shirt, wrapping it around my eyes and tying it behind my head. "Is that okay?"

The lack of sight heightens my other senses, and my skin warms. "Yes."

I can hear the guys move around and I can't tell who is where. Fingers trail all over me. My lips, my breasts, my stomach, my legs. Just as I squirm, they disappear and I feel bare. Strong hands grab my ankles and bend my legs, separating my feet so I'm completely exposed. I tingle everywhere and suddenly there's soft, cool breath being blown onto a nipple and my core at the same time. My back arches and someone grips my jaw lightly. I take the cue and open my mouth wide.

Working in unison, someone slides their cock into my mouth, someone else pushes their fingers into my entrance, and a third clasps their mouth over my breast. Their pace is slow and sensual, torturing me with the many sensations. It all stops at once, and I can hear them swapping places. The same delicious torment starts up again as my orgasm builds and my stomach tenses.

Atlas is normally the one who likes to make me beg by going slow, but they're all working in a torturous rhythm and it's driving me crazy. They stop again and switch. Every time I think I figure out who is where something changes my mind. The constant, steady friction with the relentless pleasure on my breasts and the heady feeling of someone sliding down my throat is too much and

I moan around them, clenching as my body hums with satisfaction.

This is clearly what they're waiting for as I'm flipped over, now straddling, and someone brings me down hard, impaling me with a groan. Atlas. Hands at my rear spread my wetness over my hole and I would bet money that's Maxton. He holds me still while he presses slowly in from behind, and they both move in rhythm. A hand on the nape of my neck warns me before Quincy's tip hits my lips, coating them in salty pre-cum. I lick them clean and then open my mouth, ready with my tongue out.

"Fucking hell," he groans, confirming my guess as he slides into my mouth. He keeps his hand on the back of my head and thrusts hard back and forth, fucking my mouth. Atlas and Maxton get the message and start moving properly, pleasure flooding my body as they fill me completely. The pace picks up as they watch me enjoy them all.

Maxton finishes first, clutching my hips with his fingertips and emptying himself into me. Quincy is next, pouring himself down my throat before slipping out. Atlas takes the opportunity to flip me back over to underneath him, pounding into me as his pelvis grinds against my clit.

I clench around him, moaning into his neck as he stills a few seconds later, joining me in bliss. We all lay haphazardly on the bed until Maxton heads to the bathroom, returning with a washcloth and cleaning me up.

We shuffle around so we're all back in bed, well and truly tired out. Maxton climbs in next to me, hugging me from behind.

"Happy Birthday, *belle*," he murmurs against my hair.

I close my eyes and smile. *Best birthday ever.*

BONUS CHAPTER

by debut author

Rachelle Anne Wright

CAUS

As the sun lowers in the sky the sound of my bike drowns out all noise except for the thoughts running through my head. I really fucked up this time. I knew keeping the Vipers from Lia would come back to bite me in the ass! But I wasn't expecting to meet her when I did. I wanted to keep an eye on Lai, and then Lia waltzed into my life. If I'm honest with myself, it was nice to not have to be Causus, son of the Vipers President, for a while. Now Amelia is everything to me and she won't pick up the phone, barely answers her text messages. I've got a bad feeling some shit's about to go down.

When she was kidnapped by that fucking psychopath Leighton I was beside myself, blinded by rage while doing everything I could to remain calm on the outside and get my girl back. Of course, the Titans didn't bother to tell me, they swooped in and saved my girl before I even knew what was happening. We have an alliance for now, a truce, but they'd better start treating me with respect if it's going to continue. I'm going to have to step up and be President soon. We're already running all but the darkest shit for the club, the type of shit you catch a felony for. I'm nobody's bitch.

I lean into the curves of the road and the vibrations and growl from my bike help calm the storm inside me. I can get my girl back. It's been two weeks since she left for her parents' house, two weeks since I've had her in my bed, by my side. It's time my baby girl comes home. I know I fucked up, but I'll do whatever it takes to make this right. I need my baby girl. *Come back to me, Lia. I need you.*

LIA

Looking out the front window, I hear Caus's bike before I see it pulling up the driveway. I'd recognise that sound anywhere, that was my favourite sound for years. Not so much anymore. I walk out the front and close the door behind me, praying that my Dad gives us some space. I hear Dad moving at the front of the house upstairs and know that he knows Caus has arrived. *Please, Daddy, just give us a few minutes.*

Caus parks his bike and takes his helmet off, rubbing his thumb across his bottom lip with a smirk. I can't help a little smile too. I'm happy to see him, even if my heart is breaking. Time seems to stand still while we stare at each other. Suddenly, Rue runs around the front of the house, speeding towards Caus and barking her head off. I guess she missed him too. She's jumping up on his legs and scratching at his jeans, barking and wagging her tail like she's about to take off. He leans down to scratch behind her ears, whispering sweet things in Spanish that I can't quite catch from here. I'll miss that.

He kicks off his bike and walks over, stopping at the bottom of the steps leading up to the porch. I lean my arms over the railing, looking at his face and down again, afraid that if I look at him for too long, I'll break. God, I've missed him. Why does it have to be like this?

"Hey, baby girl," he says, shoving his hands into his pockets. He's wearing his usual look: a crisp, white t-shirt under his leather jacket, his dark jeans bunching above his boots.

"Where's your cut?" *Ugh, Lia.* I'm such an idiot. I haven't seen him for two weeks, told him I needed space, and the first thing I say is 'where's your cut'?

"In the saddlebag. I only wear it on club business, baby. Too dangerous otherwise."

"What are you doing here, Caus?"

"I've come to bring you home. I miss you, Lia. I need you." My chest hurts. I know breakups are hard, but why does it have to physically hurt? My grief sits like a weight on my chest, crushing the air from my lungs.

"I'm not going back, Caus. I've given up the lease on my apartment. Since everything that happened, I...." I trail off, not wanting to say the words. *I don't feel safe. I see movement in every corner, danger in the shadows. I'm too scared to be alone in my apartment.* "I want to stay here, with Mum and Dad. I'm moving back home for a while, until I can get back on my feet."

"It's not that far, I'll ride out here whenever I can. Come and stay nights with you until your Dad kicks me out. If that's what you need, baby girl, then I'm here."

"Caus, I can't do this, not anymore." I wring my fingers, trying to will the gathering tears away before they run down my cheeks. Because I know that once they start, they won't stop.

"Can't do what?"

"Please don't make me say it."

"Can't do what, baby girl?" He rubs his hand across his face, scratching the scruff on his jaw. "I don't like where this is going, baby. I need you to spell it out for me." Those gorgeous dark brown eyes that I've seen looking back at me in every emotion look into mine, concern written all over his face.

"Caus, I care about you, you know I do. But I can't see you anymore." At that moment time stands still. Rue has disappeared, off running around the property somewhere. The birds sing in the trees and the sun slowly dips lower over the horizon, but our world just stopped spinning. Caus *tsks*.

"I get that you need time, Lia. Fuck, anyone would need time after what you've been through. I can be there for you, baby. I can keep you safe." He's not getting it.

"I don't blame you for what happened, Caus, but you also can't promise me that I'll be safe. Look at what happened to me! Please, try to understand where I'm coming from. You and I have been dating for three years, Caus. *Three years*. You never took me home to meet your family. I thought you had issues with your Dad but I didn't know he was a fucking Viper, that *you* are in the Vipers. That shit is dangerous! Now Lia is dating the Titans. Is anyone in this town not involved with something criminal? What is it that your club does, Caus? Because I've heard the rumours, but I want to hear it from you."

"Baby-"

"*What. Do. They. Do.*"

Caus sighs, hanging his head and kicking the dirt in the garden bed. "You know I can't tell you that, baby girl."

"It's over, Caus. I can't do this." I turn, and while my heart shatters, I slip back into the house.

CAUS

It's over, Caus. I can't do this. Her words ring through my ears, repeating, even after she's gone back inside. *It's over, Caus.* Fuck that. It's not over until I say it's over, and I'm not ready to give up yet.

"Lia!" I yell, desperate for her to come back to me. I pound up the steps and reach for the doorknob. "LIA!!" Just before I grab it the door swings open and I'm stopped in my tracks by a fucking wall of muscle.

"Fuck!"

"It's time to go, Causus." Of course Amelia's Dad is here. I didn't see his truck in the driveway, it must be around back.

"Officer Hale, I need to talk to your daughter." I'm face to face with the one person in this town I can't sweet-talk, bribe, or intimidate. I look him up and down, weighing up my options. He's still in his tac gear from work. Black cargo pants and shirt, his holster still around his waist. One gun on his hip, another on the side of his thigh. Police badge still clipped onto his belt. Maybe not the best time for this conversation. I probably couldn't even take this bastard on *mano a mano*. We might be around the same height, but he outweighs me by at least 30 pounds of pure muscle. I rub my eyes, trying to keep my cool. "Please. Just let me talk to her."

"Causus, I appreciate that you kept her out of your Dad's shit for as long as you did, and I stayed out of your relationship with Lia because of that. But you have to accept her choice now. Your choices are your own, and they hurt my daughter. You're lucky I'm not taking you in, just for the fun of it. Should let you sit in a cell and think for a few hours." Fuck. *Fuck!* What am I going to do?

"She ain't up for visitors right now, and I suggest you leave before I make you." With that, he steps back and slams the door in my face. Fuck.

Heading back to my bike I slide my sunglasses on and throw my helmet in my saddlebag with my cut. Fuck the helmet, I only wore it for Lia anyway. My blood is boiling. I need the wind on my skin to cool down. I hit the throttle and peel out of the driveway, spinning dirt as I go. My mind barely sees the road around me, all of my thoughts on Lia and what I just lost. I can't believe it. I can't do this. Is that really how our relationship ends? I'd die for her, and kill any motherfucker that wants to try it on with her, no doubt. She'll come around, and until she does, I'll have to make sure no other fucking guy goes near her. We've got Prospects, I'll make it happen.

Fuck. I hit a patch of gravel on the road and my bike wobbles. Concentrate, *idiota*, or you'll get yourself killed. I've driven all the way back to town without seeing anything. I slow down as the streets get more crowded and I have more cars to contend with. What do I do now? Fuck it. I head through the centre of town and out the other side, heading to The Lounge. I can't face anyone I know right now and our new business seems like as good a place as any.

I pull up outside and head into the bar, dropping my ass into a seat and lifting a hand to the bartender. His hair is so red he could be Lia's brother. *Fuck, are even the bartenders going to remind me of her now?* I ask for a bourbon and he drops a glass and a bottle in front of me before moving on. Good man.

I'm half a bottle in when I look to the side and see a curtain of long, brown hair, tattooed arms, and just a hint of cleavage peeking out from a white wifebeater tucked into skin-tight blue jeans. This girl has an ass like my Lia. *Fuck, Lia.* She turns, and her deep brown eyes meet mine.

"Gia? What are you doing here, shouldn't you be with your sister?"

She smirks. "I checked in but she needs rest. Plus, I can't face all the questions on my first night out." I stare at her a little too long for someone who's been single all of an hour. It'll take more than half a bottle to get me drunk, but clearly, I'm getting there.

"What would you rather do?"

"Drowning out the last three years of memories with tequila seems pretty inviting," she replies.

"I know you didn't do what you went down for. I'm real sorry for that, by the way. It sucks that they did you like that." Her eyes darken.

"Yeah, well, shit happens. I'm out now, I want to enjoy it. Live a little. If it wasn't for you, I'd still be there. So, cheers, I guess." She lifts her glass in a mock-cheers before downing the last of it and flags the bartender for another.

"You're welcome. Need a top-up, baby girl?" I raise my bottle, realising a beat too late that the nickname I use for Lia had slipped past my lips before I even had time to think about it. Shit. She slides over to sit with me and I fill both our glasses.

“So, what’s got you drinking alone at the bar tonight?” She’s not running away, but there’s a definite tone of disapproval when she talks to me.

“I lost my girl. Turns out she doesn’t want me anymore.”

“Sucks to be you then, I guess.”

“You should leave before it gets too late, you know. This area gets pretty rough after dark.”

She spins on her stool and leans back against the bar, looking at me intensely as she bites one lip. I see a decision made in her eyes. “Maybe I like it rough.”

This girl don’t know what she’s asking for, hanging out so late with me, of all people. She could find herself in some real trouble. Just as I go to speak the song changes to some weird woop woop shit. The singer croons, *I’m a bad guy...Duh*. Gia’s eyes glint as she smiles at me and at that moment I know, she *is* the trouble.

“Why don’t you go find yourself some pretty-boy boyfriends, like your sister’s got?”

“Not my type.”

“Really?” I lick my lips and run my hand over my mouth, hoping it’s not too obvious that this girl makes me feel things that I shouldn’t be feeling right now. Damn, this girl. Madelaine is like a sister to me. If I have any hope of winning Lia back, I can’t get into shit with her best friend’s sister. That would be burning that bridge to ashes and there’d be no hope of ever going back. But she’s looking at me side-on with those devilish eyes and she slips her hair back off her shoulder, showing off the profile of those perfect tits and that fuckable ass. I want to bite it. She sees me looking down her body and looks away, the smile on her face getting bigger.

“So, tell me then, Gia Noxx. What is your type?” She looks at me and I can’t quite tell through her sun-kissed tan, but I think she’s blushing. She bites her lip again, and I fight the urge to reach up and pull it from between her teeth.

“It’s Nobes. And since coming out of prison, I’m thinking I might like them bad.”

Now she has my fucking attention. With my hands in my pockets I stand up and turn, slowly heading backwards towards the door.

"Well, you're in luck, baby girl. Because apparently, I'm the bad guy."

To be continued in

Her Vipers (Ironhaven Book 2)

AUTHOR'S NOTE

So, how did you find it?! I firstly want to say thank you so much for reading this book, it was a real passion project and I loved every second of writing it. Secondly, if you enjoyed this one (and I really, really hope you did!), Gia's book will be next! It will carry straight on from the Bonus Scene, written by my incredible Editor, so keep your eyes peeled. I promise it won't be too long a wait. Thirdly, I would love for you to join me on my Ironhaven journey by following my Instagram @genjaswrites

Okay, acknowledgments time. They say it takes a village and my village is fortunately full of amazing women.

I have to start by thanking Rachelle, my very first (and only) alpha reader turned beta reader turned editor turned virtual friend! I have definitely told you this many times but this book truly wouldn't have happened without you. You motivated me, encouraged me, and hyped me up exactly when I needed it and the book is 10000% better because of your input. I'm so glad you've agreed to carry on with me because I was willing to beg and there's just no dignity in begging, is there?

To my twinny, Jessica, thank you for giving me the idea to write in the first place- your potential grooming really worked out well for me. Thank you for always being my biggest fan, even if we couldn't look each other in the eye for days after you read the sex scenes. Apologies. But Quincy finally got some, yay!

To my Mum who is always unwaveringly supportive, even if I have just written 75,000 words of pure filth. I hope you're proud but maybe don't read it.

To Sarah, my twin flame. Thank you for never doubting me (or hiding it well if you did!) and always having my back.

Here's to book number two!

Printed in Great Britain
by Amazon

68081184R00267